THE ADVENTURES OF SATAN HALL

THE
ADVENTURES
OF
SATAN HALL

A DIME DETECTIVE™ BOOK

■

CARROLL JOHN DALY

THE MYSTERIOUS PRESS
New York • London • Tokyo

Printed in the United States of America

First Trade Paperback Printing: April 1988

10 9 8 7 6 5 4 3 2 1

Library of Congress Cataloging in Publication Data

Daly, Carroll John, 1889-1958.
 The adventures of Satan Hall: a Dime detective book / Carroll
John Daly.
  p. cm.
 On t.p. the registered trademark symbol "TM" is superscript
following "detective" in the subtitle.
 ISBN 0-89296-938-5 (pbk.) (USA) / 0-89296-939-3 (pbk.) (Canada)
 1. Hall, Satan (Fictitious character)—Fiction. 2. Detective and
mystery stories, American.   I. Title.
PS3507.A4673A67 1988
813'.52—dc19   87-22699
                                                                CIP

CONTENTS

■

SATAN HALL originally appeared in *Detective Fiction Weekly,* where the stories in this volume were first published. In 1942, Popular Publications, publisher of *Dime Detective,* acquired The Frank A. Munsey Company and its subsidiary, The Red Star News Company, publisher of *Detective Fiction Weekly.* In 1944, *Detective Fiction Weekly* was combined with *Dime Detective.*

INTRODUCTION

The hard-boiled detective story began sixty-five years ago, in the June 1923 issue of *Black Mask* magazine. The lead story that month was "Knights of the Open Palm," by Carroll John Daly, featuring the first hard-boiled private eye, Race Williams. The short novelette was a big hit with the magazine's readership, and Williams returned in story after story. By the late 1920s, Daly was recognized throughout the magazine field as the most popular writer of detective stories. His only rivals were fellow *Black Mask* contributors, Dashiell Hammett and Erle Stanley Gardner.

Unfortunately for Daly, while Hammett and Gardner were able to make the leap from the pulps to the "slick" magazines and hardcovers, he remained rooted in the cheap magazines throughout his long writing career. The Race Williams short stories and novels evidenced all the faults of pulp writing—purple prose, minimal characterization, and unbelievable plots. The few examples of the series reprinted in the last few years read more like pastiches of the hard-boiled detective school than the originators of the genre.

Forgotten by most historians of the detective story is that Daly wrote numerous other hard-boiled adventures featuring heroes other than Race Williams. These stories, featured prominently on the covers of *Dime Detective* and *Detective Fiction Weekly* during the 1930s, did not rely on the first-person narrative and wisecracks of Race Williams, and thus aged much better than that series. Daly could write tough, gripping melodramas when he tried, and during the Depression he tried very hard.

The very best of Daly's several hundred hard-boiled thrillers are the adventures of Satan Hall. The original series of novelettes appeared in the early 1930s, during the height of gang warfare and political corruption in America's cities. However, Satan Hall proved so popular that Daly later brought him back in a new series of adventures in the 1940s. All of the stories reprinted in this collection are from Satan's earlier exploits.

Daly wisely abandoned sinister masterminds and oriental villains in the Satan Hall stories. Villains, instead, were crime bosses right off the newspaper headlines. Crooked politicians and influence-peddlers filled the pages of every adventure, and more than one crooked cop lurked in the shadows. Daly described a police force unable to cope with criminals hiding behind political connections. His writings reflected the realities of the time. And, with Satan Hall, he offered his own solution.

Hall was Daly's avenging angel—the grim reaper of the law. Daly cut loose with Satan, pulling out all stops. If the villains were ordinary criminals wrenched off the streets, their nemesis was not. Satan Hall was the most hard-boiled character ever to appear in the pulps, and one of the most memorable.

His name came from both his appearance and his attitude. Detective Frank Hall was nicknamed ''Satan'' because of his slanting green eyes, the sharp hook nose, thin lips with a curve at the corners, and jet-black hair swept back behind nearly pointed ears. Satan Hall resembled a man out of hell. Tall and thin, he walked with a steady, measured gait that seemed to promise uncompromising death to lawbreakers. Criminals shuddered when they heard the eerie sound of Hall's approach. They called his walk "Footsteps of Doom." The courts might forgive, but Satan Hall never did.

More than his looks earned Hall his title. Both criminals and lawmen feared him. Satan Hall was a killer—as ruthless and unrelenting as any crook, and twice as deadly. The look in his eyes was enough to shock a crooked politician to silence or cause a crooked cop to break out in a cold sweat. Satan Hall's eyes blazed with a lust to kill. While he never went outside the law to get his man, Hall rarely worried about bringing in his quarry still breathing.

Just as Race Williams served as a prototype for the tough, hard-boiled detectives who followed, Satan Hall worked equally as well as the hard-boiled cop who taught criminals the meaning of fear. In these days of *Death Wish* and *Dirty Harry*, his fifty-year-old adventures seem as fresh and exciting as the day they were written. For those readers unfamiliar with Carroll John Daly's work or know him only for Race Williams, meet his greatest creation, Satan Hall, "The Man the Police and Gangdom alike feared."

—Robert Weinberg

SATAN SEES RED

A NOVELETTE

■

CARROLL JOHN DALY

*He Hunted Men—His Law Was His
Own—and Police and Gangdom
Alike Feared and Hated
Detective Satan Hall*

ONE

BETWEEN THE EYES

■

Detective Satan Hall dropped to one knee and fired twice. His movements were so quick—just that sudden, dropping twist of his long body—that the sharp staccato notes of the Tommy gun died almost before it had begun to play its tune of death over the edge of the galvanized ashcan at the end of the alley.

A black touring car, with curtains tightly drawn, which had been moving slowly along the deserted street, suddenly increased its speed, reached the scene of hostilities and slowed down, the high-powered, high-priced motor purring softly.

The thickset man hidden behind the ashcan came to his feet, tottering slightly. The Thompson machine gun balanced for a moment on the edge of the can, then toppling forward, fell with the clang of metal to the sidewalk.

The gunman, his left hand dripping red, his right clutching a heavy automatic, half backed, half ran toward the slowly moving car. His gun wavered slightly—uncertainly and menacingly—toward the little hallway where his intended victim had taken refuge. Twice he squeezed lead toward that hallway. A side curtain of the car flapped back and other guns roared in the same direction as that of the wounded gangster.

Then, with a quick dash the killer ran into the street, clutched frantically at the nickel handle on the rear door of the getaway car, slipped once, and with an audible groan of relief pulled himself to the step. He turned then, as a hand stretched from between the curtains and held him, his back pressed against the side of the car. Evil, ratlike eyes pierced the darkness; and taking careful aim as the car increased its speed, he fired at the face he now saw peering from the hallway.

Two guns roared as one; two spurts of orange-blue flame split the blackness of the night.

The killer slumped against the side of the car, his knees sagged, and his heavy body was held only by the clutching fingers of a hand.

Another hand came from behind those curtains; fingers grabbed at a gray jacket. The car swung suddenly. The gunman sank to his knees on the running board—hung so a moment. Then, as the car swerved back, his body twisted, broke loose, and plunging to the pavement turned grotesquely over and lay in the gutter. The black touring car turned a corner and was lost to view.

There was the shrill blast of a police whistle and the distinct pounding of heavy feet. Detective Satan Hall stepped from the hallway, brushed the dust of the sidewalk from his right trouser leg, and mumbling something about "the street cleaning department," faced the patrolman who came running up.

"Hall. Satan—Frank Hall." Patrolman Leary corrected himself as he remembered Detective Hall's lack of enthusiasm for the title "Satan." "They didn't get you, then." And with a shake of his head that bespoke long and observant duty in the lower city, "They will, though. That's sure."

"Maybe." Satan Hall's green, slanting eyes narrowed, giving the peculiar cut of his hair an even more pronounced *V* shape upon his forehead. "But *there's* one lad who won't get me." He jerked a huge hand, with long, strong fingers, toward the inert form in the gutter.

For the first time Patrolman Leary saw the body of the gunman. He snapped erect, and raising the service automatic that was already clenched in his hand, stepped carefully toward the silent figure.

"Is he dead?" he asked in a whisper. Despite his years of service Patrolman Leary had never lost his superstition—or, as he would have explained it, his first feeling of reverence in the presence of the dead.

"That's for the medical examiner to decide." Satan shrugged his broad shoulders. "My duty is only to produce the body. His, to permit the burial."

"He's stiff as a mackerel." Leary came to his feet after kneeling for a moment by the body. He whistled softly as he saw the round hole almost directly in the center of the dead gangster's forehead. He looked at Satan again, trying to make out in the darkness those pointed features which gave him his name. And they seemed clearer now. The sharpness of the chin, the decided points to the ears—or at least, to his left ear, which Leary could see plainly because of the tilt of Satan's soft black felt hat. Yes, it was all there. And Leary gulped. There was a tiny hole in the dead man's forehead. It was more than a rumor, more than just a superstition, then, that Satan's bullets were generally found right between his—well—his "dead men's" eyes.

People were on the street now. Windows were going up. A sergeant had joined Leary, and with his hat in his hand was scratching his head and looking down at the dead, white face.

"It's Ed Graff," said Sergeant Clifford, as Satan came to him and looked indifferently down at the man he had killed. "He was Bowers' man. It'll raise an awful smell."

"Won't it!" Satan nodded.

"I wonder," said the practical sergeant, "what Bowers will say."

"I wonder," said Satan, just as slowly, "what Bowers will do." And he smiled to himself. "Maybe I'd better go and ask him."

"Maybe," said the sergeant, very seriously, "you'd better go and report to Captain Mullery. Oh, I know you're sort of the lone wolf of the Department. But, after all, you're working out of his precinct. I've sent Leary to call in. But maybe Mullery oughta hear it from you."

"Maybe he ought to." Satan pulled at his pointed chin.

"It will be a surprise to the captain," offered the sergeant.

"Yeah, it will," Satan agreed. "And it'll be a surprise to John Bowers—a disappointment, too," he added with a grin.

"Don't underestimate Bowers." Sergeant Clifford laid a kindly hand upon Satan's shoulder. He liked Satan's direct way of doing things. He liked the easy indifference with which Satan cut departmental red tape with a few well-directed shots from his service automatic. But he knew, as well as every cop on the force soon learned to know, that being a part of the system meant promotion, and promotion meant more money for an underpaid policeman.

T W O

THE SYSTEM

■

Detective Frank Hall walked down two blocks, turned left, did another block and a half, and passing under the green light, entered the station house. The lieutenant on the desk looked at him and nodded toward the room in the back.

"He's in there, Hall." And then, as Satan passed to the door to the left of the desk, "It was Ed Graff, wasn't it—he's dead, isn't he?"

"Uh-huh." Detective Satan Hall stuck the end of a match in his mouth. "It was Graff—and he's dead." And swinging on his heel, he thrust open the little door and stepped, with that even, measured tread of his, into the presence of Captain Mullery.

Captain Mullery took his cigar from his mouth and laid it carefully on the edge of the flat desk behind which he sat. Then removing a bit of tobacco from his lower lip, he looked at the detective. But it was Satan who spoke first, and his words were not the desired apology or the explanation that Captain Mullery hoped for, but did not really expect.

"Did the warrant come?" Hall asked lazily, as he threw himself into a chair.

Captain Mullery leaned far back in his seat, tucked the cigar into his mouth, took several draws upon it before making sure it was out, and then as carefully placing it upon the desk again, said abruptly exactly what was on his mind.

"You had to kill him, eh?"

Satan shook his head, then grinned. At the best, his grin was unpleasant. To Captain Mullery it seemed even sinister.

"No," he said, "I didn't. I could have let him kill me. Might have saved you a lot of embarrassment. I did my best to let him live." Satan shook his head. "It was wasted effort. Ed Graff didn't have any nerve, besides being a remarkably poor shot."

"I hope you had to do it." Captain Mullery shook his head. "Bowers is a powerful man in the district. And don't grin, Frank Hall. There always has been and always will be politics and influence. You can't afford to offend people, make trouble for the big boys, if you want to wear the stripes of a sergeant."

The captain came to his feet and, passing around the desk, looked down at Satan Hall. "And you should be sporting the shield of an Inspector. Look at me! Not half the nose for crime you've got. Not half—" His hands came far apart. "You've got to play the system if you want to get anywhere. You grin—and you're mighty proud of yourself. But you haven't others dependent on you. I've got a wife and kids, and I've got to swallow certain irregularities."

"I'm not criticizing you." Satan pulled himself erect in the chair. "And I don't expect you to criticize me. I've lived a flat-foot and I hope to die a flat-foot. Maybe, if I had a wife and kids, I'd excuse—" He came to his feet suddenly. "I've known you for years, Mullery; pounded a beat with you in the old days. We can't all think alike. Did the warrant come?"

"Yes." Captain Mullery gulped. "It's a mean break for you, Satan. The murder ain't hot any more, but every so often it bobs up that Ferago is back in town. One lad has been killed who saw that murder, and a cop that—"

"Yeah," Satan said impatiently. "But Ferago is in town now. You know, as well as I know, who committed that murder. Ferago had only a small part in it. Bowers beat in that old man's head five years ago. It was a brutal affair. Now—Bowers is a big shot. He's got money, so he's got friends and influence—and he's got votes."

"You can't do anything to Bowers—get anything on Bowers. That's just talk—and five years is a long time, Satan."

"Ferago's yellow. Ferago will talk before he fries. And if Ferago talks, Bowers burns—money, friends, influence, and what have you."

"But the rumor of Ferago being back is just gossip."

"Bowers knows it's true. Ferago's here under the name of Randolph. Bowers knows I want him—and Bowers is afraid I'll get him. More afraid, now that Ed Graff got kicked over."

"Anyway"—Captain Mullery shook his head—"the Commissioner, or whoever shoved that Ferago warrant on you, gave you a bad break."

"Maybe." Satan stretched his hand out for the envelope the captain lifted so reluctantly from the desk. "But I asked for it."

"You asked for it!" Mullery gasped, as Satan dug into the envelope, unfolded the warrant and nodded his approval.

"Yeah," said Satan. "I don't like Bowers."

"No." Mullery pulled at twin chins. "No, you don't.

It's that girl, then, Mary Rogers—that you—that all the—
that they—'' And Captain Mullery stopped dead.

Satan Hall was leaning over the desk now, his green eyes
points of flashing steel, his long tapering fingers twisting
spasmodically, his thin lips a single straight line, but for
the sinister curves at either end.

"I knew her father," he said almost viciously. "The
girl's straight. She has no friends. The police see in her
only the daughter of a dead crook."

"Bowers likes her," Captain Mullery said reflectively.
"Your trying to drag in Ferago won't help you none with
Bowers. He'll find out, and—"

"He's already found out, else why the shooting tonight?"

"Look out he don't take it out on the girl to get even, if
you—if you live. And if you die"—Mullery spread his
hands far apart—"she won't have you then. It's helped
her, Satan—the boys knowing you take an interest."

"If he harms the girl," said Satan slowly, "I'll pop him
over."

"That," said Captain Mullery, "would be murder."

"Sure," Satan agreed. "Bowers is welcome to what
comfort he can get out of that thought."

Captain Mullery followed Satan Hall to the door.

"Well," he said, "I wish you luck. At least, as to your
physical well-being. It's a big city for a cop working
alone, without the Department at least officially behind
him. How do you propose to start hunting for Ferago?
Where will you look? If he is in the city, they'll smuggle
him out quick enough."

"I'll start tonight. Now!" Satan's V-shaped jaw set
tightly. "And I'll look exactly where you'd look. Where
every dick in the city who's paid attention to underworld
gossip or stool pigeons would look. Right smack in the

John A. Bowers Club, or whatever the official label is for
Bowers' speakeasy and gambling joint. Good night.''

"Just a minute.'' Captain Mullery stretched out an arm
and fastened it on Satan's arm. "You're not going there
now. Listen, Satan"—when Satan would have shaken him
off—"Bowers is still mighty fast with a gun. The place
simply reeks with high-class racketeers. If you did get in,
if you did get Ferago—why, any one of the dozen might
kill you. There would be ten witnesses to swear that you
drew a gun; a lad without a record who'd take the blame
for knocking you over. Bowers' political friends to help
him beat the rap. I wouldn't—''

"No, you wouldn't.'' Satan shot the words through set
lips. "But you know, as well as I know, that Ferago is
there. That he plays cards with the boys, drinks at the bar,
struts in and out of the game rooms—and the only compliment he's paid the police force is to shave off his mus-
tache. It's a disgrace to the force. He's yellow, and he'll
talk. Talk, as soon as he realizes Bowers can't spring
him.''

"But the evidence?''

"A man and a woman who both saw Ferago at the time
of the killing. You didn't know that, eh? But Bowers must
know it, or guess it—though he don't know who they are.
Not even the Commissioner knows who they are.''

"I'm not thinking of Ferago or Bowers, but of you,
Satan.'' And as Satan jerked his arm free: "I could send a
couple of cops to stand out front. Nothing official, understand—
but they'd act as a—well—a sort of a restraint if Bowers
decided to give you the works. More, I can't do. It's the
infernal system, Satan. Bowers knows big guys—politicians.''

"Yeah. I know. I'm working alone and won't embarrass
you. The Commissioner's a straight-shooter. If Bowers has

anything on you, put your house in order. I'm going to get him.''

''Me? Good Gawd!'' Captain Mullery was more surprised than offended. ''I only know that big people told me he was 'right,' and to lay off him; leave him alone.''

''Good!'' said Satan as he jerked open the door. ''Leave him alone tonight, then.''

And he was gone, pacing slowly and evenly across the floor before the desk. At the outer door he hesitated, turned back, and approached the lieutenant on the desk.

''You've had occasion to visit Bowers. Yeah, John A. Bowers,'' he added as the lieutenant stiffened. ''Oh, I don't aim to accuse you of being over-friendly. But they say he always sits a lad under a lamp, in a big overstufffed chair, so he can watch him. Is that right?''

''Why—I—So I've heard.''

''It's truth, isn't it? Isn't it!'' Satan was leaning over the end of the desk now, his face very close to the lieutenant, his hot breath upon his cheek. His hot breath! And the lieutenant straightened. Like the man himself—the uncanny resemblance to that gentleman from hell. Yes, even the breath.

''Yes,'' said the lieutenant, ''that's true.'' He realized too late that he was a lieutenant and Satan simply a first-grade detective. He watched the tail of Satan's coat disappear through the door.

''There goes a man to his death,'' said Captain Mullery, coming from his private room. ''He's going to Bowers' to arrest Ferago.''

The man behind the desk whistled softly and felt for the phone.

''Better,'' he said, ''give Bowers a jingle.''

Captain Mullery hesitated, then shook his head.

''No,'' he said. ''Not this time. After all, Satan is

working out of this precinct, though we're not officially cognizant of it.'' He stumbled over the word he had culled from the Commissioner's short note that the official messenger delivered, together with the warrant for Satan.

Satan Hall's measured, even tread was well known in the underworld. But, contrary to general opinion, it was not slow. It moved his long angular body quickly.

Now—he walked two blocks uptown, three across, and another uptown again. His steps became slow only when he approached the John A. Bowers Athletic Club. That he could gain admission to the club he knew. But he knew also that his entrance would be delayed; that a bell on the side wall would be pressed, and Ferago quickly smuggled from the place.

Bowers didn't know—or couldn't know yet—that Satan carried a warrant in his pocket for the arrest of Ferago. But Bowers would know before the warrant got cold. Bowers had a way of knowing what went on, even within the department itself. But Bowers did know that Satan was hunting up information on the killing five years before. And Bowers had shown his knowledge, at least to Satan's satisfaction, when early in his investigation Satan had stood in the City Morgue and looked down at the dead face of a young girl—a girl who had promised to talk.

Satan set his lips grimly. A girl who wouldn't talk now. And his thoughts, somehow, went to another girl, Mary Rogers, the shabby tenement, and her fight against the odds of a dead father who had been a criminal.

To one side of the little hallway which gave entrance to the John A. Bowers Club, Satan waited. Several guests passed in—knocked on the unsuspicious and simple-looking wooden door which was lined with steel, and after passing the inspection of the man who peered through the square in the center, entered the club.

Honest folks, many of them. Satan nodded his satisfaction. That was good. That was John A. Bowers' cupidity. There were not enough high-class crooks to make the place pay. Besides, this honest public lent the club an air of semi-respectability.

Satan let several couples—two groups of four and one of six—pass into the club. Then he shoved a hand far into his overcoat pocket and stepped briskly from the shadows as a single individual climbed somewhat unsteadily from a taxi and passed into the darkened hall.

Wood moved, a small square opened in a broad door, a white face appeared for a moment in the light beyond— and as the door swung open, Satan took three quick steps down that hallway and was through the doorway before the astonished attendant even realized that something had barred the closing of the door.

Mean eyes glared at Satan, trying to peer beneath his slouch hat or above his turned-up coat collar. Thick lips parted, yellow teeth showed.

With a single movement of his right hand Satan swept the slightly inebriated customer back out that door, closed it, and shoved the bolt into place.

Though his sudden entrance was entirely unexpected, the experience was not without precedent to the efficient watcher at the door. Instinctively he sensed his visitor was a detective. If it was a holdup, the man would not have come alone. His right hand slipped slowly beneath his left armpit, his left hand shot swiftly toward the button on the wall—and Satan acted.

Satan's hand came from his pocket; steel flashed by the astonished attendant's arm. He felt a sharp pain, and red showed on the knuckles of his left hand as it fell to his side. He felt his right hand gripped in viselike fingers; and as he opened his mouth to shout, Satan raised his head—and the man on the door looked straight at those slanting green eyes, that sharp nose with the slight hook to it, the thin lips with the curve at the corners—and the shout died to a gurgling sort of a whisper in his throat. He was close to death, and he knew it. Satan was a killer.

THREE

THE JOHN A. BOWERS CLUB

∎

John A. Bowers, in the luxury of his private office, leaned far back in his overstuffed chair and tried to keep the end of his cigar from getting in the telephone mouthpiece.

"Yeah? He did! Uh-huh! You don't know what judge signed the warrant?" came at intervals to the attentive ears of Carpey Marks, his first assistant, who sat and waited for the conversation to end. "Judge Quailey, eh? Yeah. No, I never did business with him."

There was no expression on the thick jowls of Bowers as he put the phone back in its cradle and eyed Carpey Marks from small, round pink eyes that seemed even smaller set in such a large face.

"Know Judge Quailey—Francis X., I think? Anything stirring his way?"

"No." Carpey Marks pulled at a tightly set jaw. "He ain't regular. I know that. We've kept out of his court. All the boys do. They say he's straight. A sap!"

"Yeah?" Bowers let his huge head roll from side to side. "Well—see that mouthpiece, Jacobs. Tell him to get after Quailey. There musta been somethin' fishy, to set him on the bench. He always was a stench. But he let me alone and I let him alone. Now—"

"Yeah?" Carpey Marks leaned forward eagerly.

"Satan Hall's got a warrant for Ferago. There's been many warrants for Ferago, but this one reads, 'alias Randolph.' What do you think?"

Carpey Marks cleared his throat and spat in a corner.

"If Satan's got a warrant, he'll serve it. That's what I think." Then more slowly: "If he's got anyone to serve it on. Even Satan can't serve a warrant unless he's got someone to serve it on."

"And you suggest?"

"The same thing I suggested when I heard Ed Graff got it. You're trying to give it to the wrong guy, Chief. A dozen Satans might bob up who'd like to hear Ferago talk." And leaning far over, "But there's only one Ferago to talk, chief—just one."

"Huh—huh." John Bowers spread his huge hands across his ample front. "If there was a reason, Carpey. Not a personal one." He raised a hand when Marks would have cut in. "John A. Bowers takes care of his boys—none better. You know that. They all know that. Ferago counts on me—trusts me. Knows no harm can come to him while I—"

"Yeah. He goes up and down the avenue, buying drinks as if he were running for office. He's yellow. He got into trouble down in South America and came prancing home, scared stiff. Now look here, Chief. If Satan gets him and puts the screws on him, he'll squawk. Oh, don't shake your head. That cop ain't human. I'm telling ya truths. He'll lay a gun against my belly. Yeah, and your belly."

"Not me—not me." Bowers shook his head.

"Yeah—you. Your belly, and pull the trigger—and explain afterwards. And if he wants Ferago, he'd come here and get him, and—"

"Not here—not to the John A. Bowers Club."

"Yeah—here. The John A. Bowers Club, and—"

"I see." Bowers' little eyes got smaller. "Look here, Carpey. Satan will come here with that slip of paper—that warrant. You might wait in the hall, and—What's the matter with you? It's dark at the end. He'll come in under a light. Oh, hell!" Bowers came to his feet and paced the floor. "I'm always thinking of the organization, Carpey. I've got to. It bears my name and all that name stands for. If Ferago, now—if there was anything that would affect the organization, why—why—"

"Ferago takes dope," said Carpey for about the tenth time that night. "You've often said that a lad who sniffs the powder ain't to be trusted. If they put the screws on him, he'll wilt. He'll squawk for a whiff of snow. He'll— What's the matter, Chief?"

"Carpey"—Bowers stood above his assistant now—"I understand your feeling of loyalty to a fellow member, but your loyalty should be first to the organization as a whole. You have seen how I put aside all personal—thoughts of personal danger with regard to Ferago. I thought only of the organization. No, don't explain." Bowers raised a huge hand as Carpey's mouth fell open. "A drug addict is a menace to the whole organization. I like Ferago—you like him. We must both be above that. We must sacrifice individual friendships for the good of the whole. You may—"

"Yeah, Chief." Carpey Marks, who had no illusions, nodded vigorously. "I'll attend to everything."

"It's unpleasant," said Bowers with a frown. "And unpleasant things are best quickly over with."

"Sure, Chief. I'll tell him about the warrant and Satan

and that we're moving him uptown. I'll tell him about
some girls; nice personal ones, that you picked yourself,
and—''

"Do—do." But John A. Bowers was already thinking
about something else. "And, Carpey, there's that Mary
Rogers. You've spoken to her?"

"Yeah. And she ain't the type. At least she ain't—yet.
You'll have to make her the type, if you—''

"Me?" said John A. Bowers. "I wasn't thinking of
myself. She'd fit in nicely downstairs. Pleasant sort of a
girl—wistful smile. I was thinking she'd be an asset
downstairs.''

"Better to have her keep the books—up here with you.
You need someone, Chief, and she does that sort of a
racket—or did.''

There were times when Carpey Marks was a valuable
assistant. John A. Bowers smiled all over his huge, heavy-
jowled face.

"You're very thoughtful, Carpey—very thoughtful. You
say she *did*; did keep books and that sort of thing."

"Yeah." Carpey nodded. "She lost her last place. I
thought it for the good of—of society to tell them a little
something about her old man.''

"How's she fixed for money? Satan Hall, now. It's true
she's Satan's woman?''

Carpey Marks grinned.

"True enough for those that want to believe it. But it's
gospel that she ain't. She wouldn't take a cent from him.
She's that way.''

"I see—I see. And her father being a crook—even a
dead crook. Dead!'' He swung his head suddenly and
looked straight at Carpey Marks.

Carpey nodded.

"The finger's on Ferago." He was quick to sense the change of subject. "Don't worry, Chief." He came to his feet. "It's a bit of a drive, but in an hour I'll dump the body out by the old reservoir up Kingsbridge way. I'll take along a couple of—"

Carpey Marks paused. Both men turned toward the little glass-enclosed indicator on the wall. There had been a sharp buzz, and behind the soiled glass a tiny light showed red.

John Bowers started toward the door and paused.

"Trouble downstairs Carpey." His little eyes were like two round holes in a blanket. "Better go down and give it a look. It'll look better if I'm up here. Much better, if it's a big shot."

But after Carpey Marks had left the room, John Bowers paced restlessly up and down. One killing—one murder out of the past that might come back on him. Ferago! He should have put him on the spot long ago. It was Ferago who had held the old man when he—Bowers—beat in his—Bowers shuddered slightly. He was younger then. A fool for "courage," he thought. But the old man had looked straight into his face and called him by name. No one else knew. It was Ferago who had raised his head almost directly beneath the street lamp and been seen. And now—

Why the hell didn't Carpey Marks come back? Why the hell hadn't he done for Ferago long before? He was too soft-hearted. That was John A. Bowers' trouble. Ferago had been a brother to him; they had gone through the racket together. Those that said he let Ferago come back so Ferago could see what a swell guy—what a big shot he had become—were liars, dirty liars. But it was pleasant to talk to Ferago. Ferago was a good pal. Wouldn't stick at anything. Wouldn't—But that was before he took to snow. A dope! Carpey was right. Never trust a doper.

Besides, Ferago was younger, much younger. And Bowers looked in the glass at himself. There were wrinkles down to his mouth, heavy pouches under his eyes, and his jowls were—He leaned forward and ran a finger across the ridges in his face. That wasn't age. That was his early living—hard living. Now—well, an hour in the barber chair, and any woman would look at him twice.

He wasn't really old. On the good side of forty. He had fought his way up in the racket. Any woman—even a girl—even Mary Rogers—Damn it! What did he see in that little white face, that frail, delicate body? Spirit, that girl had. The name John A. Bowers must mean something to her. She was class. Destined to be a big shot—for a big shot. Well, John A. Bowers was a big shot, and it wasn't the name that made him that. He used a gun in those days—could still use it.

He jerked a hand beneath his armpit and a heavy German Luger snapped into it. Quick, that! He wondered if Satan could do any better, and he bit at his lip. Satan, eh? He'd knock off his men—he'd kill Ed Graff! He'd— But what had become of Carpey Marks? And the door opened and Carpey Marks burst in.

The easy indifference of the man was gone. That nonchalant carriage and the drawl to his voice were missing when he spoke. He simply shot the words through his teeth.

"Satan—Satan Hall has been here. And he knocked Ferago on the side of the head and dragged him from the place."

F O U R

A FIX

■

John A. Bowers stopped his pacing and looked straight at
Carpey Marks. There was nothing to read in his face. No
sudden twitching of his lips, no tightening of his eyes—no
rise to his voice when he finally spoke. Nothing to show
the emotions of the man; except perhaps the sudden color
that came to his cheeks, to vanish almost at once and leave
them that soft powdery white.

"And what," Bowers said, very slowly, "was Henderson
doing? What was Longman doing? Where was Richards—
and Prague? Even Gunner Rant was downstairs tonight.
What were they all doing?"

Carpey Marks shrugged his shoulders. But it was not a
movement of indifference. More, of resignation to the
inevitable.

"I suppose," Bowers still spoke very slowly as he stood
in front of Marks, "the memory of Graff—Ed Graff—was
with them when they saw Satan."

"It ain't that, Chief." Carpey Marks read wrongly that
calm before the storm. "It's Satan. It's his face—his eyes.
The slant of his eyebrows, the cut of his chin. Most of all,

his walk. That slow, even tread when he comes for a man. There's death in it, Chief. Them boys ain't yellow. They never expected he'd dare to come here. To the John A. Bowers Club. They had faith in—in—in the name of the organization, the pull you pack, the—''

''They knew—maybe, not as you know—but they suspected or guessed what Ferago is—and they knew that to lose Ferago was to lose me. I told them that—you told them that. Ferago, the lousy little skunk, told them that. Seven or eight of them. All 'guns.' All heavily armed. All seeking the patronage and protection of John A. Bowers. And not one, Carpey, even to pull a rod. If you had been there—would it have been the same?''

''Me? Well, I knew, Chief—and I'd've gunned Satan out like *that*.'' Carpey snapped his fingers and shoved out his chest. There were few who could stand up to Satan like he would, or like he told himself then that he would. Besides, the boys weren't altogether to blame. Bowers had taken too long to see things in the right light. Bowers should have—But Carpey explained it, or started to explain it in detail.

''You was slow to act, Chief.'' He stuck his thumbs in his vest. ''Don't say I didn't warn you—advise you. Ferago should a been put out before. Yesterday—a week ago—even a couple of hours ago, when Ed Graff was croaked. And I put it up to you strong. The trouble is, Chief, you don't think fast, like you used to. You don't strike when—''

''No!'' Bowers' roar of rage shook the room. For one instant all the fury that the big man held pent up in his body broke loose. Little eyes popped, great blue veins stood out on his forehead and cheeks, thick lips opened. Then his great body half turned and a huge right hand swung through the air, the back of the great knotted hamlike fist striking Carpey Marks on the side of the face and across the jaw.

Just the single crack as bone hit bone, and Carpey Marks hit the soft carpeted floor with a suddenness of a steer in the stockyard.

When Carpey Marks first opened his eyes Bowers was placing the phone back in its cradle. When Carpey Marks next opened his eyes it was from the splash of water in his face. John A. Bowers was standing above him, and he was talking.

"Get up!" he said. "I've had Satan on the phone, and he's coming over to see me."

"Yeah—yeah?" Carpey Marks staggered to his feet, felt of his aching jaw and wiped the blood from his lower lip. "I'm to tell the boys? We'll gun him out, and—"

"You're a fool!" John A. Bowers went to his desk and sat down behind it. He raised a pen and pointed it straight at Carpey Marks. "Satan put Ferago in, and Satan can get him out. See? It's not guns now—it's brains. And brains is money. It's a 'fix.' "

"But Satan can't be fixed. That's why he's still a dick. That's why—Gawd! Chief, I ain't trying to tell you how to run things. But I know. It's been—"

Bowers waved his hand.

"I know. Every man has his price. Everything in the world is for sale if the price is met. I'm going to meet Satan's price."

"And if he won't—"

Bowers came across the room and took Carpey Marks playfully by the shoulder.

"Then," he said, "we'll change positions. I'll be the seller and Satan the buyer." He whispered for a long minute in Carpey's ear. "Mind you—the men I name go with you. If I press the bell here, act—and act at once. This time, you see, it's for the good of the organization."

"She's a nifty dame." Carpey nodded when Bowers straightened again. "And Satan would give his life for her."

"Just so." Bowers nodded. "And he'll give my life for her, too. So you see, Carpey—after all, Satan's getting all the breaks in this visit. I—"

Again the buzzer on the wall rang. This time the light through the glass showed green.

"That," said Carpey, "will be a copper. Satan!"

"Exactly. Bring him up personally. And, since I'm doing the inviting, it would be stupid to try and enforce my rule—that no man to see me enters this room armed. Still—you might try it."

"Yeah. I see." Carpey smiled, and then grimaced and felt of his lip. It was like the man, that he held no animosity against his chief for that blow. "You ain't losing none of your—your strength, Chief."

John A. Bowers patted him affectionately on the shoulder.

"Nor you none of your lip." He looked down at the deep cut. "I'm speaking theoretically now." He grinned.

"Are you? Yeah, Chief?" Carpey Marks smiled, but as he left the room, he frowned. That last doubtful humor of Bowers' had been entirely lost on him. But Bowers knew that, and didn't care. He didn't mind enjoying one of his little jokes alone.

John A. Bowers stood in the center of that room. Then he moved the big overstuffed chair slightly to the right and straightened the shade of the electric lamp so that the light would fall full upon the face of the man who sat under it. Not that John A. Bowers was a great student of men. It was simply that he thought he was. He had read somewhere that great men—at least, some great men whom he had admired—did study men under a brilliant light. But the bright light had at least one practical purpose. It helped him to read men's hands—watch men's hands. Brains are all right. But they won't help you much if a man can move his hands fast, has a keen eye for distance and a steady finger upon a trigger.

John A. Bowers owed more to physical action than to mental power. It was the brute in the man that led him to the top. The shrewd brains that he had which kept him there. He didn't need to have proof of a man to "get rid of him." Suspicion was enough.

Now—Satan was coming to see him. Coming armed. There was little doubt of that. He'd never think of looking on any other copper as a danger. Bowers frowned. That was the trouble. He never had looked on Satan as a copper, as an upholder of law and order. He looked on Satan as he would have looked on any gangster—racketeer— gunman. Bowers didn't respect or fear the police. They never shot a man down—just like that. But Satan was different. Satan was a killer. Like any gunman, he killed ruthlessly. There were times when Bowers felt that Satan even killed for—for pleasure. What a man he would have made in the racket!

And the boys talked about Satan's feet. That slow, measured tread of his. Well—Bowers never watched a man's feet. Never feared a man's feet. Even in the days when he was winning his spurs by the quick and accurate use of a gun, he watched a man's hands. That was it. Feet? Hell! A child wouldn't be—

FIVE

HUNTER OF MEN

■

John A. Bowers raised his head and listened. Plainly he heard the steady tread of feet. Slow and even, just like the boys already said. Measured, too, as if Satan had practiced it. As if—Bowers grinned. But he listened nevertheless, and caught that unexplainable eerie something that others had caught. Footsteps of Doom, those feet were called. Footsteps of—Yes; they were like the slow tread of the last march—through the little door to the electric chair. Just like that. Just like—But it couldn't be. Bowers had never heard a man walk to the chair. It was like—like he thought those feet must be—those final steps to death. But, why? They were too steady for a lad going to the hot seat. Such steps would falter—must be uncertain. Of course! But yet they were like those last steps to death. Like he thought—

And the door opened—and Carpey Marks said: "Hall. Detective Frank Hall, Chief. And he's—well—he's got everything on him he had when he came in."

"I'm sporting a rod, if that's what he means," Satan said easily. And as Carpey Marks closed the door and stayed on the outside: "This isn't another of your warnings, is it?"

"Warning?" John A. Bowers' smile was friendly as he motioned Satan to the big chair beneath the light and watched him drop into it. "Well—maybe a hint or two was dropped your way. For your own benefit, Hall." And after a moment's pause, while he went and sat behind the desk, "You didn't benefit by such friendly hints. I see you're still just a detective."

"Always likely to be. Just a flat-foot." Satan's eyes narrowed and his lips curved at the ends. But Bowers couldn't tell if it was meant for a smile or not. If it was, it was a most unpleasant one. But then, beneath the light Satan's whole expression was unpleasant. Bowers shook his head and ran his hand across his mean little eyes, as if to clear his vision and change the picture before him.

"Well—" Satan said, after a bit, when Bowers drummed on the desk and made a pretense of studying the detective, "let's not waste time. You want to see me. It's about the Ferago pinch, eh?"

"Randolph!" And when Satan's lips parted again, Bowers went on, "We'll call him Ferago, then. You've got a clear case against him, eh? What's the charge? What are you holding him on?"

"No charge—just suspicion. No charge—yet."

Bowers' thick eyebrows seemed to thin.

"You know, of course, I can have him out with a habeas corpus writ in less than twenty-four hours. A great thing—habeas corpus, if you don't make a formal charge—a real charge."

"Yeah." Satan nodded. "If I don't. But somehow, Bowers, I don't think you'll try any habeas corpus this time."

"No?" Bowers hesitated. Satan was no fool. Habeas

corpus is the poor man's greatest protection against injustice. But it is also the racketeer's greatest weapon against the law. And Bowers had used it many times. Now—Bowers stroked his chin and said, "No?" again—and let it ride.

"No." Satan shook his head. "For the moment you do, I'll make a formal charge of murder against Ferago. Listen, Bowers." He leaned forward, both his huge hands with their long slender fingers upon his knees. "As soon as Ferago knows that turning State's evidence will save him—as soon as he knows that his own life will be saved if he names the man who beat in that old watchman's head five years ago, he'll talk. I've got no warrant for you now. I'm naming no names now. But you and I know who Ferago will name. You can't help him—you can't save him. All your influence; all your pull; all your bribes won't beat this rap. Bowers, I've been on your heels for years. Now—I'm going to see you fry. Get that! You're going to burn."

"Yeah?" John A. Bowers tried to smile, but it was a sickly grin. A dry tongue came out and licked at drier lips. His thick jowls turned a dull white. He coughed once and put his hand over his mouth. He laid both his hands on the flat desk and came slowly to his feet.

"Hall," he said, in evident great frankness, "you've been straight with me, and I appreciate it. You've got me wrong. You've got Ferago wrong. But there is some danger of—of—" And suddenly leaning forward, "You put Ferago in—how much do you want to get him out?"

Satan shook his head.

"It can't be fixed," he said.

But John A. Bowers only smiled at that. He had heard the same line before. From big men in the city—big shots in politics. Big bugs on the police force. And yet—He spread his hands far apart.

"You've been trying to put the finger on me for years. And—well—you can get Ferago out, can't you?"

"Yes," said Satan, "I can."

"And you've come to see me, to talk about it. You've come to warn me—to give me an out. All right. Ferago goes free tonight—and it will be worth just five grand to you."

Satan laughed, and John A. Bowers laughed with him.

"Just my fun—my little joke." He rubbed his hands together. "Come—we won't quibble. We'll make it ten grand. Cash on the spot. No checks—just bills. And after that. Well—you've been a long time on the force. We'll make you a lieutenant—a captain. Six months or a year would cover it. You've got a good record—too good a record. We could make an inspector out of you in time— make you a rich man."

Satan shook his head.

"It's not enough," he said quietly.

"Ah!" Bowers was in his line now. This was talk—this was putting the screws on him. This was the sort of thing he understood. "So you want to squeeze me, eh? You think you've got me in a jam and I'll have to pay. You've gone straight all these years—waiting, watching for the one big haul. Just one, and out! Others have thought that. But you can't do it. Money! It'll get into a guy's blood— into his mind. He can't get enough of it. I—There, there—" Bowers changed suddenly as he saw those narrowing green eyes of Satan's. "I might double it for you. But it wouldn't be nearly as much in the long run as standing in with John A. Bowers. There's gravy enough for all of us. Just let me pin the shield of a captain on you, and then—

Gawd! Satan, with a man like you in the racket, I could point out—''

"It's not enough," Satan said again, and his lips curled. "You see, Bowers, it isn't in my blood—or in my mind. There's nothing I want that money can buy. It's not honesty—not morals. I just don't get a kick out of money. That's why I'm a detective—just a common dick. It's my racket—my kick—to hunt men. And, now"—he leaned forward—"one man, Bowers. Just one man." Satan came to his feet and, taking two slow steps, leaned over the flat desk and pounded a long finger against Bowers' chest. "I've waited some years for this. You understand—the finger on you!"

Bowers had seen what he thought was viciousness in a man's face before. Bowers had seen the threat in a man's eyes—the hate and lust to kill far back behind glaring orbs. And he had nodded his head and jerked a thumb toward such departing enemies. They died later—the finger was on them!

Now he thought he read that same lust to kill—that same hate in behind the green shining globes. He had never seen it in a copper's eyes before—he never expected to see it. The look that he feared in men's eyes; the look that made him kill—and kill quickly.

His lips trembled slightly and his lower one hung down. His right hand moved toward his left armpit. He didn't think of money then—he didn't think of a fix then. He thought only of drawing a gun—and using it. His fingers were on his chest now; almost beneath his coat—not far from his shoulder holster and the German Luger it contained. And Satan's hands never moved from his side; just hung listlessly there. Yet, Satan must have known of Bowers' quickness with a gun, his reputation, and—

God in heaven! Why didn't Satan move his hands? Was

he a fool, or—? And little beads of sweat rolled out on Bowers' forehead, hung so and dripped slowly down his face. Satan's lips slipped back and his eyes narrowed slightly, and—he was laughing. Or was he? Was he just marking Bowers for death, as Satan had marked others for death—others, who had been mighty fast on the draw—as fast as Bowers? Witnesses had said that Satan's hand had never moved before that sudden burst of flame came from his gun, and the tiny hole appeared in the forehead of the dead man—the dead man whose gun hung clutched in his hand. A gun that was never fired—never—never—

Bowers' hand dropped limply to his side. Someone spoke. A voice that sounded hollow and distant said, "You—you devil, you—you've come here to murder me." And the words were out and dully registering in John A. Bowers' mean little brain before he fully realized himself that he had spoken them.

Bowers was careful now to turn his side and gently take a handkerchief from his breast pocket to mop his moist forehead. But as he stood erect and faced Satan again, the thumb of his left hand slipped below the desk and pressed the button there three times. Peculiarly, it took an effort to do that—and he wondered whether the effort showed on his face. He wondered that as Satan spoke.

"If you've rung for help—if someone walks in that door in a way I don't like, John Bowers, it'll be just too bad for you."

Bowers nodded very slowly.

"Our talk is over," he said in a husky voice. He had no more thought of bribing Satan. He had only one thought now. To see him go. "I wondered why you came, but I—I never guessed. It's personal, then."

"Very personal." Satan nodded. "You're a wise man, if

not a brave one. You had your chance—if you had any nerve.'' Satan's shoulders moved up. ''The state would have been saved an electric bill. But you were right, Bowers. I came here—well—if not with the purpose, with the hope of killing you.''

''I see,'' said Bowers. ''Hunter of men, eh? Hunter of just one man now—that's it.''

''That's it. You've given me many warnings. I'm giving you a warning now. Just one man!''

''Sure—sure.'' John A. Bowers was relieved as the door opened and one of his bodyguards stood there. ''But you can't help—'' He hesitated, with the name of Mary Rogers on his lips—and decided not to use it. ''You can't help the girl if you're dead, you know.''

''No, and you can't harm her if—if you're not alive. That's a nicer way of putting it, Bowers. At least, I think Ed Graff would appreciate that. By the way, I knocked Ed Graff over tonight.''

''Graff! An impetuous youth! He didn't—didn't attack you?'' John A. Bowers' eyebrows went up. There was nothing vindictive in his voice—in his face. He was himself again now and on his guard.

''No—no.'' Satan shook his head. ''I wouldn't go so far as to call it an attack. Perhaps 'annoyed' me is a better way to put it.''

''I see. I see.'' John Bowers spoke now with the steel-lined doors half closed upon Satan. ''Glad you called, and one bit of final advice. Don't do anything about Ferago until tomorrow. If he's as susceptible to violence and as yellow as you think—'' Bowers shook his head before withdrawing it, ''well—if he talked tonight, you might be just as sorry about it as I'd be. Good night.''

''Good night,'' said Satan lightly.

But he was a bit worried as he carefully descended the

steps to the hall below, and passed down it and out onto the street. There had seemed something ominous in John A. Bowers' "Good night." Just what, Satan couldn't lay a finger to. It was queer how it got him, though. And Satan was not given to conjuring up queer psychic warnings. But he was glad that, unknown to Mary Rogers, he had placed a private detective in her tenement house that night. His name was Finneran, and he was a good man.

S I X

SATAN'S DUTY

■

Back at the precinct Captain Mullery was pacing his room when Satan walked in. He didn't wait. He blurted right out with it.

"It's happened," he said. "Quicker than you thought. A private dick called Finneran was gunned out—"

"And Mary—Mary Rogers. What of her?" Satan fairly shot the words at Mullery.

"First thing I asked when the report came in. Ginsburg, on duty there, went back and had a look-see. The shooting took place on the stairs. All the tenants accounted for but—"

"But Mary, eh?"

"Well—she wasn't in her rooms." And getting up, Mullery took Satan by the shoulders. "No use to lie to you," he said evenly. "Her bed had been slept in; her room was—Well—she's gone, Satan. You've crossed the big boy, Bowers, just once too often."

"All right," Satan said very slowly. "Now—I'm going to kill him."

"That won't bring the girl back. Besides, you can't—

won't be able to even see him, armed. There, there—Frank. Things are not so bad. It wouldn't be to Bowers' interest to harm her, for you've got Ferago.''

"Yes.'' Satan was trying to think, and failing miserably—except for thoughts of violence, sudden death, and the huge body of John A. Bowers sprawled upon the thick-rugged floor, with a purple hole in his forehead.

"Well''—Captain Mullery stroked his chin—"they've got the girl, that's certain. You've got Ferago. It's the very system that you object to. You've got to give as well as take, Satan. I've preached it to you for years.'' And more kindly, as he reached up and put a hand on a broad shoulder, "Sometimes, Satan, it's a guy like me, wanting to be a captain; wanting to give a girl a good education. Maybe another guy wants a high-priced car. It's the system. It's the racket that crooked politics, stupid laws, and human nature caused.

"Sometimes it's just an ambitious lawyer digging out coin for a judgeship. Now—it's a man and a woman. You let Ferago go, and Bowers returns Mary. It's an even break, Satan. There—there, I know you've watched over her since she was a kid. I'll see Bowers. Oh, he won't admit it, of course—but we'll come to an understanding that Mary goes free when Ferago goes free. I'll fix it for you.''

"Fix it for me!'' Satan suddenly jerked his shoulder free and faced Mullery, his green eyes flashing like thin points of sparkling steel beneath an electric drill. "I don't need a 'fix.' I never had a 'fix.' I'll get Bowers, and I'll—''

"Yes, I know,'' said the older man quietly. "You'll kill him. That's all right if you see him—see him, armed. He's fussy about that.'' And when Satan only grinned evilly: "Oh, that's all right—when he wants to see a guy. But when a guy wants to see him, it's another matter again.

This time, Satan, you've got to make a 'fix.' If you killed Bowers, it wouldn't help the girl any. If Ferago stays in, Bowers gets the juice. You ain't aiming to give him any choice—except how he dies." Captain Mullery shrugged his shoulders. "Besides, you've got to get him before he gets you, and either way Mary—It's a tough spot for a cop—a cop with an honest record."

Satan looked up quickly. If he had suspected sarcasm in the captain's voice, he found none in his face. But Captain Mullery was studying Satan carefully. The man of iron. The man who lived for nothing but to hunt criminals. The man who could not be bought, frightened, or swerved by any influence from his duty! "Duty." Well—Mullery had always thought, with others, that that word did not fit Satan Hall at all. *Passion*, would have been a better word, or perhaps *obsession*. But the real word was in none of these. The Commissioner had called it a fetish.

"Well," said Mullery, "what are you going to do? Let Ferago go?"

"I can't—I can't." Satan's voice was very husky, and then very low. "I want to. I should. But I can't."

"Why not?" Mullery stuck his thumbs in his vest. He had never seen Satan suffer before. Had often wondered, when the big moment came, just how it would hit the man. Now—well—he had always half hoped for such a time, when he could talk to Satan as man to man—show him how his ideas didn't always fit, and let him know how the shoe felt when it pinched the other fellow. And Mullery was surprised.

It wasn't a question of honor—duty—loyalty to the force or the citizens he was paid to protect. No, Mullery had never looked on Satan as an honestly scrupulous man. He could picture Satan right now as shoving a gun against

the back of Bowers' head and pulling the trigger. It was
something else. It was—well—just as Satan said. He
couldn't do it. And Mullery wasn't sure if he was facing a
great strength or a great weakness—or perhaps, after all, a
simple superstition. But he tried to make Satan see the
thing right—make it look good to him.

"It isn't as if you were betraying your trust," he said.
"You were going to let Ferago go if he squealed on
Bowers. What's the difference whether he talks now or
later?" And when Satan looked at him sharply, "Maybe he
won't even talk at all. Anyway, there's others that may
know about the murder of the old watchman by Bowers.
You'll only be delaying things a little." And as Satan
shook his head and looked blankly past him, "Well—hell!
It ain't my job to argue with you against your duty. I
hardly know the girl. If she ain't worth doing a little
irregular—"

"I think more of her than I do of my own life." Satan
threw out the words. "You can't understand. I can't
understand, myself. I want Bowers for murder. I've got
him. I've—Don't you see? If he was to kill her tonight,
I'd have to go through with it. And I love her as much as
you love that kid—that daughter of yours."

"Maybe." Captain Mullery shrugged his shoulders. "But
you've got a damn funny way of showing it. If it was my
kid, I'd have Ferago out in five minutes. 'I could not love
you half so much, loved I not honor more' may make a
damn nice song in a drawing room, but it won't do Mary
Rogers any good in Bowers' hands." And suddenly standing
on his toes and almost shouting the words at Satan,
"Well—what the hell are you going to do, instead of
standing there making grimaces?"

"I'm going," said Satan very slowly, "straight to Bowers and ask him just where Mary is." And seeing the sneer

of derision on Mullery's face, "And he's going to tell me."

"Tell you! You're a fool and a conceited ass. You love the girl and won't sacrifice a little personal glory to save perhaps her life—or more than life. And Bowers—Bowers, who controls half the lower city. Bowers, who fears neither man, woman, nor devil!" A jeering note came into Mullery's voice. "You're going to make him tell where the girl is—tell you nicely, so you can take him up to the Big House and fry him. You're going to make him tell, so—"

Satan was walking toward the door when he turned suddenly, took two quick steps and stood before Captain Mullery. Mullery's words died on his lips, his jaw fell slightly and his left hand clutched at his throat, while his right felt fumblingly—uncertainly—almost involuntarily toward the drawer of the desk that held his service automatic. And that hand trembled. He was looking into a face of such diabolic fury that for a moment he did not think it could be human. A hatred so intense that it seemed to take on life, as if it darted out of those green malignant orbs and was a tangible, living thing in the room before him.

Captain Mullery's eyes bulged in—well—not in fear. Probably—more in horror than anything else. The thin straight lips of Satan moved evilly—yes, evilly, to the bulging eyes of Mullery. And Satan spoke.

"Wouldn't you tell me—wouldn't you tell me, knowing I wanted to know!" For a moment Satan's hands went into the air. For a moment Captain Mullery felt that two threatening talons were sweeping toward his throat. And Satan turned suddenly and was gone.

For a long minute Captain Mullery stood by the desk. Then he drew a hand across his forehead, snapped the moisture from his knuckles, and taking a deep breath, threw open the door and walked into the main room. The lieutenant behind the desk spoke.

"What you doing to Satan, Cap? He just left. No fooling about his name. The devil's in him all right."

"You're telling me, Mac." Captain Mullery's laugh made the lieutenant look up. It was like a coal shovel scraping the cellar floor.

SLOW STEPS

∎

John A. Bowers was rubbing his hands together as he sat behind his shining flat desk. He smiled confidently at Carpey Marks.

"Satan will be along to see me, Carpey. There's no doubt of that. But this time he'll be wanting to see me—not me, him. Search him. Strip him to the skin if necessary, but be sure he enters this room unarmed. No sleeve gun; no tiny automatic in the trouser leg. Even make sure of his fountain pen, if he carries one."

Carpey Marks nodded his approval, then frowned.

"If he puts up a stink, tries to shoot his way in, will we let him have it? You've got to have him alive for the Ferago spring."

"No—no." Bowers closed his little eyes and tapped the telephone pointedly. "While you were slipping the girl across town I did a little phone work. No one but Satan knows the two witnesses who promised to put the finger on Ferago. Satan promised them not to tell anyone. He's kept that promise." Bowers frowned. "If he had even told the commissioner, I'd know it. My information comes from a reliable source—a lad who has to talk to me. A lad who made one slip. A well-thought-of lad. But that slip would give him a mighty long stretch. These honest guys, Carpey—these church guys are like us, only they ain't got the nerve and they ain't recognized as public enemies. Now—"

"Then Satan gets the heat. That's it, eh?"

"That is just it." Bowers nodded. "But he don't get it downstairs. He gets it here—right in this room, see? I want to talk to him first. I want—"

"You want to see him die, eh?" Carpey nodded. He could understand that and appreciate that. Satan had been a thorn in Bowers' side for some time. Besides, there was the girl.

"Right!" said Bowers. "I'll take his life and his woman. No—no, it ain't so dangerous. He's talking all over his mouth right now about knocking me over. I'm a big man—a strong man. There'll be a struggle, and I'll shoot him with his own gun. See?"

And when Carpey's eyes went up, and he did not see: "Hell! You'll bring me up his rod. I'll get him to talk, name them witnesses. I'll ride him with what will happen to Mary Rogers if he don't talk—which won't be no kidding. Then, after he talks, I'll go over and shoot him through the stomach—close like—maybe twice. If we can plant his body uptown, all right—we'll let it ride that way. If we can't—well—then the story of the struggle and—"

"Why in the stomach?" Carpey was of a practical turn of mind.

"It hurts like hell, in the stomach," said Bowers simply. "And I want it to hurt like hell."

"You think he'll come up here without a rod?"

"Sure—" said Bowers. "It's his woman. He'll want to make a deal."

"Okay, boss." Carpey stroked his chin. "I was only thinking that—that Satan might not come, and—"

Both men turned together. The little light was flickering.

"That," said Bowers, "is Satan. Go fetch him up. No hardware—and slip me his rod at the door." John A. Bowers rubbed his hands together. Things were working fine. Satan never would suspect, at least the full significance of his reception. Just a "fix" was what he'd think; a little deal. The girl free for Ferago free. As for the killing. Well, that would be a natural outcome. It wouldn't be hard to find witnesses who'd swear Satan was looking for a chance to get Bowers. Good witnesses. It wouldn't look so bad along the avenue either. Bowers beating Satan to the kill! Satan, the fastest, the most ruthless. A killer. A—

And Bowers stepped quickly to the door.

"Carpey," he said, "be sure about that gun. Be sure he ain't—"

"Don't worry," Carpey threw back over his shoulder. "He won't come up here armed. Not him."

"And Carpey." Bowers clutched at his lieutenant's arm. Despite his assurance he wiped tiny beads of perspiration from his forehead with a large linen handkerchief. "It looks sure, doesn't it? You'll stay in the room, hand on your gun—just as a witness to the attack, you know."

"Yeah, I know." Carpey nodded. And what's more, he'd keep a hand on that gun. "Satan'll be a fool to come up."

"Other guys have been fools over a woman. Go on." And unconsciously stating the fear in his own heart, "There ain't no other way. It's Satan's life or mine."

"Yeah," said Carpey, as he started down the hall. "If you'd take my advice, you'd let me plug him in the back on the stairs."

"No—no." Bowers shook his head. But after Carpey had disappeared around the bend in the hallway he opened his mouth twice to call him back. Then, with a shrug of his shoulders, he returned to his private office, rearranged the light over the big overstuffed chair, and opening a small cabinet, took out a bottle of whiskey.

It was a long drink and Bowers took it neat, shook his head, blew out his cheeks and shook his head again. Somehow, Satan got under a guy's skin. That charmed life of his—those slow, measured steps—his quickness with a gun. He'd had the breaks, that was all. Yet Bowers did himself another drink and straightened slightly. Quickness with a gun, eh? That wouldn't do a lad much good if he didn't have a gun.

John A. Bowers laughed a bit at that and paced the room. He guessed, in his day, he was as quick as Satan ever was—maybe quicker. And now—his right hand shot under his left armpit and out again. He looked now at the flat bit of blue steel. Pretty fast, that. Damn good and fast, when the other lad didn't have any rod.

No—the thing was in the bag. Satan, the feared Satan. Satan, the killer. Just like *that*, he'd go out. He'd die as others had died. With a bellyful of lead. Satan, the same as others. Yeah—all guys with a bellyful of lead die. No difference. But would he come? That was it. Wouldn't he—? But he couldn't guess the truth. Still—

And Bowers stopped pacing the room and listened. Down the hall, outside, was coming the steady tread of feet—even, slow beats. Just a single pair of feet. What about Carpey? What the hell did Carpey mean by letting him walk that way? Was it possible that Carpey wasn't with him? Could Satan have—? John A. Bowers dabbed at his forehead.

One, two, three more steps—then silence. And a rap on the door. Just a single rap, but a peculiar one. Bowers sighed with relief. It was Carpey Marks.

"Yeah!" said Bowers. "Okay, Carpey. Come in."

E I G H T

UNARMED

■

The door opened and Satan Hall stood in the doorway. Bowers' little eyes slipped over his shoulders and his tenseness slackened somewhat. Behind Satan was Carpey Marks. Bowers nodded, but involuntarily his right hand played across his vest, his fingers just under his jacket.

And Satan walked across the room and straight to the big chair with the light over it. And the feet were still slow and measured. Bowers felt a desire to count—one, two, three—but he didn't. He liked the way Satan dropped into the big chair. He was going to be peaceful then. Follow the custom that everyone who visited Bowers knew about.

"Well—" Bowers crossed to Carpey, took the gun he slipped him, and going to his desk, sat down behind it. He looked at Carpey and nodded when he closed and locked the door. He liked, too, the way Carpey's right hand was sunk into his pocket. He even rubbed his hands together after he carefully laid Satan's gun in his desk drawer.

Satan didn't speak for a minute, then he jerked a thumb toward Carpey.

"Is our talk to be private, or do you want that punk to listen in?"

Carpey Marks straightened and his right jacket pocket bulged. He was not an imaginative man. He blurted out: "Can that stuff, Satan. Can that stuff."

Satan put slanting, green orbs on him.

"I'm marking you, Carpey," he said. "You see, when Mary Rogers disappeared Bowers was right here with me, and you're his—" Satan bit at his lip and gripped at the arms of the chair, but he didn't speak further.

"Come—come!" Bowers didn't like Satan's hostile attitude. It didn't fit in with his idea of things. He tried his dignity; a line he culled from the life of—well—some lad he'd read about. "Why am I indebted to you for this visit? We've closed up downstairs and I was just—"

"All right," said Satan. "I want to know where the girl is—where Mary Rogers is. And I want to know now."

"Rogers—Mary Rogers?" Bowers raised his eyebrows and looked at Carpey. "Not—She isn't the girl I wanted to help; offered the cigarette job downstairs to. Don't tell me she's disappeared. But then, that's youth; that's—"

"I'll come to my point," said Satan slowly. "If you don't tell me where she is, I'm going to kill you—Bowers."

"Really!" Bowers tried to smile, but it was not very successful. There was such a deadly earnestness about the man; a feeling that he spoke the truth despite the fact that he sat there unarmed. "You don't think I know where the girl is. But, I see—and you're right. I meet a lot of people—see a lot of people, and it's just possible that I could learn where she is. You want a favor, eh?" Bowers leaned forward now. "You want me to do something for you, and in return you'll do something for me."

"No—" Satan shook his head. "If you don't want to die—tell me where the girl is."

"And, of course, Ferago goes free. That's it, isn't it?"

"No!" said Satan, "that is not it. I know you had the girl taken and I know why. To make a deal with me. And I know Carpey did the actual kidnapping, because he's the one you trust—and he wasn't here when I left, earlier. I know."

"If you know so much, it's a wonder you didn't call a cop; a real cop," Carpey sneered from the door.

Satan turned his head slowly and looked at him. Then he looked back at Bowers.

"What goes for you goes for the punk, too, Bowers. I haven't much time. Where's the girl?"

"I think," said Bowers, who liked to cloak his words, "that Mary Rogers is disappointed in you. She told me you won't see her again until Ferago is free, and you tell me the names of the two witnesses who saw that—that killing five years ago. I want a good lawyer to question them, and see who paid them to lie. I"—and as Satan would have cut in—"no—no, you want plain speaking. The price of the girl's freedom is just that."

Satan's hands dug deep down at his sides. His fingers seemed to clutch spasmodically at the heavy upholstery of the chair. At least, it seemed that way to Bowers, who couldn't see that far down from behind the desk. When Satan spoke, his voice seemed tired, yet there was a certain undercurrent to it—as if, far back, an obstruction held back pent-up force. A force that Bowers could feel, but could not lay a name to.

"You misunderstand me, Bowers. I'm not threatening to watch for an opportunity to kill you—hunt you down like a rat, in some alley. When I say I'm going to kill you, I mean just that. On the open street—in the lobby of a hotel—at Forty-second Street and Broadway. In plain words, the first time I see you, no matter what the place. Even in this room here.''

''So that's it, eh?'' Bowers looked at Carpey Marks and moved his right hand nearer to the open drawer. ''So that's it.''

''Yes,'' said Satan, ''that is it. That's why I came to see you. I wanted to let you know. It will be the first time I ever shot a man down in cold blood, but it's fact just the same. I'll give you time to talk—while I count ten.''

Bowers leaned over his desk now, his left arm upon it, his right hand in the drawer, clutching Satan's gun. His little eyes blinked evilly, his thick lips slipped back—and he spoke half through his teeth.

''So you'll count ten, eh? Well—begin. You're right, Satan. There'll be death at the end of it. Death for you. You've tried to hang something on me for years. You've made it personal because of a woman—a girl. Well—I always get what I want. Now—you're just a fool, like any other dick. You've threatened me. Every cop along the avenue knows that. Mullery knows you came here tonight. They'll know you came to threaten me—to kill me. Get that! Understand that! But they won't know that you were fool enough to meet me unarmed.'' He waved Satan's gun across the desk. ''This is your rod. There's a struggle—a shot or two. See?''

Satan nodded his head very slowly as he looked at Bowers. There was no fear in Bowers' face now. Just elation, hatred—and perhaps the lust to kill. John A. Bowers, the big racketeer, was simply Johnny Bowers again. Johnny Bowers, the gangster and gunman, who had hunted his enemies in the dark alleys of the city.

Satan looked at the gun in Bowers' hand and spoke very slowly and very distinctly. Bowers was rising from behind the desk. The gun which he held in his hand was dropping slowly from a line on Satan's head to a line on his chest—to his stomach.

"It won't work." Satan half shook his head. "You see, I sort of suspected you'd work it this way—with my gun. And since I knew you wouldn't want me up here, heeled—why—I took the cartridges out and—"

"You did, eh?" Bowers sneered. "Well—I won't have so much trouble finding another gun around here." He half glanced at Satan's gun, in his own right hand. "You're on the spot, Satan. You're going to get it right through the stomach. And then—Mary and me—or Carpey, if she don't—"

And it happened.

Satan's whole face changed suddenly. He threw himself out of the big chair. The green eyes had again become malignant, burning things of hatred. Bowers saw a clawlike left hand darting across the space before him. He dropped the gun he held and shot his right hand to his left armpit. Then he saw Satan's right hand, and the thing in it. He screamed to Carpey. Hope, fear, uncertainty—and, finally, stark terror made the words a screech in his throat.

"Give it—Let him have it, Carpey."

Bowers' little eyes bulged till they nearly popped out of his head as the shot came. He saw Carpey jerk the gun from his pocket, heard the shot—two of them, almost at once. He saw too the spit of orange-blue flame close to his face, saw Satan's body half twist and his arm move across his chest. Then he saw the tiny hole in Carpey Marks' forehead; saw it widening before Carpey spun and crashed to the floor.

It seemed to Bowers that it all happened in a split second; in that fraction of a second when he dropped Satan's gun and clutched for his own, under his armpit.

Yes—clutched for it and reached it—and held it—held it just so, tightly in the shoulder holster. For at the very second he gripped his Luger, he had seen the blue steel in Satan's right hand—the blue steel and snub nose of a rod, and even the belching flame as Satan swung his hand across his chest and "got" Carpey.

Bowers cried out once more as he saw in that face before him all that Captain Mullery had seen a short time before. Then Satan's hand had gone up and down, the barrel of the gun cutting deep across Bowers' forehead—across the bridge of his nose and down to his mouth.

Bowers squealed out something as the gun struck again then sank slowly to his knees. The next instant Satan was around the desk. Fingers were reaching for Bowers' throat. Satan was talking softly, as if to himself.

"Mullery said you wouldn't tell. Mullery said you wouldn't tell—and burn. Somehow, Bowers, I think you're going to be very glad to—to burn."

Then long talons sank deeply into Bowers' thick flabby throat—and Satan laughed hoarsely.

NINE

BEHIND THE DOOR

■

In answer to Satan's call Captain Mullery sent a detail of police to the house on East Eleventh Street. Then he burned up the tires on the police car driving to the John A. Bowers Athletic Club.

A few waiters and the club manager pointed hysterically to the floor above. None of John A. Bowers' strong-armed men were present. Above, where the men pointed—just a great silence. A young waiter sat down on the lower step and put his head in his hands and wailed: "Oh, my God! Oh, my God!"

Captain Mullery looked up the dimly lit stairs, hesitated a moment, then waved to his men to stay below as he slowly mounted the stairs—his gun drawn in his hand, his feet moving as if by a motor he did not control. The silence of the men below had been more terrifying and suggestive of what had happened in that room above than if they had spoken for hours.

Captain Mullery shuddered slightly as he reached the door to John A. Bowers' room, raised his hand to rap—

then pushed his body to one side before he brought his knuckles softly against the highly polished wood.

"It's me—Mullery," he said, and was surprised at the hollowness of his own voice.

A moment of silence from within. Then the tread of feet. Not the measured tread, but uncertain, faltering steps. Captain Mullery raised his gun, then dropped it again as Satan spoke from behind that door.

"The girl—Mary—she was there? She's all right?"

"Yeah. Sure. Open the door, Satan. Come—come! Now open the door," Mullery said again, as he heard a body lurch against it.

Twice Mullery called again before Satan answered him.

"You gave the cops the phone number here—the private phone?" And as Mullery cut in with a torrent of words, "Wait!"

Captain Mullery pleaded and Captain Mullery cursed, and talked of police discipline—and went downstairs and told a story that he could never remember afterwards to the medical examiner, and for once took the lip of a young intern.

But Captain Mullery did "wait," until—listening at the door of Bowers' private office, he heard the telephone ring.

After that he thought that he heard someone talking, but he could not be sure. Then feet crossed the room—stopped— and a chair fell over. Then feet again; lurching feet. A body against the door. The lock was turned—then Satan was in his arms—and blood was on his uniform. Mullery could not see exactly where Carpey's bullet had gone through the side of Satan's neck.

The medical examiner took one look, and said sarcastically to the young intern as he stood over Carpey Marks: "This one is mine—and the other, yours. As for the big guy with the hole in his neck, if he don't get attention quick there'll be—"

And forgetting his anger as he recognized Satan, whom he had always greatly admired, he crossed the floor hurriedly and went to work to stop the flow of the blood.

"Five minutes more and you'd have bled to death," he told Satan as he turned to the intern. "As for Bowers there—well—there was quite a struggle, and he got very badly handled—no worse than Detective Hall, though."

"No, perhaps not," said the intern as Bowers was placed on the stretcher. "But Detective Hall was just a little more systematic in—in his battle."

Satan Hall felt better the next morning, when Captain Mullery sat at his bedside and told him that Mary Rogers wanted to see him.

"And Bowers?" asked Satan. "He'll live—live to—?"

"Yes—" Mullery nodded. "He'll live—to burn."

"To burn!" Satan licked his lips. "That's part of the police system. The system! It don't seem worth the expense to keep a man alive to—to kill him. I could have saved the state a lot of money."

"You nearly did," said Mullery. "Now—tell me just what happened. Oh—I don't mean afterwards—after Carpey died. But before. It seems gospel that you went up there unarmed. How—?"

"Well," said Satan, "Bowers was to kill me with my own gun they took from me downstairs. And I told him the gun was unloaded. That gave me a moment's chance—and I took it. Shot Carpey; struck down—"

"Yes—yes, I know all that. But that gun of yours was found fully loaded where Bowers dropped it. How did you get another gun? On the level, Satan, I can't believe the story that you grabbed it from Bowers' hand. It's all right for the record—but for me—Somehow or other you got a gun in there with you.''

''No.'' Satan shook his head, but he smiled. ''They searched me too well. I went up those stairs and into that room unarmed. You see, I wanted to see Bowers—not Bowers see me. I had to see it his way. That is, the last time. Earlier in the evening he wanted to see me, so things were different. That time I went in heeled, but—''

''But—'' Mullery leaned forward eagerly.

''But I came out unarmed. Subconsciously, maybe, I had it in my mind—when I asked Lieutenant Mac about that light and the big chair. But I don't think I planned it until—well—I thought that maybe the next time I'd want to see Bowers, and have to be searched. So I shoved that gun down behind the cushion in the big chair under the light.''

''You took a chance,'' said Captain Mullery. ''It must have taken nerve to jerk that gun out, with two covering you. It must have been a tough moment.''

''Not then,'' said Satan wearily, ''not then. The tough moment was—was—It was hard not to kill Bowers when I had him like that—the hole in my neck, to go on the witness stand with. But I didn't kill him—and I don't know, Mullery, if that was strength or weakness on my part. Send Mary in.''

SATAN'S LAW

A NOVELETTE

■

CARROLL JOHN DALY

*When Detective Satan Hall Hunted Crooks,
He Made His Own Law. And Under
That Law the Sentence Was
Always—Death!*

O N E

SATAN TIPS HIS HAND

■

Detective Satan Hall sat in one of Captain Logan's stiff-backed chairs and cleaned his service guns with methodical care. His green eyes seemed even brighter; the slits they looked through even narrower as he clicked home the cartridge clips and laid the guns with a sigh upon the table. Then he smiled, but the smile seemed rather to accentuate the *V* shape of the hair upon his forehead, the sharpness of his ears, and the decidedly sardonic point to his chin.

Satan was still staring with satisfaction upon his work when Captain Logan walked in. Logan was a big man, whose shoulders had crept up—or his head settled down—so that his neck was lost somewhere between the two. He had a huge head, a large, coarse mouth, and a great, thick nose. But his eyes were small in contrast to the rest of his features. They were two round, mean little brown balls, which—if you were to accept Logan's word for it—threw abject terror into those they settled on.

Logan shot a bit of cigar from between his teeth, eyed the guns upon the table and spoke in a deep, throaty voice.

"Business, eh?" And when Satan did not answer, he

jerked a thick thumb toward the two guns and repeated. "Looks like business."

Detective Hall nodded slowly, stuck a cigarette into his mouth, put a match to the end of it, and finally said: "You might call it that."

"Rattigan?" Logan's voice was affable enough, but his eyes were rounder and smaller and meaner.

"Maybe," Satan half agreed. But there was nothing to read in his face, and Logan prided himself on reading faces.

For a minute or two Captain Logan paced the room, then he paused before Satan, spread his heavy legs far apart, took the cigar from his mouth, and pointing it at Satan's middle, said: "You've got one thing to remember, Hall; one thing to keep in mind. You're working out of this precinct now—out of my precinct. We have no favorites here—no pets here. Them that know Logan know that. You're working out of my precinct now." Logan felt that the showdown was coming and was willing to force matters.

"Sure!" Satan smiled, or at least his lips parted, and Logan imagined it was meant for a smile. "I'll remember that, Logan. You remember it, too. I'm working out of the precinct—not in it."

"Yeah." Logan stroked one of his flabby chins. "The commissioner's pet, they call you. One precinct after another." A sneer came into Logan's voice. "The hard-boiled dick makes good where the system fails! The Lone Wolf of the Department, the papers call you. But if you knew what some of the boys call you! A dirty, rotten spy. A two-timing—" Logan had leaned over the desk now; his thick lips had parted and were quivering; his eyes were round points of twin steel. When Logan started to have his say he had it out. He was a hard man; a tough man; a brutal, unrelenting man—yet he paused.

There was something in Satan's face that stopped him. For the life of him Logan couldn't tell what it was; wouldn't admit it if he could tell. But for a moment he saw all that he had heard about Satan; all that had given Satan his name on the force. He didn't think that Satan's face had changed, though it must have. He couldn't see that Satan's lips had moved any. He thought it must be Satan's eyes. Not the outward, physical appearance of them, but something back in their sinister, green depths. But Logan knew that he had looked through and behind those eyes and seen something that he had never seen in a man before.

Logan was a brave man. There was nothing behind those green balls that struck him with fear. Logan feared no man. At first he couldn't lay a name to it, then he thought it must be horror. Anyway, Logan drew back with a soft curse, and rubbed a hand across a moist forehead. He felt as if he had looked down into the depths of hell. Sinister, cruel, malignant, unnameable things had glared out of those eyes at him. And now Satan was coming to his feet. Very slowly he was stretching his six feet odd above the floor.

Then a great hand with long, delicate fingers shot out, rested for a moment on the guns upon the table. Logan's eyes bulged. Satan seemed to make a single motion from the table toward his coat—just a single quick motion—and both guns were gone and Satan's arms hung at his sides. But Logan knew—knew, just as if Satan had thrown back his coat and shown him, that both those guns were now parked beneath each armpit.

Satan was speaking.

"So that's what some of them call me, eh?" Satan was

slowly caressing a pointed chin. "Some of them, Logan—some of them." And leaning suddenly forward—"You, for instance."

"I'm only repeating what I've heard," Logan said, somewhat stiffly. He would have given a month's pay to say that they were his thoughts, but the words would not come.

"I see. Well—I'll be moving," Satan went on slowly, as Logan, somewhat recovered, set those gimlet eyes upon Satan in a final halfhearted effort to stare him down.

As Satan turned toward the door Logan stretched out a hand and placed it on his shoulder.

"After all, you're a cop, Satan. Like Patrolman Shay, myself, the Inspector, even. You got certain privileges that the rest of us can't quite understand. You've got information through the commissioner's secret channel that I don't have access to. I've given you the run of the house, all the information you wanted. It wouldn't help me or the boys none if you pulled off a—a stunt right under our noses. You might—might—" Logan gulped. "Give a guy a break."

"All right." Satan nodded very slowly. "I'm a cop—just a cop, and it isn't pleasant or profitable to step over authority. I'll tell you this. It's Rattigan and Gunner Swartz, and someone—someone else."

"Someone else!" Logan let his little eyes wander about the ceiling. "You can't do anything with Rattigan. I've raked him over the coals a dozen or more times. He's got connections; got a good mouthpiece. He's a high-class racketeer."

"You didn't get him for the right thing."

"And the right thing?" Logan was slightly sarcastic.

"Murder. An accomplice to murder."

"And the real murderer?" Logan was puffing on his cigar now. There was indifference in his voice, but his little gimlet eyes never left the green, sinister ones of Satan. He felt that the long-awaited break was coming.

"It isn't pleasant," Satan spoke very softly, "but you've asked for a 'break' and I'll give it to you." A long finger came out and pounded slowly against Logan's chest. "Captain Logan, put your house in order."

Logan laughed hoarsely.

"You're not referring to those apartments that I easily explained before the commission!"

"Your rich brother." Satan sneered. "But there are some things your rich brother won't be able to shoulder for you."

"And they?"

"A rotten conscience, Logan. The dead eyes of the women who killed themselves. The living accusations of mothers and sisters. Oh, don't grin. You've been a copper long enough; you've played the game long enough to know the truth. You can't get away with it."

Logan gripped Satan by the shoulder and swung him viciously around. He didn't think of what was back of the green eyes now. Anger shook his whole body. Hate blazed in his little brown eyes. He shot the words through the side of his mouth. He didn't bother to deny Satan's accusation. He didn't try to laugh it off. They were alone in that room. He spoke out his mind—at least, enough of it.

"It's not a new story." He had hard work making the words articulate. "But it's the first time it's been spoken out like that. It's been hinted before; gone into before. There was—" And Logan stopped short, biting his lip.

"Yeah—" said Satan, "I know. Clarey and Cohen. Honest cops, both of them—and they died hard. Cohen, the night you were dining with Inspector Frank. Clarey, while you were at your sister's in Peekskill. Rattigan and Swartz gunned him out. All very clever, Logan. But, in the end, all very futile."

Logan had stepped forward now and fastened the thick fingers of his left hand tight into the lapels of Satan's coat as he put those little round eyes hard on Satan's green ones. His voice shook when he spoke; every word breathed a threat—a threat that Satan must know was not an idle one.

"Suppose it were all true—every word of it, what then? What would you do? What could you do? Knowledge and evidence are two different things. I'm marking you, Satan. I'm looking at you, Satan."

"Well—you can keep those eyes for frightening women and children. You asked me to talk out, and I did. There'll be evidence. A witness who saw Cohen die."

"All right. All right." Saliva ran over the edge of Logan's thick lips. "Remember, Satan, I'm often asked to dine with Inspector Frank, and my sister at Peekskill is glad to see me anytime. She entertains a lot. Good, sound, substantial country people. I don't know why you talked. You're just a fool, I suppose."

"Maybe," Satan shrugged his shoulders, "it isn't pleasant for the force. It gets me in the stomach every time I read about a copper gone wrong. It shouldn't, because there aren't an honester bunch of men as a whole in any profession." With a single downward motion Satan knocked Logan's fingers from his coat. "You know the racket, Logan—you know the law. Not the law of the state, but the law of the criminal." Satan jerked a hand forward and pounded a finger against Logan's chest. "The finger's on you, Logan," he said simply. "The finger's on you. I'm out to get you, Logan."

Then he turned abruptly on his heel and passed out of the little rear room and by the police desk.

Logan hesitated a moment, wiped his forehead with a big linen handkerchief, looked at the phone once or twice and finally, lifting the receiver, gave a number to the operator in a low, hollow voice.

"It's me, Rattigan," he said softly. "He's leaving now. Is Swartz ready?"

"Ready, boss," came a whispered answer. "The car's around the corner."

Captain Logan sighed easily as he dropped the receiver back on the hook. Detective Satan Hall would be attended to.

TWO

MACHINE-GUNNED

■

Satan stood for some time chatting idly with the lieutenant on the bench, then he passed out under the light, to the street. He cupped a hand and felt a few drops of rain spatter into it. Turning up his coat collar, he proceeded slowly down the street.

Just why had he tipped his hand to Captain Logan? There were two reasons. One was the hope that Logan might pack up and leave the country. The Department could smother that, and perhaps, after all, it was the best. Satan's life was the force—the hunting of men—loyalty to the badge which he wore. Neither friendship, money, nor threats could drive him from his purpose. That was why, after ten years as the most relentless hunter of men in the system, he was still a first-grade detective. The other reason! Well—Logan might be frightened into some kind of action. Action! Satan's right hand slipped beneath his coat. He liked action.

At the corner Satan ran into Patrolman Shay—three years on the force. A young man soft of skin, the enthusiasm for his job still sparkling in his clear blue eyes, still in the strong eager fingers that gripped his nightstick. And now Satan saw the shadows beneath those eyes; noted the way teeth drew in the lower lip. He stretched out a hand when Shay would have passed on; held him so a moment; looked straight into the soft blue eyes. Satan was like that once. New—enthusiastic—raw. Ready to rush anyplace for the honor—the glory of the force.

Patrolman Shay reddened slightly but did not speak.

"Anything to say?" Satan said abruptly.

"About what?" The red deepened and the upper teeth again took in the lower lip.

"About Cohen," Satan said almost viciously. "Stabbed to death in a back alley. A fine fellow, Cohen. A straight shooter, Cohen. A guy who knew too much. And you were off your beat; dragged off your beat by Logan."

"Afore God, Hall, I didn't know." There was a touch of horror in Shay's face. "Logan took me off. It was his order—his authority. I had to go, and now—"

"Now—" said Satan, "are you willing to go on the stand and swear to that?"

"I can't—I can't," Shay stammered. "I reported as on duty. Logan fixed it on the books. When Cohen 'went out,' Logan thought it would look bad, my being off the beat. He told me to say nothing—more than hinted he'd deny his part in taking me off. They wouldn't believe me, Hall. They'd break me. I can't do it! My father was killed on the force. My mother couldn't stand the disgrace that—"

"You can't hide a yellow streak behind the name of your mother," Satan said brutally. "You may be broken and you may not—but you'll be a man. The hooks are in Logan. I need your testimony. Your father wanted you to be a cop; your mother bred it into your bones. And now what? You're one of twenty thousand—twenty thousand of the finest men that ever walked the streets. Twenty thousand fine men, whose names stink to high heaven because of a few—a few like Logan—a few like you, who are puppets in Logan's hands.''

"Don't—don't!" Shay half turned his head. "It's too late. I'm in it now. And, Hall—" Shay looked furtively up and down the street, "they've been watching you. They're afraid of you. They're marking you." And in a voice that Hall barely caught, "Logan's going—going to kill you. And you can't get a single thing on Logan."

"Not a thing on him, eh?" Satan's green eyes sparkled slightly. "But it's possible—just possible—that I might kill Logan first."

And Satan moved quickly to the protection of a pole. Over his shoulder he saw the shadow of the car; his sharp ears had caught the sudden roar of the motor as a foot pushes in the clutch and advances the gas.

It happened. Above the roaring motor were the sharp, staccato notes of a machine gun. He saw the black, belching nose of it from between curtains. He saw the white face; the ratlike eyes and mouth below a peaked cap. Satan fired once. Just a sudden quick movement of his right hand, a single roar and a single spit of flame.

The machine gun came to sudden silence. The white face seemed to be a shade whiter. Then red appeared over a thick lower lip, and the face disappeared behind the curtain.

The clutch was released, the roar of the motor took on life, and Satan stood on the sidewalk and emptied both his guns into the rear of the fleeing car. He cursed softly. Then, as the big car suddenly swerved, he smiled.

There was a crash as the juggernaut mounted the sidewalk, turned suddenly, just missing the stone balustrade of a brownstone front, careened across the sidewalk again, and striking a fire hydrant, jumped into the air and turned upon its side. Satan nodded as he watched it, and mechanically shoved fresh clips into his guns.

Logan was on the street now. A half dozen officers, hurriedly slipping into their coats—guns in their hands— were running by him, toward the overturned car. But Satan was kneeling beside Patrolman Shay, looking into his eyes. Satan had lived close to death and he knew. No coroner had to tell him. Shay was dead.

Satan straightened and half lifted his hat. A shadow came from behind him. He recognized Inspector Frank, saw him kneel beside Shay, lift Shay's hand and let it fall to the pavement again.

"Twenty-four, and dead," Inspector Frank said in a low voice. "What a bad break for the boy—what a bad break for his mother!"

Satan spoke half to himself, but Inspector Frank caught the words and puzzled over them for some time.

"What a good break for the boy—and what a fine break for his mother," was all that Satan said as he turned and walked toward the overturned car.

Two men were dead. The man with the machine gun had been shot straight through the mouth. There was a bullet right through the back of the driver's head. Another gangster lay unconscious in the wreckage; a fourth had been thrown clear and was writhing on the sidewalk. Captain Logan was looking down at him, telling a sergeant he'd watch him.

Satan nodded down at the twisting gangster and said: "Gunner Swartz. I wonder why he didn't work the type-writer." Then he turned and watched the cops drag the other man from the wreck.

"A good boy—Shay," he thought. "A good boy, swept up in the maelstrom of corruption by a single man."

Satan never posed as a super-detective. He admitted quite frankly that he wouldn't recognize a clue if he met it face-to-face. He didn't believe in hunches. If he wanted information he went straight to one of two dozen stool pigeons and bought it. He believed in breaks and waited for them. Waited for them just so long, and then went out and stirred up his own. But he did believe in instinct. He didn't put it down to long association with the criminal. He put it down to instinct, and called it that. Living close to death, instinct warned him of danger. That is the only explanation of why he turned suddenly to face Logan— face Logan and Gunner Swartz, who lay upon the sidewalk. Gunner Swartz, whom Satan had distinctly heard Captain Logan tell a police sergeant he would watch.

And Logan was watching the gunner. Watching him with eager, unblinking little brown eyes. Watching him as Swartz steadied his shaking right hand with his left, and drew a bead about the middle of Satan's back with a jet-black German Luger.

As Satan turned, Swartz fired. That turn saved Satan's life. Even in his condition, Gunner Swartz could not have missed such a perfect target as Satan's broad shoulders, not ten feet away from him. Gunner Swartz fired just once. The heavy-caliber bullet tore through the sleeve of Satan's half-raised arm, and leaving the tiniest red crevice across Satan's forehead passed on through his hat.

That was all of that. Gunner Swartz was chain lightning with a gun. But it is doubtful, even if he were on his feet and in the pink of condition, that he would have fired a second shot.

Satan's hand made a single sweep. There was a roar, and Gunner Swartz was dead, shot through the head.

"That's one for Clarey," Satan muttered, and he smiled.

For a moment Satan looked down at the dead body, the smoking gun still in his hand. Then he swung slowly on his heels and faced Captain Logan, those green eyes boring into the mean little brown ones.

Logan looked straight at that hard, pointed face; at the gun that those long strong fingers held—at a gun that was slowly rising; rising until the black snub nose had drawn a bead where an ordinary man would wear his heart.

Logan gasped once, tried to step back, and felt the stone balustrade against his shoulders. He opened his mouth to speak but no words came. He had seen death in a man's face before. He saw it now in the face of Satan. Saw it mostly in the hand that held that gun; in the long finger that caressed the trigger; in the nose of the automatic itself. Then, as the sweat rolled down his forehead, a voice spoke. A distant, faraway voice that Logan did not recognize, then realized that the voice was his own.

"That—that," Logan's voice was saying, "will be murder."

And Satan grinned, and his green eyes shone, and the gun dropped to his side. The spell was broken. Inspector Frank had laid a hand upon his arm and was talking to him.

Satan nodded, and crossing the street with the inspector, passed through the iron grating of the door of a speakeasy. They found seats in a dingy side booth.

THE HOLD OF THE PAST

■

Inspector Frank was a tall, loosely constructed man. He didn't believe in wasting words. He put his elbows on the table and said: "Satan, what's the racket? Logan suspects that you're hunting up information for the investigation. I don't believe that. Logan would like to know where you stand. He wanted me to find out."

"He knows now." Satan moved his head as if it were on a wire. "He asked for the truth and got it."

Inspector Frank stiffened.

"I've done twenty-two years with the department. Logan's a good officer. We've all had temptations, and there are irregularities, of course. It's part of the system. But he's an efficient officer. He has a record for cleaning up his district that stands out in the city. Logan has friends who'd stick to him in trouble," and very slowly—"who'd have to stick to him. Me, for instance. What do you think of me, Satan?"

"I don't think. I know. You're the straightest man on the force."

"That's it." Frank nodded slowly. "The straightest man

on the force. I saw the possibilities in you years back,
Satan, and dragged you off the pavement and put you in
plainclothes. Now—'' Inspector Frank leaned far over the
table, ''I'm not making a squawk; I'm not asking for
favors. I'm simply stating facts. If you get Logan—you
get me too.''

''You!'' Satan straightened. The thing seemed impossible.

''Yes. It goes back some years. But it's there just the
same. It would break me the same as if it were yesterday.''
Inspector Frank laughed harshly. ''Break Logan and you
break me. You see, the past sometimes remains the present.''

Satan's eyes became two slits.

''If Logan were dead,'' he said slowly, ''he couldn't
talk.''

''That,'' said Frank, ''would be murder. You're a killer,
Satan, but you don't go in for murder. Besides—'' and
hunched shoulders shrugged, ''Logan's a clever man.
You've been at Rattigan's Park Avenue Casino; you've
seen that safe. In the third drawer from the top, on the left,
there's an envelope nicely labeled *Inspector Frank*. I saw it
placed there and knew what it meant. Now—how big is it?
Just what do you want Logan for?''

''I want him,'' said Satan slowly, ''for the murder of
Detective Cohen. For the murder of Cohen while Logan
was having dinner with you.''

Inspector Frank prided himself on his poker face. Emo-
tion never showed there. But now that impenetrable coun-
tenance became readable. Fear, disgust, horror chased one
another in quick succession across his face.

''I can't believe it,'' he said. And after a moment's
pause, ''I can't believe it.''

''You've got to,'' said Satan. ''Logan dined with you.
Did he leave? Did he tell you you had to cover him on
something—on murder?''

"Good God! No—not murder." Frank was on his feet, leaning on the table, breathing heavily. Satan cautioned him not to speak so loud. After a bit Frank said: "Yes, Logan did leave me. But he's done that before. He was a careful man. He had to see Rattigan."

"He used you because your reputation for honesty and straight shooting is the best on the force. And he didn't go to see Rattigan, but went straight to that alley—met Cohen and stabbed him to death."

"But why Cohen?"

"Because Cohen was working with me. Because Cohen had discovered that goods were being fenced through Jake Hearn. Because Cohen was to meet Mattie Hearn, Jake's daughter, and she was to talk—talk about Rattigan and Logan, though Cohen didn't suspect Logan then. That's why he died like he did—smiling. He still trusted his captain."

"But—Logan and—murder!"

"Yes. Logan and murder. Jake Hearn told Logan of the meeting of Cohen and Mattie. He didn't know that Mattie was going to talk; he simply thought Mattie would work Cohen into the racket. But Logan knew, and Logan killed him. Cohen told me he was to meet Mattie."

"Can you prove this?" Inspector Frank's hand clenched.

"Not a word of it," Satan said, truthfully enough. "I knew that Cohen was to hear something from Mattie—he told me that. She was to tell him the name of the big gun behind Rattigan. I knew it would be Logan, but Cohen didn't—else he'd have died with a gun in his hand. Cohen was quick."

"I can't believe it," Inspector Frank said dully. "Crooked, yes—but that Logan would go to murder, no."

"You know the racket. It always leads to murder. Logan had to kill, and he killed."

"Logan was gone half an hour—maybe, forty minutes." Inspector Frank was figuring mentally. "You prove that, Satan—and evidence against me or no evidence against me, I'll go on the stand and swear that Logan left me."

"No." Satan shook his head. "I'll do what I can for you, Frank—but Cohen was working for me. Clarey was working with me. We don't want others dragged into it. Just Logan and Rattigan. Why not take a vacation? In Mexico, maybe—until we see what breaks."

"No!" Frank's lips set tightly and his eyes knitted. "I've made my bed and I'll lie in it. I've never taken a run-out powder yet. I've been an honest cop for fifteen years." And thoughtfully, "There isn't any past in crime— just a present. I'll help you if it's true. How will you prove it?"

"By the evidence of an eyewitness to the murder."

"Someone saw it?"

"Yes. I found a glove in that alley, under a window. Mattie Hearn saw the murder. She's disappeared. Everyone in the underworld has orders from Rattigan to find her. But if I find her she'll talk. She loved Cohen. I've got to find her first."

"Yes, yes—that's right." Inspector Frank was talking with his head in his hands. "Logan asked me to put the dragnet out for Mattie Hearn. He—he—You think he wants to ship her out of the country?" But although those were Frank's words they were not his thoughts. Satan voiced his thoughts.

"They want to kill her," he said simply. "They wanted to kill me, and got Shay. Logan has to clean up the books, and only death will do it."

"God!" said Frank, "I could strangle him with my own hands. To think I covered him for murder—murder of one of my own boys!" And again, in a weak voice, "I don't believe it. I can't believe it. Logan says the Sicilian gang killed Cohen, and that Mattie Hearn will be found with a wire around her neck, strangled to death, like those other girls.''

"That's right." Satan came to his feet and put a hand on the inspector's shoulder. "If Logan finds her, the wire will be there all right. I thought I'd let you see how it is. Take care of yourself.''

Inspector Frank raised his hand and pressed the button as Satan left. Then he ordered a shot of rye and drank it neat.

"God!" he cried out inside himself, "if I'd only kept the record clean!" Inspector Frank was seeing the end of a glorious career. But he had no misgivings or doubts as to his actions. He'd take the murderer of one of his boys down with him. The past, that he thought he had buried many years before, had crept up on him.

F O U R

RATTIGAN GETS SLAPPED DOWN

■

Satan walked down to Sixth Avenue, hopped a taxi and ordered the driver straight to Jake Hearn's little pawnshop. He settled back in the seat and thought. He knew Jake fairly well, and his daughter, Mattie, slightly. And he felt that, like most of their race, Jake and Mattie in trouble would be drawn very tightly together. He felt certain that Jake would know Mattie's hideout—had even suggested it. Satan looked at his watch. It was exactly nine o'clock.

As he neared the shop Satan spoke to the driver.

"Stop here," he said. "I'll walk."

As he walked toward the shop Satan paused and stepped into a doorway. The back of the big black car before him attracted his attention. He peered at it closely through the drizzle. The license plates; the peculiar thickness of the glass; the straight, stiff back of the man behind the wheel. Then he nodded to himself, retraced his steps to the side street, passed down a few doors, entered an apartment, pressed a couple of bells at random, and when the latch clicked, opened the door and stepped inside.

Satan moved fast, yet the measured, steady tread of his

feet never gave the impression of hurrying. Now he passed down the ill-smelling hallway, carefully avoided the rubbish in the back, found the rear door and entered the court beyond.

A couple of wooden fences gave little trouble to his long legs, and at length he found himself in the court behind Hearn's shop. He could have entered it directly from the alley but he didn't want to come that way. Someone might be guarding the rear entrance and he wanted his visit to be a complete surprise.

There was a light in the back room of the shop; a light that shone plainly through the worn pale shade with the many rents in it. The shade waved slightly, too, where a pane of glass was broken in the musty window. Satan grinned. He knew that Jake was very rich; must be very rich, since he had been fencing furs by the vanload. And he knew too, though he could not prove it, that Logan's protection had made Jake Hearn the most daring fence on the avenue.

Voices came to Satan through the broken glass. No words exactly; just a mumbled drone. He drew close to the window and listened.

"Mattie's got to take a trip, Jake—free—all expenses paid and the highest class travel. We'll do things right for her. This dick, Satan, wants to make trouble."

"She's went, I tell you," a squeaky voice answered, which Satan recognized as that of the fence. "By boat she went out of the country."

Satan found a rent in the curtain and glued his eye to it as the first voice spoke again.

"What boat? To what country?"

"I don't know. Just her note. It said, 'I have left the country on a boat. Mattie.'"

"Where's the note?"

"I burned it, like you tell me to keep nothing."

Jake Hearn was a hard man to pin down. But now that Satan had a fair view of the room he saw that Jake's questioner was a harder man to avoid.

He had a sharp, evil face, with a long nose that earlier in life had been battered slightly to one side. It gave his eyes a peculiar twist, as he had the habit of centering his gaze on the end of his nose. He was wearing a hundred-dollar suit, a twelve-dollar hat, and sported light yellow spats above brilliant tan shoes.

The man was Rattigan, the racketeer, and the stamp of the gutter was on his face, in his shifty eyes, and in the twist of his lips when he talked. Satan had been right. The big black car out front was Rattigan's. There were two hard-looking men with Rattigan.

Rattigan came close to the trembling little fence, crouching in the big chair. Jake Hearn's eyes watched Rattigan and the two men who leaned against the door which led to the shop. He rubbed his hands together and made chuckling little noises back in his throat.

"She didn't leave by a boat. That's flat." Rattigan shot the words through his teeth. "She didn't leave at all." And twisting his lips and narrowing his eyes. "So you won't tell me where she is!"

"I tell you she's gone. She—"

"Stand up when you talk to me." Rattigan fairly bellowed the words, so that his companions glanced apprehensively toward the front of the shop.

Jake Hearn came to his feet. His shifty eyes sought escape, and one of the men moved to the side door.

"Now—" said Rattigan, "where is she?"

"I tell you she—"

Rattigan closed a hamlike hand, let the fist fly forward

and struck the fence flush on the mouth. It was a brutal blow. Jake Hearn was not expecting it, but even if he were, it would have made little difference. Rattigan stood six feet tall and weighed a hundred and ninety pounds, while the little pawnbroker was an old man, bent at the shoulders, his slender frame covered with parchmentlike skin.

Jake fell back into the chair. The chair slid across the room, twisted slightly, balanced for a moment on its back legs, then crashed against the wall.

"Well—" Rattigan crossed the room and glared down at Hearn. "Where's Mattie?"

"No, no, no." All the fence's shrewdness was gone. He was frightened now, in a panic. "I can't tell you. You'll kill her. You'll murder her. She—"

"Stand up when you talk to me," Rattigan said again, and the two men laughed. "No—" And to the rougher looking of his friends, Rattigan said, "You, Joe—hold him up. I have an idea Mr. Jake Hearn is going to be glad to talk—if he can."

The man called Joe crossed the room, lifted the wizened little form out of the chair, held him on his feet as Rattigan closed his fist again. And there was an interruption.

The shade shot up with a snap, an arm came through the broken pane in the window—and Satan spoke, his gun moving slowly.

"I think that will be about all of that, Mr. Rattigan. Unlock the window and open it, Joe."

Three pairs of eyes sought that window at once. The little fence dropped back in the chair and buried his head in his hands. Three hands hesitated, half moving to armpits when Satan spoke again.

"I think you're making a mistake, boys. It's Satan talking. Now, Joe—open the window."

* * *

There was no order of "Hands up!" There was nothing melodramatic in Satan's words. Yet three pairs of hands shot into the air. Joe walked toward the window. The name of Satan had been enough. Rattigan and his bodyguard knew that Satan shot first and explained afterward.

"Keep a little to the side, Joe." Satan's voice was soft and low. "I like to look at your friends. You wouldn't want me to shoot a hole in you to look through. That's right!" as the lock clicked loose. "Now—my gun is only an inch or two further back. Fine!" And as the window creaked up on long unused pulleys Satan threw a foot over the sill and climbed into the room.

"Back against the wall!" Satan ordered Joe and the other thug as he faced Rattigan. He stood very close to the racketeer, his green eyes burning balls of fire.

"We're all armed, Rattigan," he said. "Three against one." And he shoved his automatic easily under his left armpit and let both hands fall to his sides. "All armed—all even." He spread his empty hands wide open. "Rattigan, the feared gunman—the big racketeer! Rattigan, the rat who hid behind an ashcan with Swartz and shot Clarey in the back. Three to one, Rattigan—all armed. Why don't you do your stuff?"

Rattigan's finger twisted at his side. His tongue came out and he licked at his lips. He tried to cast furtive glances back at his two companions.

"Don't do it, boss," Joe warned from behind. "Don't you see? He's come to—to kill you."

Three to one. Three gangsters. Three gunmen. One the most feared gangster on the avenue. All armed; all known to use a gun; all willing to shoot it out anytime, anyplace— and Satan's hands were empty, both empty, both hanging loosely at his sides. These men who lived by the gun and expected to die by it. But they knew Satan. They knew his reputation. They remembered that Little Ricco had stood so, facing Satan. Little Ricco, the fastest drawing gunman the city had ever bred. And Ricco had smiled and reached for a gun, and died with it half drawn from its holster.

They remembered, too, the Ballast brothers. Quick, viciously cruel gangsters who feared neither man nor devil. Satan had been walking from the room when they drew together. And they had died—both of them—on the floor of their own nightclub. Rattigan shuddered slightly. He had been there that night; he had seen the little round holes directly in the center of their foreheads. Almost as if Satan had taken a compass and drawn a circle, then placed the bullet right in the center of it.

So Rattigan never moved; only his fingers twisted at his side. His lips quivered, and his two men stretched their hands higher toward the ceiling.

"So you won't play, you dirty rat." Satan leaned closer to Rattigan, so that his hot breath was on his face. "You'd rather beat up old men. All right." And little Jake sat up in his chair and gasped. Satan was pulling the act he had become famous for in the underworld.

He simply raised his left hand and smacked Rattigan across the face with it. The blow did not seem a particularly hard one and Satan's hand was open, but it rocked Rattigan. Then Satan raised his right hand and smacked him on the other cheek. Just a moment's pause—and it happened. Satan's closed right fist started some place below his knees, flashed up and landed on the point of Rattigan's chin.

Without a word Rattigan folded up like a jackknife and sank to the floor.

Jake Hearn gasped as he wiped the blood from his lips. He knew Satan. He feared Satan. He had even seen him

perform his favorite trick of "slapping" desperadoes down.
But Jake Hearn had never expected to see the day when
Satan or anyone else would dare to so treat Rattigan.
Rattigan, whom the biggest men on the avenue feared.
Rattigan, who could get a boy out of the Tombs almost
before the wagon had dumped him there. Rattigan, who—
But Satan was talking.

"Take him out, boys, and throw him in the car," Satan
said to the gaping gunmen. "Then on your way—unless,"
those green eyes slanted, "either of you object to the way
I treated the big boss."

"We don't intend to get mussy." Joe faltered the words.
"But we're armed. You—you know that." Joe had visions
of a bullet in the back when he left the shop. "You
want—our guns?"

"No." Satan shook his head. "I never interfere with the
law, and I know you both have licenses duly signed by a
magistrate, allowing you to carry them." And narrowing
his eyes, "If you want to use them on the way out, that's
all right with me."

Rattigan was coming to and cursing under his breath as
they helped him through the curtain and across the shop
toward the front door.

"I'll get you for this, Satan. I'll kill you for this!" he
said over and over as Satan stood by the little curtain and
heard the front door click closed.

Then he stepped back into the little room behind the
shop. Stood listening a moment, half expecting that a
fusillade of shots might be fired into the shop. There was
the roar of a motor, the hum of gears, and the black car
shot from the curb.

Rattigan was worried. He trusted his two companions;
had faith in them. But they were only human, and he knew

that the story would get around. Also, that it would lose nothing in the telling.

"I'll get him for this—the lousy, yellow dick," Rattigan cursed. And his conversation all had to do with the sudden and violent death of Detective Satan Hall.

"Sure, boss—sure!" His two friends agreed with him and patted him on the back, and explained how they saw Satan strike him when he turned his head. But over Rattigan's head they exchanged glances, and each had the same thought. Rattigan, the feared Rattigan, was slipping.

FIVE

THE LAW OF THE GUN

■

Back in the shop, Satan turned to Jake Hearn. Jake had recovered now and his shrewd little brain was working again. He had been saved from the brutality of Rattigan, the racketeer—but was he now in for a worse time? He watched Satan from the sides of shifty eyes and wondered if Logan would protect him. Then he wondered if Logan had sent Rattigan, and he wished he had been satisfied with the money he had saved and had returned to Poland.

Jake Hearn bathed his face carefully in the sink, and bemoaned the greed which had kept him in the city.

"Well," Satan questioned, "where's Mattie?"

"She took a boat and—"

"Yeah—" Satan nodded. "I heard that one and don't like it any better than Rattigan did. It's not my line to slap down old men, Jake. I'm not going to put the hooks into you. I'm just going to talk words—real words. You're in a tough spot. If you tell them where Mattie is, they'll bump her off. If you don't, they'll take you for a ride—a one-way ride, Jake.

"They'll find Mattie anyway. The dragnet is out for her.

You know the ropes, Jake. I don't have to tell you. A body in the park; a bit of wire around her neck—like those other girls. Black eyes—glassy, Jake. Young body—cold, Jake. Mattie—your kid. Your kid, whom you let be murdered. Your kid, who—''

"Don't—don't!" Jake cried over and over as he clutched at Satan's hand and held it tightly in his two parchmentlike claws. "She's a good girl, Satan—a fine girl. All I've got since her mother died. You won't let them. You'll save her. You'll—''

"I can't." Satan held the old man half erect as he tried to fall on his knees at Satan's feet. "I can't unless I know where she is. Rattigan's through. Logan has the skids under him. If Mattie talks out, they won't bother you any more, Jake.''

"But me—me!" Jake moaned. "If I take a jolt, what of Mattie then? There might be things I've done. Things—''

"I don't want you, Jake. I don't want Rattigan and Logan for stolen furs. I'm not interested in your racket. I want them for murder, Jake. Mattie saw Cohen killed. You won't be in it. I want her to put the finger on Logan.'' Satan clenched his hands. "I've got the evidence. I only need Mattie. They won't bother you any more. They won't be able to bother you any more. I'm going to fry them, Jake. Clarey was working with me. Cohen was my pal. They've got to fry, Jake—they've got to fry.''

"Yeah—yeah." Jake had a faraway look in his eyes. "They gotta fry. Mattie's got to turn the trick. Mattie—'' And suddenly, as his eyes widened with fear, "She didn't see it. She wasn't there. She—''

"Then why did she disappear—why did you hide her out? Why has Logan got the dragnet out for her? I tell you she was in the room by the alley. She was looking out the window. She saw Cohen killed. They'll find her, Jake.

They'll rake the city with a fine-toothed comb. They'll watch your friends. They'll—''

Satan paused. The old man was trembling. Satan wondered. ''They'll watch your friends!'' That was the line that got Jake. Those were the words that cut deep. Cut deep, because they were the truth. These Jews stuck together. They protected each other. The thing was logical, reasonable. Mattie was being hidden away by one of Jake's friends. Who were they? Which one? Satan should have thought of that before. Had Logan thought of it? Probably he had. Crook—murderer—yes. But Logan was an efficient worker. Jake's friends! That was it.

''Your friends—they'll find her, Jake. Will you talk?''

''I don't know. I don't know!'' Jake moaned, and then suddenly, ''I can't. They'll kill me.''

Satan shrugged his shoulders and turned toward the door.

''All right, Jake. It's your funeral—not mine. Or maybe it's just Mattie's. You know, Jake. There's a slab—just a cold marble slab in the morgue waiting for Mattie.''

Jake followed Satan out into the shop, clutched at his coat when his hand rested on the knob of the door.

''Suppose—suppose I want to talk, what then? Where can I find you? I might—might find out where Mattie is.''

Satan looked down at the old man. He knew what was in his mind. Jake was going to put out a few strings—find out how close Logan or Rattigan were to finding Mattie. If the thing was hot—looked bad—Jake would talk to Satan. If it didn't look as if they'd find Mattie, Jake would chance it. Instinctively, Satan knew his man. Jake would not talk—not just then.

''Headquarters, Jake. Ask for O'Brien, nights. Sullivan, daytime.''

"And the message? O'Brien don't know. He might talk to Logan. Logan has a way of—"

"Yeah." Satan nodded vigorously. "Just say, 'There's a guy who wants to talk.' I'll know, and give you a jingle here at the shop."

For a long moment Satan hesitated. Then he jerked his gray Stetson tightly down over his forehead, moved a gun from a shoulder holster to an overcoat pocket, and swinging open the shop door, passed out into the night.

Dark, deserted streets; dark doorways. A dismal, rainswept night. Satan sniffed disdainfully as he kept close to the gutter. The slapping down of Rattigan would rankle in that gunman's chest. He would plan vengeance, but would he act on it? Would others of his kind—of his mob—care to act on it? Would they gang him there on the empty street?

"Rats—all rats," Satan muttered to himself as he walked. Yet his right hand caressed the butt of the heavy service automatic in his pocket. Rats were dangerous when cornered.

Satan jumped a taxi and rode straight to police headquarters. He didn't waste time hunting up his information. Downstairs he leaned over the desk and spoke to the bent-shouldered, gray-haired Sergeant Oberheim.

"How long will it take to get me a list of Jake Hearn's friends? He's a pawnbroker over—"

Oberheim grinned.

"I know," he said. "It'll take me just as long as it'll take to open that cabinet over there and lift it out."

"Ready, huh?" Satan stroked his chin. "Fixed it up for Logan, eh?"

"Yeah. Captain Logan." Oberheim returned from the cabinet with three legal pages closely clamped together. "The names with the check marks are 'pretty close friends.' The lads with the X's—kisses—after them," Oberheim grinned, "are relatives. Them with the lines under them are known to be shady. Double lines are guys who have been in trouble with the cops."

"Quite complete." Satan glanced through the three pages.

"Too complete." Oberheim ran a finger down a card index. "Some of them probably just speaking acquaintances, but Logan wanted it that way. We've got a surprising lot of stuff about Jake Hearn, too. Amazing, considering he's never been in the lineup." And after a moment's hesitation, "Someone likes him a lot, I guess."

"I guess so." Satan nodded, shoved the list in his pocket. And he thought, as he left the room, that would be Logan's way. It would look okay if Mattie was found strangled someplace in the city. It wouldn't be a bad story anyway, from Logan's point of view. Logan would have the same purpose in looking for Mattie that Satan did, as far as the law was concerned. Mattie was a witness to Cohen's murder. It would be natural for Logan to find her dead.

Satan's lips set grimly as he leaned against the corridor wall under a light and looked the names over. He had to find Mattie. Yes, he had to find Mattie—alive. If she was found dead, then what? The whole case would fall. Frank wouldn't talk unless he was sure it was murder on Logan's part. And if Mattie was found dead! Satan's sharp, white teeth bit into a thin lower lip. He wondered if he would kill Logan then, and if he did—would it be murder? Murder! Yes, in the eyes of the state. But what of the other law? The law that the criminal recognized; the law that Satan had even come to recognize. The only law the criminal knew. The only law the criminal feared. The law of the gun! The criminal's law. Satan's law.

SIX

LOGAN GOES TO KILL

∎

Satan told O'Brien where to get in touch with him if a call came in; then he left the building, jumped a taxi and rode directly to Logan's precinct. It might be a good thing to keep an eye on Logan. It wouldn't take Logan long to cover that list; not with the mob he'd have working on it.

Satan didn't enter the precinct. A thin, emaciated, shabby little figure with a cap pulled down and a cigarette hanging from his lips stepped from the shadows and nudged Satan as he passed him.

Satan paid the driver, looked up and down the block, then followed the bent figure to the corner, around it and entered the doorway of a tenement. The man spoke without removing his cigarette.

"Logan took a cab and went to Jake Hearn's. I spent my last four bits tailing him. He's there now. He was alone. I spent my—"

"Yeah—" Satan shoved a bill into the eager outstretched fingers and left the tenement. Ten minutes later he reached Jake's shop, found the door open and walked in.

A voice was speaking. It was Logan's. There was

elation in it. Logan said, clear and loud: "That's fine. That's great. I'll be right over and—and see to the removal."

As Satan parted the curtains and entered the little back room Logan laid down the phone. He frowned slightly as he saw Satan and let his cigar run across his mouth. Then he smiled.

"See what you can do with the old goat, Satan," he said easily and friendly. "I've got a feeling that Mattie could tell something about the murder of Cohen." Then he shook his head. "I've got a feeling, too, that we'll find her dead. That'd be too bad—just too bad for me. For you, too, I guess, Satan. Cohen was your friend."

Satan looked at Logan steadily.

"That's right," he said. "Cohen was my friend."

"Tough!" Logan straightened his coat and pulled it tightly about his neck. "But that's the way things happen." He grinned now and his cigar jarred up against his nose. "Be careful of yourself. Don't go and get yourself a shovelful of dirt."

"Not me." Satan chewed on his lower lip. He thought he knew Logan. But Logan in a facetious mood puzzled him.

"Well—I'll have to trot. Just got a buzz on a raid. Work on Jake, here. Mattie's an important witness for the state. There's nothing you can do about the murder without her?"

"No—" Satan said very slowly. "Nothing legal."

"Nothing legal, eh?" Logan caressed one of his chins. "So that's how it is." Brown, round balls grew smaller.

"That," said Satan, "is just how it is."

"The boys aren't overfriendly to you, Satan. They don't understand you like I do." Logan buttoned his coat carefully. "But they're mighty proud of you—proud of your record. I wouldn't be surprised if they gave you an inspector's funeral.'' A moment's pause, then—''That is, of course, if you should get yourself killed.''

''That,'' said Satan, ''is a threat?''

''Hell, no!'' Logan grinned. ''You're working out of my precinct now. I always look after my boys. That's a warning; maybe a prophecy. Uptown the neighbors think I'm psychic.''

Satan simply nodded his head.

''I'm glad to know where I stand. I think Cohen would like it better just that way.''

Logan paled suddenly and looked at Satan's hands— Satan's empty hands. Logan's right hand half crept toward his left armpit, then dropped quickly to his side again. He thought Satan would like it that way, too—just that way. Logan jerked back his shoulders. He didn't want to die now. Just when he was getting the break—just when he was sure that Mattie wasn't going to talk.

And he brushed by Satan, muttering: ''Got business. Bye!''

The front door closed behind him; the rain bit into his face. He breathed in the cool, damp air and felt better. A few minutes now—an hour at the most, and it would all be over. All over! Rattigan was a punk. Why didn't he do it himself? What did he want to get Logan in deeper for? And as he turned the corner Logan wondered—wondered if it would be any different, any harder to kill a woman.

Satan turned to Jake Hearn, who sat silent in the big chair. His hands were clasped before him, held tightly between his knees, and his eyes, wide and staring, settled upon the phone.

''Well—'' Satan shook the little fence roughly by the shoulder, ''you know now. You saw Logan. How did he act when he came in? Like that?''

''No—no.'' Jake picked out a spot in the corner of the

room now to center his unseeing eyes upon. "He threatened. He wanted Mattie—and he told me to get my hat and coat and go with him. He was in a terrible rage. Then the phone call."

"Sure!" Again Satan shook him. "You're not just dumb, Jake. You know and I know just what that call meant. You've waited too long. They've found Mattie."

"No, no!" Jake was on his feet, clutching at the lapels of Satan's coat. "They haven't. They couldn't. You're just telling me that. You want to know where she is. You want her to tell about Logan. You want—Don't—don't look at me like that. It's not true. It's not true!"

"Just as true that an hour from now—two at the most—they'll give you a call to come to the morgue and identify the body. You know Rattigan and you know Logan, and you know Mattie loved Cohen. If Mattie lives, they die. If Mattie dies, they live."

"That's right—that's right." Jake jerked his head up and down. "But they can't know. They—"

"And Logan left you here. That's like Logan, with the hot seat staring him in the face! He left you because he didn't need you anymore, Jake. They telephoned him where Mattie is. He's going now. On his way now! She had a pretty neck, Jake. A soft, white neck. The wire will cut and twist, and Mattie will make funny sounds. Then they'll cart her up to the park—a side street. And Logan will curse to the papers, and say that the man who got Cohen killed her. He'll be right, of course, but they won't know just how right he is." And as the old man clung to him and moaned and muttered in Yiddish, Satan pointed to the worn old alarm clock on the rough, homemade shelf above the shabby couch.

"There's time yet. Time for me to reach her before

Logan; before Logan starts the job. Before the wire burns
its—"

"I'll tell—I'll tell!" Jake Hearn fairly screamed the
words. Satan placed a hand across his mouth and looked
toward the door. But through Satan's slowly parting fingers that were across Jake's mouth he caught the words,
gasped out now in husky whistling notes.

"She saw it. Mattie saw it," Jake said. "And she
wanted to talk. I—I sent her to Aaron Rostan's." And as a
dry tongue licked at drier lips, he rubbed the back of his
hand across his mouth. "She's locked up in a room on the
third floor. She's—God of my fathers! I had to do it. She's
chained to the bed, and—"

"Chained to the bed!" Satan half drew back from the
old man. "Chained there—fastened there for them to kill
her. No chance. No—You fool—you brutal fool!" And
grabbing Jake roughly and shaking him so the old man
could hardly talk, "The address? Aaron Rostan's address?"

And Satan got it. Over on the east side. A private house;
an old house that Aaron lived in alone.

He didn't listen to the old man's prayers and entreaties to
save his child. He didn't listen to the lamentations and the
cries to Father Abraham to save his daughter. Satan only
knew that the old man knelt upon the floor, his head in his
hands, his hands upon the floor. A pitiful heap of old
bones and skin. A father who loved his daughter. A father
with the false idea he was protecting the last of his own
flesh—his own flesh, who was chained to a bed. Chained
there, helpless to escape, while even now rats of the half
world and a degenerate police officer who had broken faith
with millions were on their way to find the girl.

Satan dashed from the room, through the curtain and out
the front door. A cab was passing. The driver shook his

head and jerked his thumb toward his fare in the back. But Satan was out in the street; had swung aboard the cab; was talking to the driver.

He brought the cab to a stop, swung open the door and ordered the fare from the cab.

"But I've got—" the indignant man started, and stopped.

The door swung wide and a hard voice spoke.

"Outside! Before I throw you out. Police business. Murder."

And the bewildered fare stood on the sidewalk, ran a hand through his hair, repeated once or twice the word *murder* and watched the taxi dash from the curb.

Twice they passed a red light and once a motorcycle cop started to force them to the curb. Satan didn't know the officer, nor had that particular officer met Satan. But he recognized Satan the moment he thrust his head from the cab. The glaring, green eyes; the pointed ears and chin; and now the pronounced sardonic twist to his thin lips.

"Jeez!" The motorcycle cop stopped by the curb and spoke to the patrolman who'd run up from the corner. "It's Satan Hall, and there's death for someone tonight."

SEVEN

BULLETS IN THE DARK

■

Satan stopped the cab just around the corner from Aaron Rostan's house.

"Wait here!" he told the driver. "Keep your engine running, don't leave your seat—and don't open your yap to anyone. There'll be more in it for you than just glory."

The driver grinned and said: "That's all right by me. I ain't proud."

Satan walked quickly around the corner, and a lump caught in his throat. There was no big car before Aaron Rostan's door; there was no car even on the block. The car would be on the street behind. Satan knew the racket and understood what that meant. They'd take the girl—yes—the body of the dead girl out the back way.

And Satan's thoughts were sharp and clear, but unpleasant. Was Mattie dead yet? Had Rattigan found her or had one of his men? Was the murder committed before the telephone call; probably Rattigan's telephone call? Had he killed the girl and wanted Logan to turn the trick of planting the body someplace uptown? Did Logan go straight from Jake Hearn's to Aaron Rostan's?

There was no time to waste. Mattie would be murdered as quickly as possible. Satan was running down the block toward the house.

There was no light showing in the front of Aaron's house. Satan reached the alley and turned into it. Caution was forgotten. His rubber-soled shoes made no noise on the hard flagging.

Satan was a keen, clever hunter of men. He knew how to stalk his prey. He knew how to creep up on the man who must now be watching the rear of that house. But if the man was there, there wasn't time to be clever. The man could only be waiting for the girl to be carried out. Satan would have to chance a surprise attack. So he didn't slow down as he reached the end of the alley which led to the court behind the house. He turned the corner on the run, a gun in either hand. This wasn't the time for caution. This was the time for action. And Satan liked action. He was going to blast his way into that house—a spitting gun in either hand.

He turned that corner. The man in the court saw him, of course. He was there to watch that no one entered. But he was there to watch for skulking figures, or listen for the long, weird song of a police siren. He wasn't expecting a sprinting man to turn from the alley and hurtle toward him. What's more, the gunman recognized that running figure and stood so, his hands at his sides, a gun dangling in the right one. He didn't raise that gun and he didn't fire. It was the sudden paralysis of his muscles that saved his life. If his gun had raised the fraction of an inch, Satan would have killed him where he stood. But the gunman didn't think of that. He only saw that devilish, sinister face and was frozen to the flags.

As it was, Satan fairly leaped across the few feet that divided him from the bewildered and thoroughly frightened man. He raised his right hand once, swung his gun viciously downward. There was a dull thud as steel hit bone, and the watcher dropped to the stones like a steer in the stockyard.

There was a flight of wooden steps, a locked door at the top and a window about waist-high. Satan didn't think—didn't figure it out. It was time that he feared now more than anything else. Minutes—even seconds—counted. Maybe a split second would turn the trick.

He raised his gun, knocked a pane out of the window, heard it fall with a clink into a sink, and thrusting his hand through the hole, slipped back the catch and hurled up the window.

If anyone was downstairs they would hear him, of course. But not in time to stop him, Satan thought, as he climbed over the sill, balanced for a moment on the wooden side of an old galvanized sink and dropped to the floor.

No footsteps there on the main floor. Just silence—and Satan's flash was out. He was through a swinging door, into a dining room, across it and in the front hall. At the foot of the stairs—thickly carpeted stairs.

And they did hear him. He was up that first flight on the second floor, turning toward the third when he heard the voices; heard, too, running feet—and then saw the light. It flashed up suddenly there on the third floor, just above the well of the staircase.

It was only a second, and then darkness but for the semblance of light someplace far back on the third floor. And a voice spoke. It was the voice of Rattigan.

"It's Satan. I saw him plainly over the banister."

Then three quick shots, but no spurts of orange-blue flame.

Satan grinned evilly. Those shots came from someone

shooting straight down into the well of the staircase, or from so far back in the hall that they must go above his head. They knew, then, his little trick of picking out those darts of flame and putting a bullet in the man behind them. Well—the shots could only be to slow him up, not to frighten him. Satan had a little too much pride in himself to believe anyone would try to frighten him.

But he was cautious now as he climbed those stairs. The gun in one hand went back into its shoulder holster and a flashlight crept into his left hand as a voice spoke above. It was a whisper, but a nervous stage whisper that carried clearly to Satan—and he thought he recognized the voice of Logan, but he could not be sure. The man was saying: "She oughta be dead, but I don't think she's quite out. You didn't twist the wire tight enough."

And Rattigan answered—high pitched—fearful: "Why take her out? Why not give her a load of lead and be—"

Then from the voice that Satan thought was Logan's: "We've got to make it look like the Sicilian job and get her out and dump her. You fool, Joe. Satan's alone. What's the panic? You've only got to fire when you hear—"

Dead silence above. The stairs creaked loudly as Satan advanced a step. Then the roar of a gun; sharp spurts of orange-blue flame as Satan threw himself flat on the steps. He didn't return the fire. He couldn't see the flashes from his position now. But he wasn't hit either—couldn't be hit unless he could see the spitting gun. He watched up the stairs, with his gun ready.

Five, ten, fifteen seconds passed. Mattie! Satan couldn't wait any longer. A door banged above. A man cursed and said: "Maybe Joe got him. She's heavier than she looks. All right. Lead on."

Then steps above, right on the landing. And Satan chanced his flash—just one quick pencil of flame.

For a split second he looked straight into the wide, staring, watery blue eyes of Joe. And they fired together as the flash went out. Satan grinned. When the big moment came, Joe didn't have the nerve for it. Satan was not hit. But above, there was the dull thud of a falling body. A moment of silence, then another thud—two in quick succession. And Satan gripped the banister for support. He knew. The body of Joe was hurtling down those stairs.

He braced himself there as the thudding thing came. He felt rather than saw it jump into the air. He twisted slowly as it struck his side. He drew his foot away as heavy shoes struck his shins. And it was gone, thudding, crashing down the stairs, to land with a sickening thump at the bottom.

"Now, Logan—" Satan gritted his teeth, "it's you and Rattigan. Drop your guns, and if the girl's alive, I'll give you a chance to hire a good mouthpiece and beat the rap. But I want the girl."

Feet beat far back along the hall. Then Rattigan spoke from the top of the stairs.

"All right!" Rattigan fairly shouted as Satan pressed the flash button again. "Here's the girl—dead. Take her."

Satan held his fire.

Rattigan held the girl in his arms; held her so for a split second. Then with all his strength he hurled her from him, straight out and down at Satan. Plainly Satan saw the slender young body—even the flesh-colored silk stockings, the blue skirt and the cream-colored sweater above it. He saw too the whiteness of her face, the slender neck—the neck, and the wire about it. The lips too. Lips that were blue—maybe black.

Satan dropped his flash—dropped his gun—and extended both his hands, bracing himself there on the stairs. He was a big man—a strong man, but the force of that body was too much. His huge frame bent back, the breath was knocked from his body. Then he turned, tried to balance himself, held the girl in his arms, and half falling, half jumping, carried her down those stairs. But he was on his feet until he reached the bottom, and was able to so direct his fall that he and the girl crashed to the floor well over to the side of the hall and against the wall.

Satan smiled grimly as his fingers tore at the wire about her throat. He had done well to throw himself and his burden clear of those stairs. There were four shots in quick succession. A moment's pause, as Rattigan must have drawn another gun, then six more shots, a half-hysterical laugh and running feet. Then pounding feet. Satan nodded. Rattigan was following Logan down the uncarpeted back stairs. He didn't have the nerve to descend the front stairs and see if he had finished Satan.

One flight to go and Satan could head them off. He couldn't fry Logan now for the murder of the dead Cohen. But if he could catch them there in the house—shoot them down there in the house, he could avenge Cohen; avenge the dead girl, who—who—And the wire came loose in his hand as he twisted it. And there was something else. A throbbing in the girl's throat—a convulsive gasp in her chest.

Somewhere far distant in the blackness a door closed with a bang. And Satan was on his feet. He groped for his flash on the stairs, found it and retrieved his gun. Then he hunted up the bathroom, found a glass. Water! The girl, Mattie, his witness—the star witness for the state was alive. He dared not leave her now.

She sucked in the water in great gulps. Her eyes had

opened, misty and lifeless. The lids began to flicker. She saw things—saw Satan—stared at him—gasped once—clutched at her throat and screamed.

The scream was one of fear, horror, terror. It echoed through the musty old house. But Satan only smiled and held her head against his arm, ran a hand through her hair and said: "You know me. You know Satan Hall. No one's going to hurt you. It's all right now, kid. The finger's on them. You want to tell, don't you? You want to tell who killed Cohen."

"Yes—I want to tell—want to tell who killed Cohen. I was at the window. I saw him with the knife." She gave one little convulsive gasp, and finished. "It was Captain Logan."

"Sure it was." Satan smiled. "Sure it was! Now, isn't that just fine?"

EIGHT

MORE DEATH TO COME

■

Logan was gone. Rattigan was gone. Only Joe—the dead Joe—lay huddled in a corner, well back from the foot of the stairs.

It was with some difficult that Satan got Mattie Hearn on her feet and had her bathe her head in fresh, cool water. But he kept her from seeing the dead gunman, yet had a look at Joe himself and clicked his teeth together in a certain satisfaction. It hadn't been bad shooting considering the circumstances, and Satan took a sort of pride in his work.

He led Mattie down the stairs, let her sit in the big chair in the hall while she told her story. There wasn't a great deal of it. Most of it Satan knew, or had guessed.

She loved Cohen, had planned to meet him and tell him about Logan. She only wanted her father protected. It was to be at a deserted place she knew of. She could sit there by the window and talk to Cohen, and he could move on and she could disappear in the darkness if anyone came by. But her father knew of the meeting; must have told Rattigan or Logan or someone. Anyway Logan came, and she drew back in the window. And Logan waited until

Cohen turned and recognized him, and then he stabbed him in the chest.

"Three, four, five times—like that." Mattie made the motion with her hand. "Oh, he didn't see me, but he heard me. I screamed as I dashed back in the old warehouse, found an exit and ran all the way back to the shop. I told father and he was frightened. He got a car and he took me to Aaron's and told me I mustn't tell. When I insisted I would, they got the chain and ran it around the bedpost and locked me there. Father said I had to be quiet or they'd kill me and him both.

"Then they came tonight, and Aaron heard them and ran away. And they broke the chain and knocked me back on the bed." She pushed back her hair and showed a bruise on her forehead. "They spoke of killing me and"—she shuddered—"and of throwing my body out up in Van Cortlandt Park. They talked and acted as if I were already dead. Then Logan took the wire and Rattigan twisted it—and you came. In a way I knew what was going on."

"Did they say why"—Satan placed an arm gently around her—"why they were going to take you from here to the park? Was it a frame?"

"Yes—it was. Rattigan was against it, but Logan insisted. He said there had been two or three such murders and a Sicilian gang was suspected, and that Cohen had been working on the Sicilian case. And Logan said something about some message, and that Sicily George would be up by the park and they could pick him up and hang the job on him, and the papers would be satisfied."

Mattie got a little hysterical then, and when she quieted down and sat back in the chair, Satan paced the room.

There was a phone in the corner. He only had to pick up

the receiver to have the hand of the law stretch out and fall upon the shoulder of the man who had betrayed it.

"A police captain," Satan said to himself, "and murder. The very stench of it will reflect back on every boy in uniform—on me, too. It isn't right—it isn't just. I should have given him the heat there in Jake Hearn's. Thousands of men to suffer—thousands. And"—he stopped walking and stroked his pointed chin—"and Frank—Inspector Frank." He recalled the day that Frank had stretched forth a hand and pulled him out of the line and taken him off the pavement. Now he was going to repay him. He looked at Mattie. If she didn't testify. If she didn't remember. If—

And Satan jerked himself erect. He was a cop—just a cop. He was working for six million people—and Frank was his friend. Well—you played the game on the level or you were just a dirty crook, like Rattigan—like Logan—like—He gulped. Like Inspector Frank.

It was tough. But the law was a machine. It couldn't cut down here and miss there. Frank had picked him because he was straight; because he was hard; because he was cruel; because he was a hunter of men.

Satan went straight to the phone, and lifting the receiver spoke a number into the mouthpiece.

"Inspector Frank," he said after a bit. "Make it snappy." He waited a long minute, then sighed with relief.

"Frank—listen." He talked sharp, quick words. "I've got Mattie, and she's going to talk. Logan fries. Now—does Logan trust you yet? Will Rattigan listen to a message from you, like it was gospel? Fine! I want you to call Rattigan's place. Act natural. Say you're tipped off that the commissioner is wise to the big safe; that he's getting Magistrate La Volley to sign a search warrant. That he'll be down there in two hours, with picked men, to open the safe—and he'd better get the stuff out. Yours especially. Act nervous. Tell him to take it to one of the night banks.''

A minute Satan listened, and then: ''No buts. I want it done now. No—they think they're sitting pretty. They think Mattie's dead. Don't give that away. Do as I tell you, and sit tight. If things break right I'll have good news for you. Fine!'' And Satan smacked up the receiver.

''Come on, kid,'' Satan said to the girl. ''We've got to go bye-bye.''

Mattie came to her feet.

''I'm ready,'' she said. ''You saved me. You were willing to die for me. I'll do what you want me to.''

''Not for you, kid. For the law—for Cohen—for the people.'' Satan looked down at her. The black eyes were steady now. The head was raised high and proud. The little hand that held his arm didn't tremble.

''You're a wonder, kid.'' Satan patted her hand. ''You've got nerve.'' And after drawing his lower lip under his upper teeth, ''How would you like to go and lay the finger on Rattigan—on Logan? You've been to Rattigan's place. You know how to get to him.''

The girl felt of her throat and looked straight into those green eyes.

''I would like it very much,'' she said. ''And I know how to get to him—his private office.''

''That's right. That's right.'' Satan patted her arm as he led her from the house. And although he talked in a dreamy voice and seemed far away, his green eyes flashed up and down the block, into the areaways on either side of the stone steps, and his right hand caressed a gun.

''We've done the trick for old John Law.'' He spoke more to himself than to the girl. ''Now we'll turn a trick for a friend. We'll turn a trick for Inspector Frank.''

"Yes," said the girl. "Both of us."

"Both of us! When Rattigan gets a load of you it'll be better than bringing out the reserves. You won't keel over on me?"

The girl's face hardened, her lips set tightly and she clutched Satan's arm firmly. Then those black eyes filled with hatred.

"What do you think?" was all she said.

"Kid," said Satan, "if I'd known you I'd have come like I did—law or no law—Cohen or no Cohen."

And even though the name of his dead friend was on his lips, Satan laughed. The girl didn't know it, but she was the first person to ever hear him laugh. And the laugh made her shiver slightly. It was as if a heavy sleigh had been dragged across dry pavement.

The taxi was waiting, the motor running. They stopped at a drugstore. The girl went in. Satan stood by the door. It was five minutes before Mattie came out. The rouge and powder and sharp, penciled eyebrows made a difference.

"That's right," Satan said. "I want you to look nice for Rattigan."

They got into the cab and drove straight to the Park Avenue Casino. Satan told Mattie what was on his chest and nodded when she spoke out.

"I've often brought him messages from Father," she said. "They always let me right up to his room. It ain't likely he'll tell them that he and Logan murdered me. The casino is run separate from the fur racket. Only the man on his door will be close enough to know the truth. Harrigan will give him a buzz downstairs that a friend's coming up. He won't know. Do you think he'll be there?"

"Where else?" Satan was sure. "It's his standing alibi. They'll all swear to his being there all evening. He'll be covered well tonight. Maybe I shouldn't bring you, Mattie."

"You can't get up without me. You want to get in. It's the only way."

"That's right." Satan agreed with her. "I'd have to blast my way in, and he'd know and slip out. He won't be expecting you, Mattie. He won't even mention you to anyone. They should let you up. What about me?"

"You'll have to hang over the cloakroom counter—at least until he's put the buzzer through. Rattigan's door is at the back of the hall. It's dark there. I often bring men from Father, who want to buy stolen furs. Harrigan will be on the first door. You can slip through if he don't know you. If he does—" She shrugged her shoulders. "You can crowd him through the door and handle him, I guess."

"Sure! I can handle Harrigan. He won't give much trouble. Anyone else?"

The girl set her lips.

"Rattigan's careful. Big Jim Ralston will be by Rattigan's office door. Used to be a major in the army. Rattigan can trust him to the death. Rattigan has him because he's faithful. He can't be bought. But he don't know too much. Thinks it's all liquor business. Used to drink around the casino before he was cashiered out of the army."

"It sounds bad." Satan shook his head and looked at the girl. "But I've got to take you, I guess. Frank's a fine guy; a good guy. Sure you'll see it through?"

The girl felt of her neck. Her black eyes blazed in the darkness of the taxi. She was thinking of Cohen—of the wire.

"I'll see it through," she said simply.

Satan looked at her and nodded. She wasn't more than twenty-five; probably not that. But she had seen life—seen death, too. And she knew the racket. But most of all, she had loved Cohen.

NINE

LOGAN GETS THE DROP

■

Logan sat in the luxuriously furnished room and chewed on an unlighted cigar while he talked. Rattigan was selecting papers from the big safe and stuffing them into a briefcase. He went to the alcove and downed two glasses of water from the porcelain basin.

"As soon as you're ready," Logan said, "I'll cart them out the back way and over to the bank. If necessary, the night manager will swear I never came in. Frank seemed nervous and fidgety, didn't he?"

"Sure! Wouldn't you?" Rattigan pulled out an envelope and laid it on the desk. "That's Frank's," he said. "It's funny nothing happened yet. I wonder if Satan is dead, too."

"It doesn't matter," Logan said. "I told you he wouldn't squawk. He won't even peep. They all know he's out to get me. It's around that he slapped you down. Judge Quinlan P. Paulson and his secretary are in the private dining room. They'll swear we were with them all evening. You've got nothing to worry you. Look at me. Spending the evening with a notorious racketeer!"

"Hell!" said Rattigan, "I ain't so bad. No one has anything on me."

"I'll say you wanted to give me a tip. Sort of line of duty. The judge wanted it that way. Tomorrow I'll raid Platz's place and pick up Ed Donahue. It'll look fine. A good cop has got to mix."

"I ain't so bad," Rattigan said again. "Some of them bullets musta got Satan." And after a pause, "I don't like the silence. Satan's a killer. If he's alive he'll have to be smoked out. Why the hell don't someone bust into that house? I tell you, Logan, it might be days, if Satan's croaked."

"Not days. Aaron will be afraid of the police, but Jake Hearn loves that dame. He'll go there in time. He won't want to, but he'll go." And very low, "I'm afraid Jake will have to be taken care of."

"Cripes!" Rattigan swung on him. "Clarey and Cohen and Mattie and Satan—and now Jake. You can't go into it wholesale, Logan."

"Jake's a natural." Logan shrugged his shoulders. "You can get it done for a couple of grand. We'll throw a banquet that night." He looked thoughtfully toward the ceiling. "We'll throw it for Inspector Frank. Great guy, Frank. Straightest shooter on the force. Yeah. That's it. We'll throw—"

Logan bit off his final words and sat straighter in the chair. Rattigan stopped halfway between the safe and the briefcase on the table. There was a slight buzzing high up on the wall.

"It's a friend." Rattigan nodded. "What a break!"

"Why didn't you say you weren't to be disturbed?" Logan demanded.

"I couldn't." Rattigan spread his hands far apart as he pushed the safe door partly closed. "I always see the boys at this time. None of them know about Mattie. I wanted things to look natural. It won't take a minute."

"Yeah. But me!" Logan frowned. "It's all right with the judge and his secretary—but up here with you!"

"I ain't so bad," Rattigan said again. "Take the back stairs there." Rattigan went over and slid back a panel. Then, "Maybe you better listen in. It might be Jake Hearn."

"Maybe." Logan nodded. "Maybe we might find out who knows he came, and—"

"Not here!" Rattigan's narrow eyes snapped. "God! Logan, I can damn near smell blood on you."

Logan shrugged his shoulders as he passed through the panel, but just before it closed behind him he looked at Rattigan with those unblinking little round brown eyes.

"It's better than smelling burning flesh, Rattigan," he said. "Much better, if the flesh happens to be your own."

Rattigan watched the panel close. He shuddered once and shook his head. Logan gave him a pain. Yes, a physical disturbance far down in the pit of his stomach. Then he picked up the phone and spoke quickly.

"Sloppy and Finnigan and the Weasel and Grouse and Hogan." He rushed the words. "That's right. Round them all up and have them back at the cloakroom." He had to do it. He couldn't get that damn house off his mind, with Joe and Satan and Mattie at the foot of the stairs. He'd send the pick of the gang there. He had to know about Satan.

He thought he heard sounds in the hall outside his door while he talked, but he couldn't be sure. Then there were two sharp raps, three slow ones, a moment's pause, and a single rap.

Rattigan grinned. Things were all right. That would be Ralston. Ralston was a white guy. Rattigan had put him on his feet. He'd die for Rattigan. There was something in this blue-blood business after all.

Rattigan crossed the room, paused long enough to see the name Inspector John Frank upon the envelope he had laid on the desk. He turned it over. Then he went to the door and opened it. Ralston would be there.

And Ralston was there. But Rattigan didn't see him at first, for Ralston lay unconscious on the floor, at the feet of—of—And Rattigan drew back into the room. His mouth was open, his eyes were wide with horror. He was looking straight into the white face of Mattie Hearn. Mattie Hearn, whose body he had hurled straight at Satan Hall upon those stairs. Mattie Hearn, whose neck Rattigan's hands had twisted the bit of sharp copper wire about. And it was there—the mark of the wire. The red, purplish welt about the whiteness of her neck.

For a moment only Rattigan had strange illusions running through his head. Then he drew in a deep breath, took another look at Mattie as she stepped into the room, and his hand started slowly toward his left armpit.

"I guess not, Rattigan." Satan stepped into the room, and closing the door behind him, locked it. "You had your chance to kill Mattie." And as Rattigan's hand dropped to his side, empty, "I want to know about Clarey, Rattigan. I want to know now, or—" Satan's raised gun finished the sentence.

"I don't know. I don't know." Rattigan fairly gasped the words, his eyes glued on Mattie's throat. "Swartz did him in. It was Swartz who did him in."

"Laying it on the dead, eh? Well—it don't matter so much. Logan will squeal like a stuck pig before they roast him. He's built that way." Satan's quick green eyes brightened as they took in the open safe.

He moved to it now, covering Rattigan with his gun. Then he called to the girl.

"The third drawer from the top, to the left," he said. And a moment later, when she found nothing, "The briefcase, then. He's moving the things, according to plans. I wouldn't try for a gun, Rattigan. You're not much use with it, you know. Now—I want that envelope marked Inspector Frank." He walked toward Rattigan, his gun raising slowly, picking a spot just above and between his eyes. "Come across, Rattigan," he said.

"So—" A voice spoke behind Satan. A voice he knew well. It was a throaty, hoarse voice, but it was calm and hard. Logan was talking as he stepped into the room. "So Frank double-crossed us. Got Rattigan to open the safe so you could cop off the evidence against him. No—Don't turn, Satan. And drop that gun."

Satan's gun lowered, then stopped almost in the center of Rattigan's stomach.

"You may kill me, Logan, but my finger's on the trigger. The shock of the bullet in my back will tighten it—and Rattigan will go out."

"That," said Logan, "will be too bad for Mr. Rattigan."

"Logan—" Rattigan wheezed the words in his throat, "don't. He's—"

And Satan dropped his gun to the floor. After all, Logan was right. Satan had played the avenue long enough to know that the man with the gun talks and the other listens. Also, things were pretty hot for Logan. He wouldn't miss Rattigan any. So far as Jake Hearn and Rattigan and Logan were concerned, that racket was over.

"Damn your hide, Logan," Rattigan said. "You'd have let him do it."

"Keep your shirt on, Rattigan. I know my business. I wouldn't let him dump you over. I just called his bluff."

"What now?" said Rattigan as Logan backed Satan against the wall and jerked his other gun from its shoulder holster; had him raise his hands high in the air while he frisked him.

"The room's soundproof, isn't it?" Logan said, and when Rattigan nodded, "Well—we simply start over again where we left off. This time there'll be two of them. Sicily George will be up in the park. Things can go through as scheduled."

"Mattie!" Rattigan licked at his lips. "She's got to die—die twice?"

"She's got to die anyway," said Logan. And turning suddenly, he raised his gun and fired.

Satan's face twisted in pain and his left hand fell to his side. Blood trickled from beneath his sleeve, ran along his fingers and fell to the floor.

"What are you doing?" said Rattigan. "By God, you'll roast us yet!"

Logan raised his arm again, and Rattigan cried out in anger.

"Cut it, Logan. Here, you fool. I'll snuff him out and be done with it."

"What the hell!" said Logan. "The room's soundproof."

"Practically." Rattigan swore. "But it ain't no shooting gallery."

Satan stood against the wall, his right hand still in the air. And there on the floor, between Logan and Rattigan, was his gun—his fully loaded gun that he had dropped there. His gun lying there while he was to be shot slowly down!

Satan didn't expect to live. He didn't expect to get his gun. But he didn't intend to be shot to ribbons either. For a split second Logan's eyes had switched to Rattigan's. And Satan acted.

T E N

SATAN SHOOTS LAST

■

Satan threw himself forward, straight toward that gun between those two men.

Both men twisted their guns quickly and fired. But Logan fired first. The bullet tore into Satan's shoulder; twisted him around; pitched him to the floor.

Then Rattigan fired—blindly, wildly at the hurtling figure of Satan. But Satan was not there. Already Logan's heavy-caliber service gun had hurled him to the floor. And as he fell, his right hand rested upon his gun—but his eyes rested on Logan.

Logan, who stood there straight and stiff, his eyes staring before him. And just above his right eye was a hole. A red hole that was widening. Then Logan opened his mouth, spun suddenly on his heels and crashed to the floor.

In a dazed way Satan knew that Logan was dead and that Rattigan had killed him—that the bullet meant for him had passed through Logan's head. Satan also knew that Mattie screamed and that Rattigan had fired again, and there was a sharp pain in his side. His head buzzed. He rolled over, jerked up his gun and looked for Rattigan.

And he saw him. Saw him struggling there with the girl. Saw him hurl the girl from him—saw the gun in his hand. Saw three guns in his hand—saw three Rattigans—three pairs of ratlike eyes—three pairs of thick sensuous lips that were curled and snarling like an animal's.

And as the stab in Satan's side came again he fired; fired at the middle one of those three Rattigans. Then he blinked his eyes and smiled. Three Rattigans were clutching at their stomachs. Three Rattigans were trying to raise three guns that hung limply in three hands. And then as the three guns came up, Satan fired again at the whiteness of a face. A single face—a single Rattigan now. Somehow his head had cleared.

"It ain't a bad way to go out," Satan muttered as with an effort he kept his eyes open long enough to see Rattigan—a single Rattigan now—give at the knees, sink slowly to the floor, then pitch forward on his face.

Mattie was bathing Satan's head, stuffing towels from the alcove beneath his shirt—against his side. There was his necktie bound tightly about his arm, and he was lying back in a big chair.

He swung his head slowly and looked around the room. Logan and Rattigan were there. But they were dead. They looked funny to Satan, and he grinned.

"A smoke, Mattie." Satan tried to move his right hand toward his pocket, but it lay still upon the arm of the chair.

Mattie put her hand in his pocket, pulled out a package of cigarettes and stuck one in his mouth. She held up an envelope before him.

"Inspector John Frank," he read.

"That's nice," he said, and suddenly his green eyes sparkled. "Light the butt with it, Mattie—that's the girl." He pulled on his cigarette and watched the papers burn. Mattie pounded the ashes in the tray.

* * *

"You got it bad, didn't you, Satan?" She ran a hand through his hair.

"Pretty bad." Satan nodded. "But I've had it worse before. It's a lot of lead, but one or two in the right place is better. Frank's a good guy, Mattie—a fine guy."

Mattie looked at him long and earnestly. Then she leaned down and kissed him.

"I've wanted to do that for a long time," she said very seriously. "I guess there aren't many girls who want to kiss you, Satan."

"No—" said Satan slowly, "not many. I guess you're the first."

"You're going to live, aren't you, Satan?" And suddenly, "You've got to live."

"Yes, I'm going to live all right. I—"

And Satan stiffened in his chair. Footsteps were in the hall without. Voices—loud. A curse, and the sound like a falling body.

"Mattie," Satan whispered, "there's the back door, there where Logan was. Take it. Remember listening at the door. Rattigan was telephoning. There'll be too many now. They'll gang me out. Beat it, kid."

"No, no!" said Mattie, and she grabbed up the phone. "Police headquarters!" she called into the receiver.

"Mattie—" Satan was moving the fingers of his right hand, finding that the arm had a little life again. "Mattie, stick that gun in my hand. Hurry!" With an effort Satan's fingers closed about his gun.

A body pounded against the door. A man called. There were loud, threatening voices—clear enough, perhaps, but jumbled words to Satan. More bodies against the door. A heavy pounding, as an ax against wood. Then a single crash and the door flew in. A single figure was framed in the doorway.

Mattie screamed and Satan's finger closed upon the trigger. Satan didn't know it then, but a bullet from his gun passed within an inch of Inspector Frank's head.

"Hell!" said Satan, when Frank stood looking at him. "I thought you'd be home in bed."

Frank came close and was whispering in Satan's ear as men in uniform tramped the room.

"Mattie told me. It's a good story and she'll stick to it. Logan and you came here to get Rattigan. He shot Logan. There's the bullet from his gun to prove it. Then you got Rattigan.

"You wanted him for the Cohen and Clarey killings. Why not, Satan? It's for the honor of the force—the boys in uniform. For the six million people you're always talking about serving. Why the stench now? Logan's dead. It's for the system."

Satan closed his eyes.

"All right, Frank," he said, and his head fell back against the chair. "But, mind you—I won't go to his funeral."

"No—" thought Frank, as he watched Satan carried from the room, "he won't go to Logan's funeral—and I hope to God he won't go to his own."

Four days later Satan sat up in his bed in the hospital and looked into the black-rimmed, sleepless eyes of Mattie.

"It's Inspector Frank," she said, as Frank came and stood by the end of the bed.

"It's over," Frank told Satan. "They buried Logan yesterday. Since you were working out of his precinct I put you down for ten bucks. It was a beautiful wreath, Satan."

Satan frowned, then his lips parted and he grinned.

"It seems hard," he said slowly. "Ten dollars to bury Logan! But I guess it was worth it."

SATAN RETURNS

A COMPLETE SHORT NOVEL

■

CARROLL JOHN DALY

*Only the Green-Eyed Man Could Punish
those Murderers Who Mocked the
Whole Police Force— Satan Hall*

ONE

THE DEAD GIRL

■

The girl was dead. She was not a pleasant sight. She lay there in the gutter, her right leg curved grotesquely under her, her left hand reaching up and clutching at her throat. Yes—you could tell it was her throat.

Lieutenant Morrisey came slowly to his feet and shook his head. He had seen many dead; some with their throats slashed just as horribly as that. She was so young to die, so beautiful, too—that is, he thought she was beautiful. Soft, delicate, "expensive" skin, Morrisey called it.

He coughed twice before he spoke to the medical examiner.

"Well, Doc." His voice was slightly husky and he had to clear it again. "Someone drew a knife across her neck and tossed her into the street! That's it, eh?"

The medical examiner lifted his head, turned it slowly and put soft, bulging eyes on the police lieutenant.

"You're almost a mind reader," he said. "You might have gone further and added that she's dead." And after a moment, "Are you going to let her lie there in the street—like that?"

Morrisey pursed his lips, ran the fingers and the thumb of his right hand down over his mouth and onto his chin. His words wiped the affected half-smile from the doctor's face.

"Yes," Morrisey said very thoughtfully, "just like that."

"Hell, man! You can't do that." The doctor waved a hand toward the thickening crowd. "The bus is here. We'll throw her in it and—and—My God! Morrisey. You, with twenty-seven years on the avenue, and acting up like a rookie with his first stiff?"

"I've got a kid about that age, maybe a year or two older," Morrisey said slowly.

The doctor came to his feet, put a hand on Morrisey's shoulder.

"The boys are beginning to look you over. Get a grip on yourself! You wouldn't want your own kid to be lying there like that! Then why—"

"Because," said Morrisey, "I know who she is. The commissioner will be down. I want him to see her like that—just like that."

"But hell! Why—?"

"Why—why?" Morrisey's laugh was not pleasant. "You're a good guy, Doc. I want you to go home and get your sleep."

"I don't get you."

"There are other gutters and other—"

"Other what?" The doctor spoke when Morrisey hesitated so long.

"Other throats. One other throat, anyway. That's right! I want to keep that other throat from being like that."

"But the commissioner can't—"

A thick finger dug into the doctor's chest.

"It's one thing to read it on a police report shoved over your desk and another thing to look right smack down on it in a gutter. I want the commissioner to see it. There's only one man to turn loose on this job."

Morrisey swung around suddenly. "Keep them mugs back, Flannigan!" He paused, looked at the long, thin-legged man who had pushed through the crowd and was standing almost directly above the body. "You reporters spot the dead better than vultures."

"Spot them but don't rob them." Kirby, of the *Tribune,* grinned knowingly.

"What do you mean by that?" Lieutenant Morrisey's words were sharp now.

"The card!" said Kirby. "The white card that was pinned on her chest. There, there! I know I wasn't in time to see it. But half a dozen other people did. Some said it had blood on it." He looked at the dead girl. "I can believe that easy enough, and I can print that."

"Print it if you like!" said Morrisey. "Now beat it."

"Huh—huh!" Kirby didn't move. "Going to let the girl lie there? Don't you know what to do with a dead body? Hell, man! There's the wagon!"

"Are you telling me my business?" Morrisey moved threateningly. Kirby stood his ground.

"Don't get rough with me, or I'll tell the world your business. I know the dame. It's Mercy Oakes. Did relief work." Slender, bent shoulders moved. "Did a little too much of it, I guess. Now, that card was there for the press. A reason for its being there, a warning, maybe; a threat. Okay, okay. Don't put your dirty mitts on me. If you want it printed that way, I'll print it. 'Lieutenant Morrisey is withholding evidence in the shape of a card which was found on—' Hell, Morrisey, you can't get away with that."

Lieutenant Morrisey's big fist fell to his side and turned into a hand again. The voice that dropped that hand was sharp and quick. A small, erect figure stood between him and the *Tribune* man.

The short man spoke.

"Well, Morrisey, what's this? And why is the body still on the street?"

Morrisey pointed down. His voice was hollow, lifeless. There was no snap to it now.

"I thought you oughta see her, Commissioner. It's Mercy Oakes."

The commissioner looked at him a long moment, then down at the body. He was a wiry little man whose shoulders jerked spasmodically and whose eyes blinked continually. If that can be called nerves, then he was nervous. But no one had ever seen him blow up.

He looked down at the body now for a full minute; turned, gave quick low orders; then spoke to Morrisey.

"Well?"

"I wanted you down, Commissioner. I wanted—"

Morrisey paused while the body was placed in the wagon. Then he looked at the medical examiner, who, after holding his ground for a moment, fumbled with his bag, muttered a "good night" and climbed into the small police car.

The commissioner walked slowly down the street with Morrisey, both men fully aware that Kirby of the *Tribune* followed leisurely fifteen or twenty feet behind. He paused when they paused and kept the same distance. Under the light, the commissioner said again: "Well, Morrisey?"

"It's this." Morrisey held a handkerchief in his huge cupped hand. The commissioner bent forward, saw the white card slightly smeared with red imbedded in that handkerchief. He made out dimly the blurred black letters upon it—typewritten letters. Then he removed his glasses, put them in his pocket and replaced them with his reading ones. Very carefully he studied the letters, read the full sentence; spoke the words much as if he thought them aloud.

YOUR DAUGHTER, NINA, WILL BE NEXT

"Well?" he said again, but this time he looked back over his shoulder at the slouched figure of Kirby against the building. "There's plenty of Ninas in New York, and plenty of them have fathers."

"You want me to play dumb on this?" Lieutenant Morrisey said. "Listen, Commissioner! That girl in the gutter was Mercy Oakes. She put every nickel she had into helping the unfortunate. She got to know a lot. She kept her mouth shut, too, and they let her alone. Until now. She knew something special, was going to talk, and they tossed her out like that. Just like that, just like you saw her. Nina Radcliff was her friend. At least, Mercy Oakes tried to help Nina."

"There are other Ninas in the city." But the commissioner's voice lacked conviction.

"But just one Nina Radcliff. You told me to keep an eye out for her. She's been going with McCray." Morrisey lowered his voice and jerked a thumb back down the street. "God! That looks like a job of Joe McCray."

"Why?"

Morrisey's shoulders moved.

"Those that cross McCray go out like that. Nina Radcliff has been playing around with McCray. Suppose this Mercy Oakes tipped her off, or thought of tipping her off? She knew things, Mercy did, yet never opened up. It was her code, her way of helping others. Mercy! An odd name."

"The papers wished it on her," the commissioner said

bluntly. "Her name was Mary." He looked back again at Kirby. "What is he waiting for?"

"He knows about the card." And when the commissioner half raised his hand as if to call the reporter, "Just 'about' it. Someone saw it on her chest. He threatened. Hell! Commissioner, if the papers get wise—"

But Morrisey's restraining hand was too late or too weak. The commissioner had already beckoned the *Tribune* man.

Kirby swaggered down the street. The cigarette that hung from his lips straightened.

"What were you waiting for?" The commissioner didn't choose words.

Kirby smiled. He knew the commissioner; knew his way of doing business. Straight from the shoulder, honest, sincere. He liked the steady eyes that watched him now.

"I thought maybe you'd want to see me, Commissioner, before the paper went to press," Kirby said.

The commissioner hesitated only the fraction of a second; then: "I do. It's about that card. Any of the other boys know about it?"

"I hope not." Kirby grinned. "I think not."

"Good!" The commissioner nodded. "That note held a threat to a wealthy man that his daughter would be treated the same way. It was worded rather weirdly. They wanted it printed, so he would understand, and either pay money or call off the law. At least, that's how it looks now. So you see why you can't print it."

"It's a good story." Kirby was noncommittal.

"Sure it's a good story," the commissioner agreed. "But it won't be the first good story you couldn't print. I want you to see the point, Kirby. It won't be so good for them, and it will give us a chance to cut in on the racket if the thugs who killed this girl have to make the threat directly to the other girl's father. It won't be as convincing as the note on this dead girl's chest."

"Who," asked Kirby, "is the other girl's father?"

The commissioner smiled.

"That puts you on a spot, Kirby, that question. The girl is Nina Radcliff. Her father is Chester Radcliff."

Kirby opened his mouth.

"The banker, eh? God! That makes the story twice as big!"

"And twice as impossible for you to use. Good night!"

The commissioner turned, took Morrisey by the arm.

"You see, George," he said, "these boys are not as difficult to handle as you think. They have a job just as you and I have. They have honor, too, and a sense of justice, just as we have."

Morrisey shook his head.

"When you read the paper in the morning you may feel different about—"

He stopped. Kirby had come down the street, clutched the commissioner by the arm. He was grinning broadly.

"Listen, Commissioner! When the break comes, don't forget. It was *my* story. You'll remember that?"

"Certainly," said the commissioner, "I'll remember that. You, too, George!" He turned to Morrisey.

"Yeah. Sure. Sure!" Morrisey was uncertain. Then the words just blurted out to Kirby. "You—you ain't going to print it?"

"Me?" said Kirby. "How the hell can I—now?" And with a laugh, "It's a wonder a cop like you wouldn't get to know your own commissioner. A great guy, a real great guy. Good night!"

Morrisey scratched his head, watched Kirby cross the street, and muttered: "He looks like he meant it, but I'm glad you did the talking. That guy and his kind have double-crossed me a hundred times.''

"That," said the commissioner, "is because you've double-crossed them. Now, you're a good cop, George, got a clear head, know the regulations. You let that girl lie in the street until I came. There's a reason. Why?''

"I wanted you to look at her."

"You could have told me the details; all of them."

"I wanted you to see her like that, because—"

"Because?"

"Because there's only one man for this case. I've got a kid her age, Commissioner; a kid like this Nina Radcliff, who should know better. There's only one man. It's—" He leaned forward and whispered the name to the commissioner. "I could have a go at it myself. But I'm too old; not quick enough, and haven't got the stuff."

But the commissioner wasn't listening. He was thinking; first to himself, then half aloud.

"You want me to turn him loose in the city; turn a killer loose in the city again! The papers—"

"To hell with the papers!" Morrisey snapped in. "I've got a kid myself."

The commissioner shook his head doubtfully.

"It will break him. You know McCray; know who's behind him. Know how powerful that backing is."

"Yes. Hollis Daggett. He came up slowly, Commissioner."

"Slowly, carefully, shrewdly. He was there on top, pulling strings, influencing judges, controlling officials before we were aware of it."

"And McCray is his pet. The new after-repeal criminal. A killer."

The commissioner's head bobbed up and down.

"I can't afford to chance it. One man against the system!''

"See what he says," Lieutenant Morrisey urged. "You can't afford not to chance it."

"By God!" said the commissioner, "I think you're right. I'll have to talk with him—now. And I'll have a talk with Chester Radcliff."

The two men stood and looked at each other. Then their hands met. They had been friends for a great many years. Lieutenant Morrisey was smiling when they parted. But the commissioner of police wasn't. His lips were set tightly, his eyes twin balls of brightness; vivid brightness.

The dead was to come alive; the buried was to walk the streets again. He was going to turn death loose in the city.

TWO

IN THE LONELY
HUNTING LODGE

■

Chester Radcliff's hunting lodge was far up on top of the hill. Below it lay the great rambling country estate which Radcliff in all seriousness called his summer bungalow. He was a stout, heavyset man and had to catch his breath several times before he could swallow the generous drink he poured out. But he did get it down, had poured himself another and was half through that before the commissioner of police had more than taken a sip from his tall, mild highball.

"By God!" Radcliff rubbed the moisture from his forehead. "It's like something out of a book." He waved a hand about the big rustic room; at the jet blackness of the windows. "After midnight. You and I alone, and I'm frightened."

"We could have talked just as well in your house below." The commissioner's voice was low. "We've been friends for years, Chester. Why not tell me about it?"

Chester Radcliff finished his drink, quickly poured another, opened his mouth twice but did not speak. The commissioner finally said: "You came to me about your daughter, Nina. You were vague, worried, and"—he pointed at the tall glass—"had some courage out of the bottle, but not enough. Now, it was your suggestion we come up here. Let me have it all."

Chester Radcliff came to his feet and paced the room.

"I'm just worried, I tell you." His voice was irritable. "It's about Nina. The company she keeps. Oh! I suppose it's part of her work in a way. But I'm—just worried."

"You said 'frightened.'" The commissioner didn't raise his voice. "Look at this, Chester. The card here."

Radcliff glanced down at the card, jerked slightly, mentally spelled out the letters.

YOUR DAUGHTER, NINA, WILL BE NEXT.

He raised his head, saw the curtains that led to the adjoining bedroom, walked toward them, hesitated, then passing quickly into the little bedroom, snapped on the light. He snapped it out again almost at once; came back into the room rubbing the back of his hand over a wet forehead.

"Where did you get that card?" he asked abruptly.

"That," said the commissioner, "was found on the dead body of Mercy Oakes. Mercy Oakes, your daughter's friend! It was meant for you—for you to read in the papers. I kept it." The commissioner leaned forward now; his voice was low. "Mercy Oakes was found with her throat cut; cut from ear to ear. You must have read that, must have heard that."

"Yes, I heard that—was told that. That's why I brought Nina up here."

"It's a lonely spot." The commissioner swung his head about as if to indicate the entire countryside. "A bad spot for a man who's afraid. Come on, Chester! Talk."

Chester Radcliff wet his lips.

"There is nothing to tell; absolutely nothing more than I told you."

"Before God!" The commissioner came to his feet. "Do you want Nina found like that? Lying in the gutter, her throat cut!"

"There is nothing to tell—nothing!" Radcliff fairly shrieked the words. Then dropping suddenly into a chair, "It's Daggett. Hollis Daggett."

"Ah!" The commissioner's eyes widened. This was big; the biggest thing in the city. Even bigger than if it were Joe McCray; McCray, who without Daggett couldn't act, couldn't move; could be grabbed up on a dozen charges, real or imaginary. But he wasn't thinking of Joe McCray, ace of public enemies, then. It was the power behind such men; the influence, the politics. Oh! he wanted Joe; wanted him more than any man in the city. The commissioner didn't think any longer. Chester Radcliff was talking.

"There's nothing to tell; nothing that the police—that you can do to help. But here it is; all of it. Daggett opened a small account in our bank. He didn't have it very long; a few months, I guess, when he came in to see me. He wanted to borrow a hundred thousand dollars." Radcliff waved his hand and for a minute or two the banker was speaking; not the man—the frightened man.

"Like others, Daggett had been hard-hit financially. His vast real estate holdings threaten to overwhelm and collapse the huge fortune he built up. I know his political influence; but his notes at present threaten to swamp other institutions.

"I explained to him the strict regulations of the state; that the bank could not accept any more real estate as security and that unsecured loans were out of the question. The bank examiners; the usual routine, you understand."

"And then?"

"Why, he thanked me, smiled, and suggested that I get in touch with him 'if the policy of the bank' should change. I didn't hear from him for some time after that. Then came threats to Nina, a peculiar accident to my car and the death of my chauffeur, and the information that Nina was traveling with—well, people that you would hardly wish a daughter of yours to travel with.

"I didn't connect Daggett with these events in any way; can't exactly now. But he visited me again about borrowing that hundred thousand dollars, listened to the same explanation from me, and smiled again at leaving. But this time he said, 'I'm a man who hears things, and I heard of threats to your daughter. I get around, Mr. Radcliff; have some peculiar but powerful associates and have used that power to protect your daughter. I'm a man who takes care of his friends—friends.'

" 'What do you mean?' I asked.

" 'About that loan,'' he told me. 'I'm not a banker, but I need a hundred thousand dollars. Manage the thing for me in your own way. Take care of my interests and I'll take care of yours.' '' Radcliff hesitated a long moment. "Would you say that was a direct threat?"

"I would." The commissioner smiled grimly. "But I doubt that a jury would; that is, if you could even reach the jury with a charge of attempted extortion."

"Now—you see how things are." Eyes blazed brightly at the commissioner. "I did nothing. This girl was killed. Hollis Daggett has shown me he is above the law. I am to pay him one hundred thousand dollars—one hundred thousand dollars out of my own pocket, and pretend that it's just a regular business deal; an investment.

"An investment in what? In the life of my daughter. Well, other men have daughters. What are they doing? Are they paying and keeping quiet? Are they appealing to the police, who can give them no protection? Or are they waiting by the phone for an only child to be found dead? There's the story. What am I to do? What can I do? Daggett's a big man in the city.''

"The biggest," the commissioner agreed solemnly. "You can't do anything, Chester. Publicly, perhaps the department can't do anything. But, privately, it can—I can. I am putting a man on this case tonight."

"A man. Good God! A man! A single man against such forces. A man against Daggett, who controls—"

"Yes, a man. A man who'll have no personal interest in you or your daughter, a man who'll have one single purpose. To protect your money and your daughter's life, and bring to justice—"

The commissioner paused, his lips twisted slightly at the left side. "Well, a man who'll demand the full penalty of the law for the death of Mercy Oakes."

"And this man?" There was the slightest semblance of a sneer; perhaps simply a doubt, for Chester Radcliff considered himself above a sneer.

"A man I've kept under cover. A man who so startled the city; the people, the press and the crooks a year ago, that—"

The commissioner jarred to his feet, swung about, faced the door that suddenly opened and the white-faced girl who stood there. She was small and slim and straight, and her nose was slightly turned up at the end. But she had keen, penetrating brown eyes; steady, eager eyes that now held a touch of fear, or perhaps just excitement.

"You're the commissioner of police," she said, closing the door behind her. "I knew that. I knew that. Father, you've done it now! There's men at the house. They're looking for me; they're going to take me away. Why did you bring me here?"

The commissioner looked once at the girl, asked no

questions; but went quickly to the phone. She was across the room before him; grabbed at the phone; was frantically calling a city number, talking to the commissioner at the same time.

"You can't do anything. You can't help. It's McCray I want. I need McCray. Everyone fears him. If they come here I'll have them talk to him on the phone, and—"

She whirled. "The phone's dead—the wires are cut!" She turned accusing eyes on her father. "Why did you bring him here? They know. They think I'm going to talk."

And flaring out, half in fear, half in defiance, "If I had kept him with me; had him here, he—"

"Who?" said the commissioner.

"Joe McCray. He's protected me. Mercy died because she wouldn't accept his help. But he's protected me. He said nothing could happen to me, and now—"

The commissioner swung her around, looked at her. He took in the white sweater, the brown riding breeches, the high boots, the windswept roughness of her wild, bobbed hair.

"Why was Joe McCray protecting you? Did you give him money?"

"Money!" The girl laughed shrilly. "Give him money? No, no. He loves me. Yes, loves me. I know! He's been in prison. The police hounded him; but he fought his way back, his way up."

The girl stopped. The door she had bolted shook behind her. All eyes turned. Glass smashed beyond the room; behind the curtains. Chester Radcliff hurled himself across the room, toward the desk, jerked open the drawer.

"Don't, Chester," the commissioner said. "Let me talk to them. You could do no good. Don't—"

A voice between the curtains in the doorway spoke.

"That's right, mister. Don't! There's another lad at the

door. It's a snatch; a quiet one if you want it that way. There would be no percentage in killing off the heavy dough. I''—voice shrilled—''the Commissioner! My God!''

The commissioner looked at the squat figure. A black mask covered the eyes and nose and the upper part of the mouth.

''That's right.'' He nodded; his voice was calm. ''You've made a mistake. The window you came through is in the room behind you. Use it.''

''Yeah?'' The man straightened the gun in his right hand, crossed his left to his right armpit and jerked another black automatic into his hand. ''Well, I didn't bargain on this, but the snatch goes through.'' Then, with a queer clicking sound far back in his throat that might have been a laugh, ''What a joke this will be!''

''Joke!'' The commissioner tried hard to keep his voice steady. ''There are twenty thousand policemen in the city. Think of it. Twenty thousand men with a single order; an order to get the man who stood in this room tonight.''

''Yeah, twenty thousand.'' The man nodded. Thick lips showed as a jaw protruded slightly. ''Twenty thousand cops that don't know who I am, and one lad who does know and knows I didn't go through with it. No, Mr. Head Cop. There's a chance with twenty thousand dumb bunnies who don't know me, but no chance with the one lad who does. Open that door, sister, we're going bye-bye. Be nice now, or I'll knock you sillier than the commissioner.''

''And when they get you,'' the commissioner went on slowly, ''when they have you downstairs at headquarters, they'll remember. Things happen to men downstairs; things you must know about, if—''

The commissioner leaned forward. ''Yes, you do know. I recognize you now. You're—''

''By God!'' the masked figure snapped. His right hand

moved quickly. The huge black nose of the automatic swung straight on the commissioner. "Those orders ain't ever going out. You want the heat, eh? You—! Open that damn door, sister, or—"

And the girl did. Mechanically her feet moved; mechanically her hand reached the bolt and shoved it back. She saw the door opening slowly, very slowly. The man in the room was still talking, his eyes gleaming slits of evil through the mask, still on the commissioner.

"So you wanted it that way? So you know me? You know me—just you. Not the dame, not the money shark. Just you! Grab the dame, Eddie." This last without even looking at the opening door. "I know it ain't orders, but I've got to give the Big Cop the works."

The man's hand steadied, his head shot forward. The thick knuckle of his index finger whitened. The commissioner straightened. He had made a mistake; he knew it now. He never expected to die like this. Cops! Yes, many of them. They had known how to take it; had taken it; died straight and stiff. Stiff! His mouth curled slightly. Well, it was his duty, just as much as it was the duty of each of the men he sent out; sent to their death many times.

The shot came. No streak of orange-blue flame; just the report of the heavy automatic. He saw the finger tighten; nothing more. His body jarred—or did it? Didn't he simply straighten himself, pull himself together to receive the lead? But there was no lead. The man had missed. The man had—had—

Good God! The man was dead. Dead there on his feet! He wasn't masked anymore. The mask hung down over one ear and the eyes were glassy; sightless. Then the man twirled suddenly; spun and toppled over in a peculiar way. Like a full-length ashtray with a weight on the bottom.

Yes, toppled over as if he would swing back erect again. But he didn't. For as he fell, the commissioner saw the hole in the side of his head; a hole just where the string that held the mask must have been.

The commissioner turned his head toward the wide-open door and the blackness of the night beyond it. But he didn't see the night. He saw a second body that lay sprawled there almost in the doorway, and he knew it was the man called Eddie. He also saw two feet, two legs that straddled that silent form. And he ran his eyes up those legs, up over the huge body; the long arms and the smoking gun that was still gripped in the right hand of the third man.

If evil was written on the dead gunman's face, it was written more so upon the unmasked face of the man who stood so unexpectedly in that doorway. Sinister, long, cruel lips; narrow lips. Green eyes that slanted upward like an Oriental's. Tapering ears. A peculiar V-shaped cut to the jet black hair gave the man the appearance of a devil, as you might see Mephistopheles portrayed upon the stage.

But there was more than just the cut of the hair that was devilish. Something diabolical was back of the green eyes; something that was fading now as the man's head turned and those green eyes settled with a peculiar satisfaction upon the dead man on the floor; the man he had just killed.

The commissioner spoke. "Hall! Detective Satan Hall." And after a moment the commissioner added, "I—I thought I told you to wait—wait down in the village."

Thin lips parted and Satan smiled. At least, his teeth showed and his green eyes took on a more decided slant. But he said simply: "I never wait."

SATAN SPEAKS

∎

Down at the foot of the hill, in the great rambling house which Chester Radcliff called a bungalow, activity was dying down. Hysterical maids had gone to bed, or at least to their rooms. The butler's dignity was still supreme but had taken on a stagelike effect, and he was blissfully unaware that he had no tie on.

"So this is the man!" Chester Radcliff said, looking at Satan, who sat uncomfortably erect in a great easy chair. "I remember something in the papers at the time. There were officials who thought his—hm—activities a little too—well, brutal."

"That's right!" The commissioner nodded; smiled over at Satan. "In a way, I've brought him out of retirement."

The girl, Nina, said sullenly: "You've forgotten me. I'm over twenty-one; I've got money of my own. I don't need anyone. I've got a friend who will protect me." She raised her head a little proudly; almost a forced pride. "I mean Joe McCray."

Satan spoke for the first time.

"Joe McCray," he said simply, "is a rat. The worst kind of a rat."

The girl turned on him. Her eyes blazed.

"You wouldn't say that; wouldn't dare say that to his face." And to her father, "I won't have this man about me."

Her father coughed.

"We are thinking of you, my dear; of your interests. Perhaps it would be better if you went away someplace; someplace that no one would know about." He looked at the commissioner. "You know the place I thought of."

The girl came to her feet, stood so a few moments, looked from one grim face to the other, turned suddenly and fairly ran toward the door. She spun the knob, pulled at the door, jerked it, turned back, faced the men.

"So that's why you brought me here; had him here." She talked to her father; pointed at the commissioner. "You're going to take me. Put me someplace; keep me there. I'm of age. You can't!" Her upper lip bit down on her lower one, her hands clenched at her sides; fingers bit into her palms. It was a full minute before she spoke again. But her words were carefully chosen, her voice free from any hysteria.

"Father." She stood directly before him. "You are three men. You've got the physical strength, the political influence and the money, of course, to do it. If you do this thing to me I'll never speak to you again. I'll have to come out sometime, and then we're through."

"But, my dear, Mercy Oakes died. It's for your own good."

Satan said: "Why not leave the girl alone?"

The commissioner and Chester Radcliff both looked at him.

"But her danger. The company she keeps," Radcliff said. "She said herself she knew something, and—"

"You can't lock up all the fools in the world, and if you could, it wouldn't stop them from being fools," said Satan. "And she doesn't know anything. She's being used as a blind. Mercy Oakes knew something; was going to tell her what it was. About McCray. Let me talk with her—alone."

Radcliff hesitated, looked at the commissioner, followed him to his feet. Then both men left the room.

"If you're trying to be kind to me," the girl said as soon as the door was closed; "if you think that will make me talk—well, I know all about detectives and their methods and how they hound people."

"Sure. Sure!" Satan nodded. "You oughta know. McCray's the kind to talk his head off. Now, if I fix it with your father and with the commissioner so that you can run your own way, will you make a promise—one promise?"

"Oh!" she straightened. "What?"

"The day you find out McCray is a rat you'll tell me so, and tell me why."

"That isn't a very hard promise." The girl smiled.

"It's harder than you think." Satan shook his head. "For a girl like you it will be a comedown."

"Will it? Well, I promise." And suddenly, "I suppose, after all, I owe you my life; at least, my safety tonight."

"No, you don't. Not tonight." Satan shook his head again. "The commissioner does, but not you. Don't you see? That was simply a plant tonight. McCray would have rescued you—saved you."

She laughed, not believing him.

"But, why?" she asked mockingly.

Satan looked puzzled.

"I don't know the plant. Maybe money; maybe gratitude from your father. He may even intend to marry you."

"Intend to! He wants to. He loves me."

"No, he doesn't love you." Again that shaking head.

She smiled in a superior way.

"But you admit he might want to marry me. Why?"

"Money. Connections. It would be a good 'in' for Daggett; a better one for McCray."

Her lips set tightly; her little nose tilted more.

"But he doesn't love me? I suppose he couldn't love me!"

Satan ran hard green eyes over her face; let them rest on her eyes.

"No," he said. "McCray couldn't love you."

"Why?" Her smile was a twisted little grimace.

Satan said simply: "You're too good and clean—and decent. McCray doesn't like his women that way."

"And you?" She didn't know why the red flooded her cheeks; why she was indignant.

"Oh! Me?" Satan shrugged his shoulder. "I don't like women at all."

She looked at his pointed face and laughed shrilly.

"I guess," she said, "women could feel the same way about you."

Satan nodded absently.

"I guess they could," he agreed. And then added, "It's a promise. I'll fix things with your father and the commissioner. Remember! When you find out McCray's a rat you come and tell me, and tell me why."

"Yes, yes." She grabbed him by the arm as he passed toward the door. "Why are you doing this for me? It can't be the promise—"

"For you?" Satan seemed genuinely surprised.

"Of course, for me. You're not doing it for yourself."

"No," he said thoughtfully. "No, not for myself. For the department. For the people. For the city."

"What—what do you mean?" Nina Radcliff had been around, but she had never met a man like this before.

Satan turned; faced her.

"I don't like McCray; I don't like him at all. I am back on the street again; back in the city again. I hope it isn't personal; certainly it wasn't personal until last night when Mercy Oakes died. She was working for the city, too; in a way we were working together."

"But what have I got to do with it? Why are you giving me my freedom?" She looked up at him. "Freedom to go straight to Joe McCray!"

Satan's laugh was not pleasant.

"You're the bait that'll trap McCray. Trap him to his death."

"You—you believe, as my father and the commissioner do, that I'm in danger—real danger? Yet you—you'd use me?"

"Yes." Satan nodded. "Why not? You're only one out of many; many who have died or are going to die." He stuck a long finger out and pointed it at her. "I'm paid to protect the whole city; paid to get Joe McCray—get him for murder."

"You—you'd kill him?"

"Just like *that*." Satan snapped his fingers. "I just want the opportunity."

"You tell me this, knowing I'll tell him—knowing I must tell him!"

"Sure!" said Satan again. "If he's half the man you think he is, he'll give me that excuse."

He turned suddenly and jerked open the door.

"The girl's all right," he told the startled commissioner. And seeing two state troopers and the officer in charge, added: "I guess that smooths out things for the rest of the household. The lad I shot was Dutch Albert. The boy in the doorway with the cracked head, Eddie Malone." And to the commissioner again, "Let's get going."

The commissioner said, uncertainly and in a low voice: "You think—you think it's the thing to do?"

"Sure. Sure!" said Satan. "I've got her promise. It would bust things higher than a kite if her freedom were interfered with."

The commissioner spoke low and earnestly to Chester Radcliff, who seemed willing if not exactly eager to have the commissioner settle the trouble arising between himself and his daughter.

At the door the state trooper stood, first on one foot and then on the other.

"It's all right with me, Commissioner, since you called us up as soon as Mr. Radcliff's chauffeur located the bust in the wire. But"—he half looked at Satan—"after all, this business isn't exactly regular."

Satan looked at the man, took in the feet spread far apart; the broad shoulders; the swarthy, weather-beaten face.

"Not regular, eh?" Satan's head shook slowly; his eyes narrowed. "It's the *regular* things that don't get convictions. There's Dutch Albert, up there now. He won't beat the rap. But I'll lay you ten to one that if you ever try Eddie Malone it won't be within a year, and then—"

The state trooper leaned forward.

"You're—yes, by God! You're Satan Hall. I—I—"

A huge hand came out, gripped Satan's, tightened upon the long, tapering fingers. The trooper was proud of his grip. He was surprised to find his fingers first give, and then soften. "I've wished," he said, "I've wished I had—well, all the boys have the guts for it, but we just don't feel the will to do it. How do *you* do it?''

"That's not the question you want to ask.'' Satan's lips parted. "You want to know why—how I can do it and get away with it. There's your answer.'' He jerked a thumb toward the commissioner. "It's not so much the guts of the man who can shoot, but the guts of the man who stands behind him when he does shoot. Good night!''

Satan pushed by the troopers and passed into the blackness.

"Damn it! Satan, if you aren't trying to be a politician,'' the commissioner said when they climbed into the car. "Patting me on the back! I brought you out and turned you loose, but now—the girl! She's—''

"She's one in six million back there in the city.'' Satan fairly blasted out the words. "You gave me my run in this thing. You want Joe McCray. You're going to get him.''

"I know Morrisey has been working through you and was in touch with Mercy Oakes. But you're sure Joe McCray killed her?''

"Just as sure as if I saw him drag the knife across her throat.'' He went on quickly when the commissioner would have cut in. "It's knowledge, not evidence. Mercy was going to spill it all to Morrisey. But you saw her! You promised to let me work it out my own way.''

"Yes, yes.'' The commissioner stretched out a hand and squeezed Satan's arm in the rear of the speeding car. "You saved my life tonight. There's no doubt about that. But I wish you could be a little more subtle; a little more—well, perhaps a little less brutal.''

The commissioner was aware that green eyes peered at him in the blackness of the car. But Satan's voice was clear enough, his words plain enough.

"You go after rats with rat poison, not warrants and

writs." And after a moment's pause, "I carry my rat poison under each arm—plenty of it."

For a long time after that the commissioner was silent. He was of the old school. Writs and raids and warrants! He had tried to change his ways with the times; that was why he was commissioner. But he was quite aware that there were still politicians, ward captains, crooked officials who could and did make trouble.

He hoped that he was doing right. He sighed once. He was a man of quick decisions; he had made his. He had turned a legal killer loose in the night. Yet Satan never went to murder. The other man had a chance—well, perhaps not a chance, but at least the opportunity to shoot first. The commissioner knew that. He smiled in the darkness. Better still, the crooks knew it. The murderers, big-timers and little-timers, feared Satan as they feared no law, no judge, no technically hampered detective on the force.

Of course he didn't have to bother about all that. He was a one-man commissioner. He had been given the office under that understanding. Still, he could embarrass his friends; those who stood behind him. Make it hard for them at election time.

He leaned over and whispered to Satan, as if he thought aloud.

"Whatever you do, Satan, you'll have to do it quickly."

And strangely enough, Satan's nod of agreement didn't cheer him as he had hoped it would. There was something grim; something even ominous about that moving head— just moving downward in the blackness.

FOUR

STRAIGHT TALK

■

Lieutenant George Morrisey pushed his chair back against the wall in the little room above headquarters, sucked on his pipe a minute, then shot the words out.

"Good God! Satan, you're not actually turning this girl loose, as bait—human bait? Sometimes I'm afraid of you; actually afraid of you."

"That's all right, George." Satan grinned. His voice was purely conversational. "Sometimes I'm afraid of myself. The thing, at first, seemed greatly involved; but, after all, it's rather simple. Hollis Daggett needed the money. Threats to Radcliff's daughter, Nina, seemed the easiest way to get it. At the end, Joe McCray could always be the one who saved the girl. I don't know just how it was to work out last night; if the snatch was to go through, and Hollis—of course at the suggestion of Radcliff—be the go-between; or if Hollis would have made the rescue through his underworld influences after Radcliff had arranged his note at the bank, or even both. You're sure Mercy Oakes had the dope on Joe McCray?"

"Well—yes. Enough evidence to roast an ordinary man

over and over." Morrisey pointed his pipe at Satan. "But we've had that before on Joe McCray—and *blooey*! Just like that, evidence disappeared, witnesses vanished or died or changed their stories a dozen times. There's no two ways about it, Satan. I've been too long in harness to be fooled. We'll never roast a man that Hollis Daggett needs; stands behind. And he'll go to bat for Joe McCray."

"He will!" Satan nodded solemnly. "While he needs him."

"He'll always need him. What do you mean?"

"I mean he wouldn't need Joe if Joe were dead. The evidence would look good then. Witnesses wouldn't disappear."

"You mean you're going to kill him."

"I hope so." Satan leaned forward.

"That would be murder."

"No." Satan shook his head. "I never went to murder—yet. Don't you see, George? That's why I turned Nina loose. She'll go straight to Joe McCray. She'll tell him what I said. He'll be expecting me; waiting for me. If he wants to marry the girl he'll have to make good."

George Morrisey bounced his chair back hard against the wall.

"Good God!" he blurted. "You're not going to slap him down?"

"That's right. I'm going to do just that; slap him down."

Morrisey was silent for a long time.

Finally Satan spoke. "That evidence! Why didn't Mercy ever give it to you? How did Nina Radcliff get in with Joe McCray?"

"The evidence!" Morrisey was thoughtful. "Mercy Oakes knew as well as I knew that Joe McCray would beat the rap. She fell hard for that kid, Nina Radcliff. She didn't want her to look on Joe as a persecuted man. She wanted to prove something to Nina first.'' Broad shoulders moved. ''She died the night she was going to spill it to Nina.''

''And Nina knew Joe. How? What influence did he have over her?''

''I don't know how they first met. Nina was only playing at welfare work. Mercy had her heart and soul in it. She did a lot of good. But, anyway, one night Nina heard two men talking over a murder they had committed. They discovered her and were going to kill her. Joe McCray walked in. She's young; she's rich; she had found a real man, hounded and persecuted. And that was that!''

''The two men talking of murder was a fake, of course.''

''Of course.''

''Didn't Mercy tell her?''

''No. She started to run down Joe, then quit. She was a woman and she understood. She saw it in Nina Radcliff's eyes. She didn't want to chance a walk-out and a bust-up of friendship. She wanted to wait until she was sure she could put it over. And when she was sure, she died.''

''Nothing in the papers about that card on Mercy Oakes' chest!''

''No, no.'' Morrisey smiled. ''The commissioner knows his way about. I'd've busted Kirby wide open. He didn't print a thing; kept his word.'' A moment's thought. ''A word he didn't even give.''

Satan nodded thoughtfully.

''The *Tribune*'s after Daggett; the only paper really hot to get him.''

''Yeah. And it will cost them plenty. Two libel suits

already. And Kirby digging up his past and guessing about his future!''

"Kirby will get it in the stomach some night." Satan jerked out a hand and snapped up the ringing phone. "Yeah—yeah. She's there, too? Fine!" He dropped the phone back on the table, came to his feet. "I'll be leaving you, Morrisey. Just got a buzz that Joe McCray is shooting his face off all over the Gilded Globe; and the bright little girl, Nina, is with him. It's working out nice. Night!''

At the door Morrisey took him by the arm.

"You're not going to slap him down tonight—now!''

"Tonight and now. Kirby's there, too. I don't like newspaper men. But I'll give Kirby a story to print that will make Joe McCray the laughingstock of the whole city.''

"He's not like the others, Satan." Morrisey still held his arm. "He's big, he's tough, he's quick. He'll go for a gun.''

"Will he?" Satan's lips smacked. "That's just what I'm hoping, George.''

The phone rang again. This time Satan seemed surprised when he answered it. The voice was low and soft, like a woman's. He didn't recognize it until the man gave his name. When he put down the phone his face was puzzled. He shook his head.

"So what?" said Morrisey.

Satan buttoned his coat.

"Joe McCray will have to wait for an hour. I've got a surprise for you, George; one for myself, too. A man wants to see me at once at his house—alone. He said he would make it worth my while. He's a man who can do it, too, George.''

"Who's that?''

Satan stretched out a long finger and pounded it against the older man's chest.

"Daggett—Hollis Daggett!" he said, and walked out of the room.

Hollis Daggett's big stone house was different from most of the others in the city. It set rather far back from the street, and had a stretch of grass behind it that led down to the river. Satan opened the big iron gate, passed through and closed it behind him. A man stood far back in the shadows close to the front steps. Satan nodded grimly. Once again, a little more grimly, when he saw another man emerge from the shadows on the opposite side of the steps, and, joining a companion, move around the corner of the large house. The first man, if alone or with a companion, remained in the same position; in the shadows, but not in complete darkness.

So Daggett wasn't above a few theatricals, Satan thought as he mounted the steps. But even Daggett would hardly have a man shot down on his front porch, especially so close to the street. In the backyard, maybe; in the front living room, yes! It wasn't so long since Hollis Daggett had come through a host of dead to lead the living.

Satan took no chances. He paused at the top of those stone steps, placed a cigarette in his mouth, calmly struck a match so that the men in the shadows could not fail to see his face in the quick, bright glare. If that was conceit, Satan was quite unaware of it. He knew that his face and his name had meant something to the criminal. He knew that it had taken long years to build up that *something*. And he wanted any man who desired to shoot at him to know just whom he was shooting at.

Hollis Daggett opened the door. He was a big man who threw his body from side to side when he walked, and though his steps were short they were quick, getting his huge bulk about with surprising swiftness. His face was peculiar; that is, if you could actually call all of it his face. It was large; almost grotesquely large, accentuated by the smallness of his features and the little space they covered. It was as if a child had made a huge snowman, then picked out a space in the center of the enormous head to dot the eyes, the nose and the mouth. The tiny ears far back on the side of his head didn't look as if they belonged to that face at all.

"Satan Hall—Detective Satan Hall! Well, well, well." Hollis Daggett moved quickly across the room, indicated a comfortable chair and a decanter of whiskey in almost a single movement as he himself dropped into a chair. "Nothing to drink, eh?" Beady eyes blinked brightly. "Well, sometimes when I'm interviewed for the press I attribute my success to that. All bosh—all bosh, of course. Funny we haven't met before!"

Satan eased into a chair, lifted a cigarette from the box on the table beside him, smelled it, rolled it slightly between his fingers and tossed it back into the box. Then, taking a Chesterfield from his own pack, lighted it.

"We have met before," he said. "You weren't coming along so fast then. I ran you in."

The big man started, then jerked erect and laughed; threw back his head and roared.

"They told me you didn't have much tact, and by God! they're right. We politicians are strange creatures. We don't say what we mean or mean what we say. It's refreshing to come across a man who likes straight talk." He leaned forward in the chair. A small round mouth puckered, beady eyes were steady. "You do like straight talk, don't you?"

"As straight as you can give it," Satan said simply.

"That's good. By God! that's good." Hollis Daggett

fumbled for a moment along the thick black ribbon that hung about his neck, finally found his glasses, placed them on his nose, and leaning forward, pulled open the drawer of the table.

Satan's green eyes never left the fingers of the pudgy right hand that went into that drawer. But his own hands never moved from their position upon the arms of that chair. Hollis Daggett chuckled, watched those hands; seemed to nod his approval. But what he took from the drawer was a folded sheet of paper. He opened it, looked it over carefully, then gave it to Satan.

"A map of the city." Small eyes became twin black coals. "Every precinct laid out; carefully laid out. The ones in color are simply a suggestion—my suggestion."

"Well?" said Satan.

"Well," echoed Hollis Daggett, "you want straight talk. I doubt if you can lay a finger on a precinct there that I can't make you captain of." Daggett went on eagerly as Satan just stared at him. "I don't mean in a day. That might invite talk. But a few months; a very few months. That little shooting up in the hills warrants the stripes of a sergeant; perhaps a lieutenant. You've been held down, Satan; held down by your own way of doing things." Daggett's little mouth puckered again, and his black eyes danced. "Killings are all right, provided you kill the right people."

Satan folded up the map and laid it carefully on the table.

"You came up from the gutter, Daggett. But you didn't come so far, unless you reckon it in dollars and cents and the higher priced clothes on the dummies you influence. You just changed your gutter, I guess." Satan shook his head. "It can't be fear. You never would have gotten so far if it was that. Why this offer, then?"

"It's you, Satan. I could use a man like you. Look at the others. I don't have to name them. Cars and wine and women. Money, Satan. All that money will buy. Look at Joe McCray. He had the stuff, but he couldn't use it."

Satan shook his head. He wasn't angry. He wasn't even offended. It wasn't the first time people had tried to bribe him. Though never before had he been offered so much. He said simply: "I'm no better than any other cop. I've got no ideals; no high opinions or copy book beliefs that honesty is the best policy. I just don't need money. Wouldn't know what to do with it."

"There's nothing you want, eh?" The soft, feminine sound had gone out of Hollis Daggett's voice; the tiny mouth was hard-set, almost square.

Satan started, and stopped; leaned forward. "Yes, there is," he said almost viciously. "I want to get guys like you. Like you and McCray."

"So that's how it is." Round eyes were sharp as a vulture's.

"That"—Satan leaned far back in the chair—"is just how it is."

Hollis Daggett came to his feet. A chubby hand came out; a stubby finger jabbed toward Satan.

"All right. I'll give you orders, then. Lay off McCray. I'm trying to be nice; trying to be easy with you. I don't want trouble on the avenue. I like McCray. I'm running things in this city. I know you; know your record. I need McCray, and I don't want to complicate things. I know just what you intend to do. McCray's built like that, too. He won't take your lip. I don't want him to shoot you to death. Not right now."

Hollis Daggett paused. He looked down at the man, so quiet; so serene there in the chair. Satan's face hadn't changed any; yet a queer sound had come from his lips.

Daggett was a wise man; he had come through a hard school, where success was achieved by first stepping on the shoulders of his friends, then standing by and watching the dirt being shoveled in on their faces. He knew men; he knew people. He had not exactly expected to bulldoze Satan. But that queer sound! Daggett told himself it wasn't true, but he knew that Satan had laughed.

"Well," said Daggett after a bit, "what do you intend to do?" He was sorry the moment he had spoken. He liked to say something and let the other man talk around it.

Satan came slowly to his feet, walked leisurely across the room and lifted the phone. He flipped the receiver into his hand and called a number. After a bit he said: "Gilded Globe? Get me Kirby. That's right—of the *Tribune*. And stick a connection in on the bar; there's nothing private about this conversation." Green eyes gleamed as Daggett half reached for the phone and dropped his hand almost at once to his side.

"Kirby? Satan Hall talking. I'm coming down to have a talk with McCray. He is, eh? Well, shoot the message right along the bar. You might say that friends will try to influence him to take a run-out powder. No, no. Open and aboveboard! Speak your piece like a radio announcer. Let him know he's got the whole city to hide out in if he doesn't want to hear what I've got to say. Sure! Shoot it out now."

Satan dropped the phone back on the table.

"You got your answer, Daggett," he said.

Daggett was a man who prided himself on never losing his temper; not even his sense of balance. But he was losing that sense of balance now. He knew it. He didn't care.

"Satan," he said, "you and I are alone. You remember

the old days when I did my own business? Well, did you ever think you might not leave this place alive?''

Satan waved his hand about the room.

''You never trusted anyone, Daggett—not a soul. You're alone in the house. It's the way you're built. Personally, you're not a hell of a lot of grief to me; not tonight. It takes too long for you to get to work. Strings—just strings.''

Daggett's voice was husky.

''There are four men outside. Four, waiting. I have only to say the word.''

Satan nodded.

''Only four. You don't flatter me, Daggett. Not by a damn sight. I thought there were six at least. I saw to it that they got a good look at me before I came in.'' He read the concentration on the other man's face. ''I thought you didn't tell them who it was. They'll hesitate when I leave—if they're still there.''

Daggett moistened his lips.

''You're a guy who thinks pretty well of himself,'' he said without much point.

''That's right!'' said Satan. ''And I don't care who knows it.''

''And me. And me!'' Daggett's voice was shrill now. ''You see only the present, Satan, not the future. Dutch Albert; Eddie Malone; even Joe McCray. He's impulsive. But, me! You can't just work that gun stuff on me. You've got something to contend with.'' The smoothness had gone from Daggett's voice, from his whole manner. He had slipped back over the years. The gangster who had become a political figure was talking. ''What about me?''

Satan shoved out a long finger, sunk it suddenly in Daggett's fat middle.

''You haven't changed so much, Daggett, and lead in

the belly, right there in the belly, is going to hurt just as much today as it did ten years ago.''

Satan walked heavily toward the front door, jerked off the chain, heard it jangle against the wall. There was a certain grunt of satisfaction that he couldn't hide when he opened the gate and stepped out onto the street, unmolested. His face was his fortune, and he knew it.

F I V E

AT THE GILDED GLOBE

■

Joe McCray carried himself well. If clothes could make the man, Joe was made. It was his boast that he never put a "rag on his back" that cost less than a sucker's wardrobe for a year. And he wore his clothes well. He had been in the money for some time. He had never taken any leading position in the days before repeal. He was satisfied to stand back and collect the heavy dough for knocking over undesirable citizens.

He was not a leader who liked to sit back and give orders. Joe liked to get out in the world and do things; do them himself. When Hollis Daggett took control, Joe came into prominence. He could be counted to go out and do things, and Hollis Daggett wanted things done. A man doesn't suddenly grab off the sugar in a big city without incurring the enmity of others; others who were used to sitting in high places.

Joe was envied. He carted two guns, had a license to carry them, and, as far as the underworld was concerned, a license to use them. Daggett stood flat-footed behind him, and Daggett controlled him. It was something, too, to control Joe McCray; the bad boy even of crime-land; the man who swaggered his way about the city; the man who did more for Daggett than he did for himself. For it was known that Daggett simply had to pass the word to Joe to start the fireworks. Joe was Daggett's right-hand man. He feared no present because he could take care of himself; he feared no future because Daggett could take care of that.

Now he leaned his muscular frame against the end of the bar and sipped champagne. He bought it by the dozen bottles when he felt in the mood, but he didn't drink it that way. He knew too many nice boys—big boys who departed this world because of the simple words, "Just one more."

"Listen, sweetheart!" Joe McCray lifted Nina Radcliff up on the end of the long bar. "You should drink champagne, breakfast, noon and night. It makes your eyes dance—sparkle. Yes, even me! I'm proud to be seen with you."

"It's this man; this detective, Joe. There seemed such hate in his eyes; in his voice. And he called you a rat. I didn't think anyone would dare, even when you weren't there. To me, too."

She threw up her chin; her little nose raised. Her eyes were bright with youth and wine. She liked this man; liked to hear him talk; liked to see the way headwaiters bowed to him and men jumped from their tables that he might give her the most desirable seat in the dining room. It wasn't money. All the people she knew had that. It wasn't just bluster, though he was loud at times and did like to talk about himself. Though it was all true. Men feared him. All men. When she was with him she was somebody. Not because her father had money, but because she was with McCray. He feared neither man, God, nor devil. He told her so.

Nor devil! She looked at Joe again.

"That's it." She nodded. "He looked exactly like a devil; as if he'd come straight up from hell." She giggled slightly at her own daring; her own almost swaggering importance as she sat there on the end of the bar.

Joe McCray laughed.

"If he bothers you again, sweetheart, back he goes to hell. As for me!" He waved a hand deprecatingly. "I drove him off the avenue before, and I'll drive him off again. Rat, eh?" He pinched her cheek, turned suddenly to the bartender. "Champagne! All along the bar. To the queen of them all!" And with a pride that he could not keep out of his voice, "To Joe McCray's girl!"

The girl liked it. At least, she thought she did. Something inside of her jarred at the "Joe McCray's girl." But she liked it. She raised her glass high and told herself over and over again that she liked it.

"And that," said Joe loudly, "means a quart for the news hound Kirby—or just hound." He laughed. A dozen others along the bar laughed. "He can't help working for that dirty sheet. What do you say, Kirby?" He beckoned the newspaperman along the bar. "A drink to McCray's girl. A drink even to Joe McCray."

Kirby took the bottle of champagne, poured out a glass, downed it with a single gulp.

"It's good wine," he said, "no matter who pays for it."

"That's you! That's your kind." Joe McCray sneered at Kirby. "You'd lie all over your face about a man and drink his liquor."

"That's right," said Kirby. "As long as it's good liquor."

"A drink even to Hollis Daggett, eh?"

"Sure!" Kirby grinned. "A drink even to Hollis Daggett."

Joe McCray dropped his air of light banter.

"Someday you'll play the lamb to my little Mary once too often. Why are you here tonight?"

"It's a public place." Kirby shrugged. And after a bit, "I want to see the fun."

Joe McCray had turned away. He swung quickly back.

"What fun are you talking about?" Thick lips curled. He was not handsome for the moment then; his nose seemed bigger, flatter, and his long, thin eyes even further apart in his head.

"*Any* fun." Kirby looked at the girl. "Having a good time, Miss Radcliff?"

If Joe McCray didn't catch the inflection in his voice, the girl did. She flushed, then kicked her feet against the bar.

"One always has a good time with Joe," she said.

McCray was following a single trend of thought: Kirby's continued presence there at the bar.

"Fun, eh?" He set those narrow eyes on Kirby. "You're thinking someone is coming here tonight? That's what you're thinking?"

Kirby moved slender sloulders.

"Satan's back on the avenue. I was just wondering."

"So?" McCray laughed. "I scared him off once and I'll scare him off again. What are you grinning at? You don't believe that?"

"No," said Kirby, "and neither do you."

McCray straightened from the bar. He knew, of course, that Kirby spoke the truth. He had tried to tell himself different for the past months, but he couldn't make himself believe it. He didn't fear Satan; he didn't fear any man. He never had; never would. His right hand closed into a fist, half raised. And the bartender spoke: "Phone for you, Kirby. Wants you to take it here." The white coat was half beneath the bar. It came up suddenly; a phone was shoved over the bar. The Gilded Globe boasted service!

It was pretty hard to faze Kirby; it was doubtful if he was fazed now. But he was surprised; perhaps even shocked, and he had trouble getting his words out when he set down the receiver. Joe McCray was watching him. The half dozen men; Joe's "close friends," for Joe would never admit of a bodyguard, were strangely silent, too—yet they couldn't have heard what came over the wire. At last Kirby spoke. The words sounded hollow to him.

"He's coming here!" he said. "Satan Hall. He asked for you, Joe. Said to tell you there were a hundred places in the city you could hide out in if you wanted to take a run-out powder. Said—said he wanted to talk to you."

Joe McCray just stood there and stared at the reporter. He didn't speak; just looked at the long, lanky figure. Then ran the back of his hand across his mouth.

Kirby started to speak again; to repeat the message in a slow, even voice. Suddenly he broke in on himself.

"What a story!" he said.

"Shut up!" The words came from deep down in McCray's throat. He raised his head; glared along the bar. When he spoke again his voice was loud. "That dick—Hall, eh? Coming here to see me; trying to square himself; trying to get an 'in.' "

Kirby looked over the bar, at nothing. Raised his glass, smacked his lips, laid his glass down again.

"Dutch Albert is dead," he said slowly. "Malone kicked over less than two hours ago. Nice boys, Joe. You remember?"

Joe McCray's right hand mechanically and perhaps unconsciously sank under his left armpit; it rested there a moment. His face was hard; tense.

Nina said: "I'd do nothing for him, Joe—not a damn thing. He said you were a rat, and when I found out—"

Kirby laughed, raised his glass, looked at the bubbles.

"It's a new one for you, Joe. On the spot! Got an appointment uptown, haven't you?"

McCray raised his hand, smacked it in a snapping motion. There was a thud. Kirby staggered backward, the glass fell to the floor. He clutched at the bar, regained his balance. A tiny trickle of blood came from between his lips.

Nina Radcliff said, "Oh!" in a funny little voice. She didn't drink any more. She put the glass down. The phone rang again.

The white-coated man said: "Want to take it in the booth, Joe? It's the big fellow."

Kirby rubbed the blood from his lips.

"He'd better take it up in Harlem," he said.

Joe McCray hesitated, stepped toward Kirby; turned back and said to the bartender: "Plug me in a rope. That's the stuff!" The conversation was one-sided. McCray seemed to be arguing, then his voice raised. His eyes wandered the full length of the bar. He said in a loud voice, "That's the office. If he's looking for trouble he'll get it. No—not me. Hell! He wouldn't have the guts for it! By God! I'd turn the heat on him."

The phone slid back along the bar and was scooped up quickly by nimble fingers before it reached the floor. Three men in a booth got up and left the place quietly; others sidled toward the door. A half dozen or more moved down the bar toward McCray. They nodded, tossed their heads indifferently, almost defiantly. The door to the bar opened and closed. Six men started; turned quickly. Hands that had been hidden came into view, hung listlessly by their side, plainly visible—empty. A waiter came in.

The bartender rubbed down the bar, spoke to McCray. His voice was apologetic.

"You ain't going to start anything here, are you?"

McCray hesitated, lifted his glass, drained it, looked at the boys, at the bartender.

"I never start anything, Jake; I just finish it," he said. "That's me, Joe McCray."

A dead silence, then the sudden babbling of voices. One man laughed; another joined him. A third said: "If Satan Hall pops in here he'll be surprised, eh, Joe?"

"And how!" Joe laughed; the others laughed; the girl giggled. But the bartender just rubbed down the bar. The talk became general; trite; even stupid. Joe threw down another glass of wine; it warmed his stomach, tingled pleasantly. He didn't drink much. He said to Kirby: "You see what happens when you open your pan too often? Sore as hell, eh? Don't feel like laughing now."

Kirby wiped at his mouth, looked at the blood on his fingers.

"Not me," he said. "I've got some sense of decency. I never laugh at the dead."

Joe McCray looked at him a long time.

"This Satan must be some parsnips, eh? It's time he was put in his place. Tough dick that's been playing around with hoods and dips. I've got a century that says he don't come. It's bluff."

A thickset man in a blue shirt and dotted bow tie said: "Nix, Joe. He don't bluff."

"Who asked you to put your face in?" Joe glared at him.

Kirby looked at Joe McCray a long moment.

"I haven't got a century, but I've got ten bucks. Ten bucks that says he comes."

McCray nodded, laughed.

The girl said: "Aw—nerts!" She was feeling the wine a bit.

After that a long silence. McCray was thinking. He wasn't afraid. But he thought of what he had heard about Satan. He called to a thin-faced man: "On your way, Frankie. Go get yourself a few friends."

Kirby straightened against the bar. He knew what that meant. Frankie was hot; he couldn't stand being dragged over the coals. He looked at Joe. It was a hard, cruel face; a mean face, but it was a determined face. He wondered if he was going to lose that ten. Joe McCray shot fast. Was Satan going to meet up with—

And Satan came. The wing door from the long, narrow hall banged open and crashed back against the wall. Men at the bar moved quickly; seemed to fade back as if opening a prearranged path. Bartenders moved quickly to the front of the bar.

Satan didn't hesitate. He walked straight down the length of that room—the length of that bar. His steps were slow, almost measured. His arms swung by his sides and his hands showed; white hands; empty hands. Joe McCray straightened. His right hand came mechanically up, half crossed a white shirt-bosom. His coat fell back; a shoulder holster was plainly visible.

His eyes dropped, rested on Satan's left hand and then his right. Both hands were empty. Joe's first thought was one of satisfaction, almost elation. Then that thought died. Stories he had heard; quick, kaleidoscopic thoughts raced through his mind. Satan's hands were always empty when he was on the kill, forcing a man into a draw.

His lips parted; he smiled. Satan wasn't bent on trouble. Satan wouldn't dare face him like that if he were.

And Satan was facing him; standing directly before him now. Green eyes bored into his.

"Hello, Rat," Satan said. His green eyes never moved to the fascinated, staring eyes of the girl. "Yellow rat! Stick a knife in a woman's throat."

Joe McCray was a vicious man and he liked viciousness in those who worked under him. That he confused it with ruthlessness didn't matter. He read, now, all the viciousness, hate, ruthlessness he admired in the green eyes of Satan, but he didn't admire it then. For he read something else in those eyes; something that he always recognized in a man's eyes and acted on—quickly, surely. What he read was lust; the lust to kill, just as surely as he ever had read it in any gunman's face.

Joe McCray tried to sneer; anyway, his lips curved. And then he saw Satan's right hand come up empty. Red lips before him were just a vivid gash; green eyes lights of fire. And he knew the truth and cried out his warning: "None of that with me, Satan; none of that. Or, by God I'll blast you out where you stand!"

Joe knew the showdown had come, and he wasn't afraid. Joe knew it, and he was going to kill. He didn't think of Daggett then; didn't think that Daggett would see him through. He knew only that Satan Hall was pulling his old stuff; slapping him down as he might slap down any common hood along the avenue. He didn't care. He was going to kill.

Satan's right hand came up open; it moved quickly. There was a slap that wounded like wood meeting wood, then the sharp sting of the open palm against his cheek. Joe's body rocked sideways against the bar, and his hand darted beneath his left armpit—and stayed there.

There was lots of time. He could see Satan's right hand still raised in the air, and still empty. He could see his left hand coming up. Why, no man could do that to him and be quick enough to duck a hand beneath an armpit and get him!

Five full seconds; seconds that seemed like hours in the stillness of that bar, passed before Satan's left hand came up, came up and struck Joe across the right cheek, rocking him back again.

Both hands empty; both hands in full view—and Joe's fingers tightened about his gun. Then two things happened at once.

Someone said: "Don't do it, Joe. He's on the kill." That was the first thing. What Joe heard. The second thing was what Joe saw.

Joe saw through Satan's green eyes and the thing behind them. It was as if he looked into the depths of hell; a hell that was waiting for him. Both his hands fell to his sides; fell there as Satan's right hand dropped, turned into a fist, and hurtling upwards, landed right on the end of his jaw.

McCray—Joe McCray, the most feared gunman in the city, folded up like a jackknife and sank to the cold tile floor. He had been slapped down like any common punk, and not one of his friends had raised a hand or a gun to help him. But why should they? The feared Joe McCray had not raised a hand or a gun to help himself.

Satan looked down at the fallen man, shook his head, looked about the room, then raised his eyes to the startled ones of the girl.

"There's your rat," he said slowly. "The worst kind of a rat. He had his chance and he wouldn't take it. Well?"

The girl said, her eyes wide: "You brute. You brute!"

Satan laughed.

"I thought you liked your men that way. Rough, tough he-men." He kicked the unconscious man in the side, turned and passed slowly down the length of the bar. Men gave him room.

Kirby was shouting into a phone at the end of the bar: "The hell I'm drunk! McCray. Yes, Joe McCray! I'm telling you Satan Hall slapped him silly, then knocked him cock-eyed with a single punch. Sure. Sure!"

Kirby nodded at the phone but looked at the disappearing back of Satan Hall. "If all hell breaks loose in the city tonight the devil's walking the streets to take care of it."

ONE HOUR TO LIVE

■

Hollis Daggett apparently sat very comfortably back in the big chair. He tapped his glasses steadily, almost in rhythm, upon the palm of his thick left hand.

For the first time in his life Joe McCray was ill at ease. He stood first on one foot and then on the other. He waited for Daggett to speak; then couldn't wait any longer. He said, thickly: "I'll kill him. I'll have every boy out looking for him. But I'll find him and kill him."

Hollis Daggett's smile was not pleasant.

"He walks into the Gilded Globe and knocks you around. He shows no gun; no weapon—just knocks you around. Now, you're going to kill him!"

"Cripes, boss! I don't know; don't know what happened, what came over me. I was just going to let him have it! Someone yelled. I think it was Frankie; he hadn't gone yet. It threw me. And Satan's eyes! I don't understand it myself."

"Then you stepped on a banana peel and slipped, eh?"

Joe got sulky, but not too sulky.

"I'll get him. I'll kill him!" he said again.

Hollis Daggett made funny little sounds in his throat.

"That's what he wants, Joe." A chubby finger came out. "He's put the mark on you. You've heard of it. Satan's mark! Your hand will tremble now. The finger's on you!"

"Not me!" Joe shot the words in; followed them with oaths. "That damn girl was there, too."

"Another reason!" Daggett nodded. "I never liked excuses, Joe. I never knew you made them. About the girl, Nina Radcliff! You've been through her rooms? I mean the ones downtown."

"She's okay."

"I know. I know." The eyes that watched Joe now were like two holes in a blanket. "But she was Mercy Oakes' friend. Mercy Oakes was working more for her than for the law. Mercy Oakes had the goods on you, Joe; you told me that yourself. We never found that evidence. You searched the girl's rooms downtown?"

"Hell!" said Joe. "I tell you she's all right. I could marry her tomorrow."

"About her rooms downtown!"

"I tell you she's all right. She hasn't even been to those rooms since Mercy died."

Hollis Daggett came to his feet.

"That's it, then! Mercy told you where you stood before—before you did it, of course. Mercy was sure then; sure that Nina Radcliff would know; that Nina would tell the police. There—don't talk. Listen!" A pudgy hand came up. "It's quite possible, Joe, that Mercy guessed our purpose and mailed that information to Nina Radcliff; mailed it to those rooms that Nina Radcliff hasn't visited since."

"Cripes!" Joe was startled. "I thought all along that Morrisey had it, whatever it was, and didn't think it was worth using with you behind me." Joe's voice was a little ingratiating; something new for him. He didn't exactly fear Daggett. It was something different from that. Daggett had a sort of power that Joe didn't have; didn't fully understand.

"I'm a businessman, Joe, and so are you. I need money. You've interfered with the collecting of that money. Get down and search that apartment of the Radcliff girl's." He leaned forward. "You've hurried things, Joe; anticipated me."

Joe nodded but didn't quite understand. He said simply: "Whatever you say, boss. I'll square things with Satan later."

"*I'll* square things with him. I've been on the phone, Joe. I've been taking care of your interests. We'll have to let the rescue come through you, I guess. It will square you with the press; the public. The officials, I'll fix."

"The commissioner! He's a tough egg, boss."

"Yes, yes. I know. But election is coming around." Daggett hesitated a long minute. "I'd liked to have had Satan out of the way first."

"I'll knock him off tonight, if—"

Daggett shook his head. His voice was very soft, like a woman's. He was thinking while he talked.

"I'll run the show. Let the boys take her to the house on Seventy-sixth Street. You know the place. I've had it planted for months. I think"—he rubbed at the rolling fat that was developing chins—"yes, I think I'll be the go-between. There'll be no ransom, Joe. That will look good for you and me in the papers."

"But I thought you needed the jack! I could use money."

"You can always use money." Daggett's mouth puckered; his little eyes twinkled. "I meant that there will be no public ransom. A demand, but no payment; no payment because of my cleverness and your—er—shall we say, altruistic heroism?"

"Yeah—maybe!" Joe never liked that kind of talk. He didn't get it. "But the jack!"

"Oh, that! That will be simply business—between Radcliff, myself, and the bank. Just a note, Joe. Very private business."

Joe laughed. He didn't know why. Then he frowned.

"Then what?" he said.

"I think you'd better marry the girl—right then. It will silence Radcliff, give the press a story of romance and heroism, and you'll have a wife that gives you an 'in' in the right places where the big money is."

"Yeah—a wife. I'm not strong for her, boss. She don't get me like some dames. Has ideas; ideals, she calls them. Blows me higher than a kite one night with her praise for being a big shot, talks about changing my life and living off in the country the next. She talks like you sometimes."

"Don't worry about that." Hollis Daggett nodded. "I've seen her; met her once or twice with you, Joe." His lips parted, uneven little teeth showed. "If you find things dull I'll take her off your hands, Joe. Entertain her."

Joe laughed.

"You're a card, boss," he said. "Imagine you—" He stopped, and looked at Daggett. Dull coals flamed brightly; burned.

"Well"—Hollis Daggett was more than sensitive about his appearance—"there was Doris Kline and Gladys Riece. Do you see any reason why women should not like me?"

"No, no!" Joe said hurriedly, and changed the subject. "You should have someone here with you, boss. I mean here in the house. Even one good man. I can fix it."

Daggett shook his head.

"The less people know about you and your affairs the

safer you are. My enemies are not close enough to bother
me; besides, they know better. Remember, Joe. It's your
friends you must fear most in life. There's a man out on
the grounds. Just one man, Joe. One man has nobody to
plot or plan with. It's getting late—almost twelve o'clock!
Get down to her apartment." And as Joe moved toward the
door, he added, "How did she take it, there at the Gilded
Globe? You saw her home, afterwards?"

"No, I didn't. She wasn't there. Don't look at me like
that! I've got that kid right smack under my thumb; you
couldn't expect a dame to stand around." He hesitated a
long moment. "I think that news guy, Kirby, chased her
out, and damn it! I think he followed me here."

"There's no harm in following you here. You're my
friend, Joe. Don't forget that. Don't forget that when you
marry the girl."

"Sure!" Joe smirked. "I think you're soft on that
skinny little trick." He dug Hollis Daggett in the ribs now;
he was quite familiar. "I'm your friend, boss."

"Yes, yes." Hollis Daggett straightened, swung swiftly
toward the door. "Give me a buzz on what you find
downtown. I'll be up until three."

Joe McCray had more to say; much more. It was all
about Satan. But he didn't say it. Marry the girl, eh?
Marry a banker's daughter! He might join a club or two. It
wouldn't be so bad to walk in and tell a bunch of those
stuffed shirts where they got off; watch them take it,
cringe.

And he laughed at Hollis Daggett's fears. Daggett was
always thinking, always scheming—never acting. If *he* had
been running the show he'd have had the girl snatched
months ago; be spending the money by now. The girl!
Queer piece of goods, that. Talked about marriage and
love; was as cold as an Arctic night. Hollis Daggett could

have her for all he cared. Marriage wouldn't interfere with a lad getting around; not a lad like Joe McCray, anyway. There were many times when he wanted to smack his fist on that tilted, high-hatting chin of hers. Damn it! You'd think she owned him.

But as he went downtown he smiled. He was figuring how much cash there would be in it for him.

Satan lay on his back and listened to the phone ring. The commissioner, probably. Things hadn't gone right. He had hoped to end Joe McCray for good and all that night; and he had given Joe a break. A break that, for a man as quick on the draw as Joe McCray, would be considered suicide by many.

Satan knew that deep down someplace inside of him Joe would be yellow; all such murderers were. Once you got beneath the veneer, the sneering exterior, behind the smoking gun, you found putty. But he had thought the yellow lay far deeper in Joe McCray. He thought he'd dig for a rod, even shoot; and Satan had expected to take a hunk of lead in the arm, the shoulder—even in the chest. Yes, by God! he would have been willing to take it right smack in the stomach, just for one shot, one single shot at Joe McCray.

The phone rang again. Satan looked at it. So Joe had already run with his squawk to Hollis Daggett, and wires were being pulled. Pulled? Jerked clear out of their sockets! That might do him a lot of harm, but it wouldn't do McCray much good. The story would fly through the underworld. And the girl!

He had rather liked the girl in an impersonal way. But he thought she had more stuff than she showed when he made a rat out of Joe McCray. The ringing was continuous now.

Well, he never ducked trouble. Commissioner or no commissioner, Satan reached out and grabbed up the phone.

"Satan talking," he said gruffly. "What do you want?"

"Detective Hall," the voice was very low, "this is Nina—Nina Radcliff." As if he wouldn't know. "I lied to you there tonight at the bar. I was too stunned and dazed to speak the truth, but I think I did know it. Anyway, I know it now."

"Yes?" said Satan.

"You see," she went on. "Maybe I'm trying to excuse myself, but I think—yes, I'm sure I would have called you, anyway, if I hadn't found what I did."

"Ah!" said Satan. "What did you find?"

"Evidence. And a letter to me from Mercy Oakes."

"Where are you, home?"

"No. An apartment down in Greenwich Village. Mercy mailed it to me here."

"Yes," said Satan. "Morrisey was working on that end of it. But he never turned it up."

"The apartment isn't under my name. Only Mercy and McCray knew of it. It gave me more freedom. The letter was there in my mailbox."

Satan had switched on the light; had lifted a pencil, held it poised over a pad of paper. Long training on the force had instilled certain rules in him. He cut in on her.

"The number of the apartment. Street number?"

And when she gave it to him: "Go on."

"It was here in my mailbox; anyone could have found it. I came here tonight to think. And I would have called you before. I opened it. You'll come down?"

"Go on," said Satan. "I'll come down, but go on!"

"It was evidence to be given to Lieutenant Morrisey, and a letter to me. Mercy was going to see McCray; she didn't think I'd believe her. I wasn't to open the letter unless she was dead. God, God!'' She started to cry. ''She was going to promise him never to produce that evidence if he let me alone. She—she died for me. He murdered Mercy.'' Her voice raised now. ''It's I who am the rat—the rat. I want him dead. I want him dead in the chair. He murdered Mercy. Joe McCray! He cut her throat and tossed her out into the street—''

A moment ot silence, a quick intake of breath, then a scream; a piercing shriek that for the moment had been held in check by terror.

After that a thud, a quick gasp that might have been a groan. Then the thump of a body hitting the floor.

Plainly came the words, ''You two-timing little twist!''

The voice was the voice of Joe McCray.

ONE HOUR TO LIVE

■

Hollis Daggett leaned over to the flat table, lifted a card from it, inserted it carefully between the pages of the book he was reading, laid the big expensively bound volume gently on the table, then lifting the French phone from its cradle, answered it.

"Yes?" he said—and jarred erect. But he listened intently and his curses were so low and soft they didn't reach over the wire. He listened and thought. And his thoughts were not pleasant. He should have known the truth; known it the minute the story reached him that Satan had given it and Joe McCray had taken it.

He knew, too, that the girl must die. He would have to stick to Joe; just as long as Joe lived. They were too closely wound up together not to; far too closely, he thought. He didn't lose his head. He was trying to think of a way to get the money also. And he couldn't. Radcliff would come out flat-footed after the girl was dead; no two ways about that. It might be better to wash his hands clean of the whole thing. Yes, the girl had to die. The longer she lived the greater the danger to McCray, the greater the danger to him.

"Listen, Joe!" he said finally. "You can't hide the body; it's too risky. You say she was talking to someone. Hall, eh? That's bad. But, after all, it's only hearsay. The state can't prove that you were there; only that Satan says the girl said you were. But we can prove that you were somewhere else. It'll have to be good; a real good alibi. Men—well-known men from widely different areas—come together through chance. Say four, or even five of them. It's difficult, but it can be done. There's the senator. You know who I mean. He won't like it, but he'll have to come through. I never used him before on anything big." The phone shrilled.

"What?" said Daggett. And after a bit, "No! I said no. Dump her straight out of the car, like the last one. A card, too, Joe. Yes, a card. Let me think! 'So die the daughters of those who have robbed the public.' Mercy Oakes' uncle was a banker in the Middle West. It'll sound like a crank. We'll tip that to the papers. She's still alive, eh?"

Hollis Daggett hesitated a long moment. He told himself it was the hope of getting that hundred thousand dollars. He cursed Joe, but it was all inside of him. He didn't exactly admit the truth to himself, but he was thinking of the girl. If he had combed the city, the whole country, he couldn't have found one more to his liking. He was a big man, none bigger. Maybe he could fix things so that she could live.

"Sit tight, Joe!" he said finally. "I want to think; yes, damn it! Think I'll call you back in . . . No, I won't. If . . ."

And he knew she couldn't live. She had to die. He didn't like to give the order, that was all. But he didn't need to give it. He finally said, "If you don't hear from me in an hour, let her have it. Dump the body on a side street and get over to the hideout in Newark. I'll get in touch with you.''

Another moment of silence.

''Sure! Cut her throat. Just the same way!''

He felt sorry for the girl. She was cute tricks. But what could he do? He sighed, set down the phone, half turned his head—and paused. Plainly he heard stairs creak. And Hollis Daggett knew, or thought he knew, that he was alone in the house.

He didn't lose his head and he didn't turn. Rather slowly he came to the edge of the chair, puckered his lips, whistled softly, and with an easy indifference, pulled open the long drawer in the bottom of his table.

Nothing happened; no one spoke. Just the creak of the drawer as he opened it. Nerves? No, it couldn't be that. Imagination, then? Maybe. Things were certainly happening quickly enough and badly enough to play the devil with a man.

But if no one was there, why didn't he look? And he couldn't look. More than that, he didn't need to look. He knew someone was there. Felt the presence even without the groaning wood of the stairs.

The drawer was open. He moved his huge body slightly so as to hide from prying eyes the thing that he sought. Why the devil didn't he carry the gun, as he used to carry it years before? Years before! Well, not so many years. He was still a young man. Soft living had filled him out, that was all.

The gun was there. He saw it; whistled a bit louder. As his hand went forward he changed the whistle to a hum. He was trying to listen, too. He'd have to grab the gun, swing and fire. Certainly the man was armed. The man! He wondered. The guard outside, the ladder down by the water behind the house. The thought that he had money in the house? But, no. The guard wouldn't dare. And Daggett's stubby fingers closed about the butt of that gun, seemed to suck it quickly into his hand. His index finger wrapped around the trigger.

Hollis Daggett jerked out the gun and swung.

There was a single shot. The gun fell from his hand, bounced upon the floor. Blood was running over his fingers as he jerked to his feet and faced the man who had fired.

"Hall!" he cried out. "Satan Hall! By God! I'll break you for this!"

Satan shook his head.

"Not you," he said slowly. "I've come here to kill you, Daggett."

"You—?" Daggett tried to laugh. It was a rattle in his throat. Then he saw the thing in Satan's face; Satan's eyes. Words he didn't want to say, never meant to say, just came out. He said: "Good God! Kill me? Why?"

"Because I want you to tell me where the girl is—Nina Radcliff. You'll figure it will roast you, and you won't talk."

"That's right." Daggett nursed his wrist, backed toward the chair, glanced toward the phone. Sometimes he wondered if this man was a little mad. "I don't know, and I can't talk."

"I heard you on the phone." Satan nodded. "You won't talk and you've got to die."

"Listen!" Hollis Daggett watched those green eyes and talked fast. "Nothing to do with the girl can be pinned on me; not a thing. I know what Chester Radcliff said; what you heard. I went to the bank to borrow money. I *did* offer my help when I heard the girl was in trouble. That help might have influenced Radcliff to grant my loan. But what good would it do me now if the girl were dead?''

"That's right," said Satan. "What good would it do you if she were dead? Where is she, Daggett?''

"I don't know. You misunderstood my—''

Hollis Daggett tried to step back but the chair prevented him. He staggered slightly, gripped at the arm, raised his hand to his head; to his face, but too late. Satan's arm had shot up, his gun down. It turned in his hand; the nose of it whipped down Daggett's face, cutting, tearing, ripping the flesh wide open.

Hollis Daggett screamed. The gun came again. His lip was torn; he fell to his knees.

Again the gun, and Satan's voice.

"You're not going to tell, and I'm going to kill you."

"I don't know! I—Before God! I'll tell."

There were two reasons why Daggett was willing to talk. The one was plain enough. He knew men, and knew he was going to be beaten to death. He didn't know how he knew it, but he knew it. The other reason! Well, the chair didn't loom up for him. There was no way to connect him with Nina Radcliff. Just the one chance—if both the girl and Joe McCray lived. He was thinking that now; half kneeling, half sitting on the floor, his huge form, with the bloodstained face and popping little eyes, giving the appearance of some particularly repulsive species of frog.

Beaten to the floor, Hollis Daggett's mind was working clearly and quickly; never more quickly in his life. Satan Hall was a killer; Joe McCray was a killer. Both of them alive, and Daggett was through. One of them dead; it didn't matter which one, it would be different. For Satan alone, without Joe McCray to talk, could not send him to jail. McCray alone would have no cause to turn on him. And he felt certain that if those two men met tonight one of them would die. Both men were killers; killers of the most desperate type. He coughed out the words.

"You and I are through—you're through with me to-night if I talk; tell you where the girl is?"

"I'm through with you tonight if you tell me where she is."

"Good. Good!" Hollis Daggett was thinking of his own position; of the future; of the attack upon him. Satan certainly wouldn't mention it, and he couldn't. It wouldn't help him in the half-world that he ruled if they knew that he turned up Joe McCray.

"Very well." Daggett climbed to his knees, gripped at the chair. It was the best he could do. For the life of him he couldn't lift his huge body into that chair. "She's in a brownstone front on Seventy-sixth Street." And he gave Satan the number.

Satan looked at him a long minute.

"That's God's truth, Daggett?"

"God's truth," said Daggett. And with some of the bitterness that was back in his mind, "You washed up McCray tonight. I didn't want to get in his thing; I'm not in it. I don't care if you shoot him to death."

"On that one thought we're agreed," Satan said. "Sure you haven't lied! You'll be here if I have to return."

"I haven't lied," said Daggett. And, taking Satan's second statement for a question, "I'll be here if you return."

"You will!" said Satan Hall as he glanced at the phone. "You certainly will."

He raised his gun quickly and crashed it down on the top of Hollis Daggett's head. Daggett sank more than fell, and seemed to spread out slowly on the floor. Then he was still; very still indeed.

EIGHT

A GUN FROM BEHIND

■

For a full minute, perhaps, Satan stood looking down at the silent hulk of the man. Once he half raised his gun, covered the body with it, picked out a place in the center of the battered face and half tightened his finger on the trigger. He was thinking of the girl; the girl with the turned-up nose and the slightly snippy manner.

He shook his head. He could kill. But he couldn't go to murder.

He let the gun fall close to his side again, glanced at the phone, seemed to measure the distance between it and the inert form. The life of the girl would depend on the ability of that man to reach the phone; the life of the girl and the death of Joe McCray. Sure! The death of Joe McCray! He'd never be taken alive, red-hot like that.

Satan straightened; jerked erect. Much as Hollis Daggett had jerked erect a few minutes before. His right hand half raised with the gun, his left slipped easily into his jacket pocket. But, unlike Hollis Daggett, he didn't have time to think things over; plan things. The voice spoke quickly.

Feet were crossing the wood of the floor, muffled by the thick, expensive rug.

The voice said: "Drop the gun before you turn. By God! Satan Hall, I know you. If you so much as turn your head I'll fire!"

Satan opened the fingers of his right hand. The gun fell to the floor. He turned slowly and faced Kirby, of the *Tribune*. His green eyes widened; his lips parted.

"Kirby!" He was surprised. "And alone?"

"Yes, alone," Kirby agreed. "I've watched this house a lot. Tonight I followed McCray here, saw him leave, saw you come, looked through the gate and saw you drop the guard outside; at least, I saw him lying there. It wasn't hard to follow you, find the ladder and climb in the second-story window almost on your heels."

"Why the gun, then?" Satan looked puzzled. "If you heard, why the stickup?"

"Because," said Kirby, "I did hear; did see. I don't want the same dose. Did you kill him?"

"Not him." Satan shook his head. "Put down the gun, Kirby. There isn't much time. The girl's life depends on action—quick action."

"That's right." Kirby moved, edging toward the phone. "I heard the address, too. I'm calling the paper. They'll call the cops. We'll have the rescue in print before the police even get there."

"You can't do that!" Satan said.

"No?" Kirby's voice was high-pitched; there weren't many guys who held Satan like this. "Who's going to stop me—you?"

"I hope not. No, I hope to God not," Satan said very seriously, and his eyes bored—deep, hard, cold eyes.

Kirby stepped back, away from the phone. For a moment he saw in Satan's eyes what others had seen there;

what he had heard was there. Yes, he was almost sure of it. It was as if Satan were making a decision; asking himself a question. And that question was, "Will I kill this man?" Or perhaps, "Must I kill this man?"

Satan spoke again.

"You can't do it, Kirby, because of the girl. You can't do it because of a possible leak. A call to McCray; a call here to Daggett. You can't do it because—"

"No nearer. By God! No nearer." Kirby almost screamed the words.

But Satan was nearer; much nearer. Kirby saw his right hand shoot suddenly out. His eyes bulged; sweat broke out on his forehead. He had never shot a man before. He had used a gun once or twice, but not even the same gun he now carried. But now! He jerked his hand up; tightened his finger on the trigger.

Kirby never knew which came first. The roar of the gun he held in his hand or Satan's hand against this wrist. Perhaps, it was simply the recoil of the gun that jarred his wrist. But, no; he knew it wasn't. He stood there, his hand empty now, the gun across the room against the wall. And he was looking into the green eyes of Satan.

He was going to die, he supposed. Satan would never want this to come out. And Satan killed; killed, if the stories around were true, just for the very pleasure of killing.

The green eyes were bright, the thin lips were parted. Kirby opened his mouth but didn't speak. Satan was smiling at him. It must be a smile.

Fascinated, he saw Satan lift his left hand from his jacket pocket; saw the gun that hand contained, and realized the truth. He finally said: "You had that gun there, like that—covering me all the time! You could have killed me any minute."

And Satan laughed.

"That's right." His head bobbed quickly up and down. "Any minute, any second, any split second. I was figuring the necessity; the chance I would have to take if I didn't."

"So." Kirby's tongue came out and licked at dry lips. "I was near death then; very near death."

"You were never nearer death before in your life," Satan said. "You see, it was your life or the girl's—and McCray's death."

"That's it. That's it!" Kirby nodded vigorously. "I read death; saw death in your eyes. What made you change your mind?"

Green eyes narrowed, thin lips parted.

"The way you held the rod; your whole grip on the gun. I guessed I could make it." Satan lifted his right hand, looked at the smudge of burned powder across the knuckles, the hole in his coat sleeve. "You were better than I thought."

"And him?" Kirby jerked a thumb down at the unconscious Daggett. "You didn't think of silencing me about him?"

"No. You can't think too much of yourself in this racket. And I knew I couldn't argue it out with you."

"You'll want my promise not to print it?"

"No." Satan looked straight into Kirby's eyes. "We both have the same job, Kirby—to serve the people. We both don't do it in the same way. A man's word is no better than his will to give it. I'm going to take you with me tonight. Daggett won't talk or make trouble for me because I'd tell why I gun-whipped him and the information I got. He turned squealer and rat when the big moment came."

"I saw it from the stairs. I don't blame him," said Kirby.

"But others will blame him. As for you! After tonight, if you think the city is better served without me, print what you saw here."

"Hell!" said Kirby, "it's a big story; a great story. But you know I won't print it. God! you could have killed me"—he snapped his fingers—"like that."

"Just like that," said Satan. "Get your gun and come on. We haven't much time."

Kirby's dilapidated coupe took them to Seventy-ninth Street and the two men walked slowly back, around the corner at Seventy-seventh Street and down to the middle of the block.

"This is directly behind the house where Miss Radcliff is," Satan said. "I'll duck down that alley, go over the fence behind and make an entrance."

"Wouldn't it be better for us to go around the block; hide across the street, and catch McCray and the others when they come out?"

"Better for us, yes," Satan agreed. "But the girl will come out dead. You wait here."

"But why?"

"Well"—Satan stroked his chin—"I didn't like Hollis Daggett. I hit him too soon; before I questioned him as to how many will be in that house. That's why I want you to wait here."

"The more in the house, the more you'll need me."

"No. The more in the house, the more people will need you. If I don't come out, tell the whole story—Daggett and all. It won't be much evidence, with you and the paper riding Daggett, and I'm not overliked by the boys. But, after all, I'm a cop, and some of the boys on their off nights may give the people vengeance, if not what the law calls justice."

"You're going in there alone! Why?"

"Why were you at Daggett's tonight—alone?"

"Hell! It's what I'm paid for."

"That's right," said Satan. "It's what I'm paid for, too. Slip into the rear yard of the house behind later, and if things look bad, shoot that gun of yours in the air." And with a grin, "You won't be liable to hurt anyone. 'Night!"

"Cripes!" Kirby said. And then "Cripes!" again when Satan's figure disappeared in the blackness of the alley.

NINE

"I WANT TO DIE"

■

Nina Radcliff sat straight and stiff in the plain kitchen chair. She had to sit straight, for she was bound tightly there, the rope wound about her feet, around her body; her hands securely tied before her. But her eyes were not taped and her mouth wasn't gagged. She used those eyes, and knew that she was on the third floor of the house. She used that mouth, and told Joe McCray what she thought of him; told him as he paced back and forth along that floor.

"Rat!" she said. "The worst kind of a rat. That's what Satan said you were, and it was the truth. Woman killer—that's all you are."

Joe McCray paused and looked at her. Then he shook her head. She wasn't a girl of his world. He knew that all along; knew it more so now. He had killed women before. Even Mercy Oakes had broken down at the end. Oh! Not like the women he knew; crying, pleading, screaming, cursing women—who went almost mad before they took the dose. He couldn't understand this girl. She certainly wasn't terror-stricken; maybe not even frightened. She just seemed angry. Peculiar, that. Anger at herself. Joe McCray had been going with a thoroughbred. The very opposite of himself. A human whose weakness was all on the outside, while Joe's weakness lay far deep inside of him. He couldn't understand her kind. He looked at her now, grinned.

"You've been a lot of trouble to me, High-hat." He nodded at her, curled up his thick lips. "You've got a nice throat. Daggett likes it. I like it for a different reason."

She looked straight at him.

"I've been thinking," she said slowly. "This Satan Hall! He hasn't got much use for women; doesn't know much about them. Yet he gave me the greatest compliment I ever had. Do you know what it was, Rat?"

Joe jarred slightly at the word. It was beginning to bother him. He looked at the tilted chin. His eyes narrowed, his fingers closed at his sides. But he gripped himself and said: "What did he say? Marriage and babies, and a home in the country?"

"No, he didn't." She seemed very serious. "He said you didn't love me; couldn't love me."

"I'll give him credit for being right in that."

"He said," the girl went on very slowly, as if she were talking to herself and McCray wasn't in the room with her, "that I was too good and clean, and decent. Maybe it wasn't true, but it makes it not so hard to die now. He thought it was true."

"You're not afraid to die, eh? You won't squeal when the moment comes? Do you know I like your throat; do you know how you're going to die?"

He was rather close to her now. He had never noticed her eyes much before, except that they sparkled and were bright and she looked like class, to cart around. Now— there was something new in them. Neither hate nor fear; just contempt—loathing.

"Yes." The girl put those eyes on him. "You're going to drag a knife across my throat."

"And you're not afraid?"

She shook her head. Her words were real; true; so sincere that they bit through even the thick skin of Joe McCray.

"I can remember it now. You held me in your arms once—for a moment. You were going to kiss me, and I jerked away. If you had kissed me, then I would have known the truth; I must have known it. No, I'm not afraid to die. You held me in your arms once." She shuddered. "I don't want to live now."

"You don't!" Joe didn't get it fully at first, and then he did. "So you'd rather die than remember that!" He jerked a knife into his hand, stepped toward the girl, half raised the knife—and saw the clock.

An hour had not passed since he spoke to Daggett. But what difference did that make? Daggett was getting too bossy, anyway. He moved toward the girl; liked the way she tried to draw back in the chair, put her chin down upon her chest. But he didn't like her eyes. They bored right through him; defiant. No terror.

"I'm afraid," she said. "But Satan will kill you; he said he would kill you. A rat; the worst kind of a rat held me in his arms."

Joe stiffened. She raised her head; her slender white throat was plainly visible. He only had to lift the knife and—and—

And in that moment Joe McCray hated her. The knife moved in the air. The clock ticked. He heard it plainly. Daggett—to hell with Daggett! But Daggett was to frame his alibi for that night; Daggett might have had some purpose in that hour's wait! What that purpose was Joe couldn't think. Then he didn't try to think. Just the flash that Daggett didn't do anything without a purpose, and he needed Daggett tonight—needed him more than he ever needed him.

Well—it was only fifteen minutes. He'd use it to advantage. She'd high-hat him, would she? She wanted to die, did she? A rat had held her in his arms! She'd die. Not like Mercy Oakes; with one squeal, like a stuck pig. He'd take that loathing, contemptuous look off her face. He would have her begging, crying, pleading.

Joe McCray did it. Did what he had wanted to do for a long time. He switched the knife to his left hand, closed the right one and let it go. It caught the girl on the end of the chin. Her head went back; the chair went with it, in a spinning, whirling motion before it struck against the wall and toppled to the floor.

Hate, anger, passion; the brutal viciousness in the man, all came to the surface then. He jerked the chair erect, laughed when he saw her eyes were still open and was glad that the moving chair broke the force of his blow.

"So you want to die?" he said. "You're going to, and how! They'll have trouble identifying you. You'll lie in the gutter for a while, then on a slab. If Satan can find anything good or fine or decent in that face of yours, why—"

"Satan will find you and kill you." The girl tried to keep her words calm, but they broke now. She tried to keep her eyes open, but the knife was very close; an evil, leering face almost against hers. She tried to tighten things inside of her; things that were all seeming to give at once. And she told herself over and over, "I never could have loved him; never could even have thought that I loved him. A rat held me in his arms and I want to die."

She heard the words, too, and didn't know at first that

she had spoken them. It was as if she were two persons. The one who was to die, and the one who stood across the room with her back against the wall and watched and nodded, and tried to help.

She didn't know if she heard the noise; the tinkle of breaking glass. But she must have, for the glaring face, with the hateful, malignant eyes and thick, curling lips, bobbed away from her eyes. Then she did hear, heard plainly the sudden roar of a gun—two quick shots and a single one, far below on the first floor, she thought. The police! Satan Hall! They were coming. There would be the tramp of feet now, many feet—shouting men.

But there weren't. Just those three shots; the two in quick succession and the single one that followed them. After that . . . silence.

She saw Joe McCray hurl the knife across the room onto the couch, saw the gun that seemed to jump into his right hand, saw his big form cross to the door; a hand jerked it open; knew that he was listening there. Finally he spoke, called loudly: "Frankie! Red! Frankie!"

And then an answer. That would be the man Frankie, on the second floor.

"It came from below," Frankie answered. "It's Red. He—Red! Red!" he called. And then suddenly, in a shriek of abject terror: "It's Hall—Satan Hall."

The girl heard the shots then. Five of them like a single blast, and again the single shot. A moment of silence; a queer rumbling sound, like a body—a falling body; a body that went over and over down a flight of stairs.

It was Satan then. Satan coming for her! Coming alone.

Something went up into her throat and jarred back again into her stomach. Had he been shot to death mounting the stairs? Was that his body she had heard hurtling down then? She was listening, scarcely breathing; and Joe McCray was listening, too. She could see him plainly in the doorway; see him start to pass out into the hall, draw back quickly, hesitate, look at her; at the single window with the boards nailed tight and strong against it.

Then McCray spoke. His voice was low; hardly above a whisper.

"Frankie," he said, and again, "Frankie!"

There wasn't any answer. Then feet; feet that moved steadily, evenly on those stairs. Slowly, too, but with no attempt to deaden the sound.

McCray closed the door, felt for a key that wasn't there, dug a hand into a pocket—into another pocket—looked wildly about the room.

"Rat" was right. Nina Radcliff knew that before, but she saw it now. Saw the furtive look of a hunted animal. Would he kill her first; would he shout out to Satan that if he came on she would die? Yes, that's what he'd do!

But he didn't. He didn't even think of her; didn't even realize she was there in the room. He thought only of himself; of escape; of escape that was barred to him through the single window closed with wooden boards.

She could have cried out with relief at the terror the man showed. And maybe she did, but inwardly it seemed as if her pounding heart had suddenly enlarged to great proportions, and blocked off all sound; jammed up into her lungs even, and made breathing difficult, almost impossible.

And now, like a rat cornered at last, Joe McCray changed. He wasn't going to be simply shot down at the girl's feet. He was going to fight. She saw the other gun in his left hand, saw his crouching, shuffling movement as he slid across the room close to the door; the door that was slowly opening.

Nina Radcliff saw what he meant to do. He was bent

low; both guns raised. Satan would have to come through that door. Joe McCray would be crouched behind it, waiting. Satan wouldn't have a chance. Just two blazing guns in the hands of a desperate killer, and Satan would die. Die even before he knew where the shots had come from.

Slowly, very slowly the door was opening, further and further. And as it opened, Joe McCray grew more confident; at least, he grew steadier. There were no furtive glances about the room now, no nervous movements of his broad shoulders, no uncertainty about the two steady hands that gripped those guns, no quivering of thick lips. Just a determined, assured set to them.

Joe had figured things out! Satan's strength was psychological, though that wasn't the word Joe's mind pictured. He just suddenly knew that it was derived from the fear that Satan had built up in the underworld for years; a superstition that he bore a charmed life; a superstition that had grown into a fetish.

The girl saw Joe's lips move and knew that he smiled. She saw both his hands raise and knew Satan was going to die. Desperately she tried to cry out a warning, but no sound came from her dry lips. Her lungs were bursting; she couldn't cry out. It was as if she were dreaming. A horrible nightmare; a horrible nightmare of reality. She didn't think of herself then; just of the man who was risking his life for her, and because of her was going to die.

Things happened so quickly after that that she wasn't exactly sure of events; that is, minor details of the events—if there were any minor details.

The door that was moving so slowly suddenly crashed in. She hardly saw it moving until it struck; struck the crouching, sneering murderer; struck him and hurled him back across the room. Stumbling, staggering; trying desperately to regain his balance, Joe McCray blazed away with both guns.

Wildly, frantically, he shot at the twin points of green that glared at him. The girl looked at Satan's face and tried to close her eyes. She couldn't see him die like that! She couldn't, but she had to. Her eyes wouldn't close; they were glued open.

Then the single spot, the single spurt of orange-blue flame from Satan's gun. The grim, vivid gash of his lips, the horrible slant of his eyes, the sudden terrible viciousness in his face!

The girl turned her eyes and looked at Joe McCray. He didn't stagger anymore. He was backed flat against the wall. His coat was open, his left hand was raised and pressed against a white shirt; a white shirt that was stained with red. His right hand hung at his side.

He clawed at his chest, cursed suddenly and jerked up his right hand. His mouth hung open. And Satan shot right through that open mouth.

Nina Radcliff didn't think she fainted. After that things were—well, "indifferent" was the only way she could express it. She knew, and she didn't know. What she knew was that Joe McCray slid to the floor, sat there a moment, then eased over on his side. She knew, too, that Satan walked slowly over to him, moved the body with his foot, hunched his shoulders, and swinging suddenly, faced the door and jerked up his gun.

What she didn't know was that the man who came into the room was Kirby, of the *Tribune,* and that it was Kirby who cut her loose and tossed the water into her face. When she came around fully and tried to sit up on the couch, where she had been placed, Kirby was talking to Satan. They weren't looking at her.

"They're both dead," said Kirby. "One in the library, and the other at the foot of the stairs. You don't waste much lead."

"It's hard times," said Satan. "The city's trying to economize. Bullets cost money."

"They'll save on Joe McCray, on the electric bill." Kirby grinned, though the hand that lighted his cigarette trembled violently. "If he hadn't been hidden behind that door when you knocked it open you'd have been completely out of luck."

"Where else would he be?" Satan shrugged his shoulder. "I slapped him down earlier, and he took it. It wasn't likely he'd stand out in the center of the floor and shoot it out, even if he did get the first shot. No, Kirby, it was in his blood; in his heart; in his dirty rotten soul to slink behind some protection when the big moment came."

"You took a chance, coming alone."

"Sure!" said Satan. "But a raid would have meant the kid's death." He jerked a thumb toward the couch. "She's a good kid, Kirby."

"Maybe." Kirby moved narrow shoulders. "She ran with a bad gang. I don't see how you figure it."

"I looked in her eyes," said Satan. "She's clean and good, and decent. Joe McCray couldn't change that in her. I saw it. All she needed was a break."

And the girl was off the couch, across to Satan, her arms about his neck. She held him tightly, crying softly.

"I don't care what they think; what they say, if you—you believe in me. I don't want to die now. I want to live; help you rid the city of—of—"

She tried to look down at the body, but couldn't. She turned up her head, looked straight into the green eyes. "I want to help you rid the city of rats like him. Like Joe McCray.''

''Sure. Sure!'' Satan spoke to her as if she were a child. But he didn't know then, and didn't know until later, just how deadly in earnest she was. And he never was sure if she really had fainted and he had to carry her from that house, or if—if she just wanted him to do it.

But Kirby smiled and winked at him, and Satan only grinned back. She was just what he always thought of her—a fine clean kid.

Later, with his story in screaming heads pounding from the press, Kirby sat down to write a feature article on Satan which the paper wanted. He wrote the first line quickly and easily. But he looked at it a long time. It began simply enough.

''I was near death tonight.''

Finally he jerked it from the machine, chucked it in the basket, and sitting back, sucked on the end of his pencil. The first time he had done that since his cub days.

SATAN LAUGHED

A COMPLETE

SHORT NOVEL
■

CARROLL JOHN DALY

*Out of a Bullet-Riddled Body, Through a Mask
of Blood, Satan Hall Laughed—Laughed
at the Horrible Irony That Forced
Him to Drag That Murderer
to Electrocution*

ONE

A LEGAL KILLER

■

The commissioner of police dropped his frail body into the chair behind the great desk and tapped his fingers continually together. It wasn't nerves. It was the tension inside the man; the energy of a constantly active brain overflowing into the body. He looked long and earnestly at Satan's face, as if it were the first time he had seen it and wished to study it.

Yet he knew every detail of those pointed features: the V-shape to the entire face, which had given Hall the name Satan. Even in repose the likeness to His Satanic Majesty was there. When not in repose—!

The commissioner shrugged his shoulders, glanced at the closed door marked PRIVATE, finally said: "I have just come from the mayor."

"Sure!" Satan nodded. "Election is coming on and Hollis Daggett has brought pressure to bear; pressure that even the mayor must submit to. Daggett wants me out, and Daggett gets what he wants. I'm not kicking. You have stood behind me. I guess it just had to come."

The commissioner smiled.

"You have done more to rid this city of crime than any other agency, single or wholesale. It's been brutal sudden death, Satan. Even made me shudder at times. But it's been effective, even if too many editorials have called your method legalized murder. Hollis Daggett has prominent, influential friends. He knows how to get out the vote. He knows where to strike the hardest and hurt the most. But I told you! My job goes with yours, and the mayor has said—"

"Sure. Sure!" Satan nodded. "I'm to go back into retirement for a while again. It's just the system. You've stood behind me, and—"

The commissioner stopped him.

"And—what? Have I given you reason to believe that I don't still stand behind you?"

"You're more important than I am, Commissioner. The city needs you. You've prepared me for today—the day when Hollis Daggett and the machine he controls, demanded a showdown. I'm out. I know it."

The commissioner grinned.

"You're not out. You're still taking orders from me. And those orders are—to clear this city of all public enemies. Of Eddie Jerome, the new man closest to Hollis Daggett; even of Daggett himself."

Green slanting eyes widened; lips opened.

"You—you bluffed Daggett? You . . . Hell! Commissioner, it can only be for a little while. You can't work against the system; the pressure he will bring. He wants me out; made a point of it. It seems a small thing to others; just the dropping of a first-grade detective working straight from the commissioner."

The commissioner frowned.

"You don't have to thank me, Satan. Lord knows what I might have done under pressure! But it was Daggett himself. There isn't any explanation. Of course we all knew that Daggett was behind the force to remove you, though the demand came through Judge Rudolph Yates. Today was the time for the showdown. The people after your scalp weren't all crooks and grafters. Good honest men were convinced that your activities were a detriment to the force; a disgrace to law and order. But the fact is—Judge Yates suddenly dropped the subject of your activities. Dismissed it as of no importance, after the great importance he had attached to it."

"But why?" Satan jarred erect in his chair. Hollis Daggett quitting? It didn't sound right, didn't even sound true. Especially as Satan recalled that night in Daggett's own house when he—Satan—had beaten the great Daggett unconscious with his own gun.

"There wasn't any 'why,' " the commissioner said. "At least any 'why' that I can understand or that you can understand. The reason, of course, seemed clear; even sensible. The judge just said it was too small a matter to disrupt a great and successful administration." The commissioner put both hands on the arms of his chair, leaned slightly forward.

"It's like this, Satan. I'm not giving you orders now. I'm going to ask a favor of you; give you the biggest job of your life. This Eddie Jerome is bad. He is Daggett's link with the underworld. Murder, death, fear and crime that Daggett couldn't control; couldn't execute without him, are his job. Jerome's a killer." The commissioner paused, made a clicking noise far back in his throat. "Like you!" he added quickly. "As the papers label you; as some of our influential citizens label you. They say—and not without some justification—that your elimination of the criminal proves the inefficiency of justice; the failure of justice to punish. Oh, I know! The criminals always shot first. You've always been in a position where you had to kill to save your life. And that's the trouble, Satan. Always! They say that it doesn't happen; that you make it happen that way.''

"You'd like me to take a bullet in the stomach to prove my critics wrong—wrong, just once?''

"No, no.'' The commissioner got up and paced the floor. "I don't mean that. I mean—can't you once; just once, to make it better for the entire city and the citizens you and I both serve, bring one man in alive to the bar of justice—with the evidence that will convict him?''

Satan's eyes narrowed, his lips set tightly.

"It would be novel,'' he agreed. "Very novel.'' Suddenly he returned to the main topic. "It's not like Daggett to quit. You think he fears me? What I've done to his crowd; what I'll someday do to him?''

The commissioner's lips tightened. He said: "Hollis Daggett eliminates those he fears. I don't know, Satan. It's hardly understandable.''

Satan's eyes closed to oblique slits, shifted slightly and looked out the window. His head bobbed up and down. It was the commissioner who spoke next.

"More trouble, Satan. I saw Chester Radcliff today.''

Satan's green eyes showed mild interest.

"And how is his daughter, Nina?'' His lips parted. "The girl detective.''

"It's his daughter, Nina, I want to talk to you about. She's young, she's rich, she's impressionable. You saved her life. She's pestered me for a job; a job hunting criminals, discovering evidence. An undercover worker. She wanted to work with you. Talked about her debt to society; of her girlfriend who was murdered when they were together in welfare work. You didn't encourage her, Satan?''

Satan's grin was not forced, nor was it unpleasant.

"She's a good kid, Commissioner; a bright, clever kid; but she doesn't belong. Don't worry. I've got troubles enough without encouraging her."

"Good. Good! But she's been running around with the wrong people; maybe trying to do things herself. I've known her since she was a child. Her father's my friend." A long pause, a frown. "I hate to do it, but she's going away."

"You hate to do what?"

"Help send her away. Oh, her father offered her six months; a year, in Europe. She refused. She's over twenty-one, and all that!" The commissioner's fingers drummed on the desk. "So we must use force. She goes away tonight." Satan only looked at the commissioner. "You know the girl. What do you think of that?"

"I think," said Satan, "that it's a grave mistake. For you, for her father, for the girl herself."

The commissioner said simply: "Maybe. But it's better than having her found some night in the gutter with her throat cut. You remember her friend!" And when Satan didn't answer. "Anyway, it's settled. She goes away tonight."

A tap. The door opened. A bald head with a pencil behind one ear ducked in; a hard mouth spoke: "It's a phone call for Detective Hall, Commissioner. Will he take it here?"

The commissioner nodded. Satan flipped the phone into his hand, and when the head disappeared, said: "Detective Hall. What do you want?"

It was a woman's voice. Satan straightened. The woman said: "This is Nina Radcliff, Satan. Are you alone? I want to talk to you now. It's important; it's big." There was excitement behind her words.

Green eyes flashed toward the commissioner, back to the phone

"As far as you're concerned, we're alone." He pushed the receiver close against his ear. "Let's have it."

"Satan," her voice was quick, shrill. She gave him a street and house number. "You didn't think I could help. You want Rusty Walsh. The police want him for murder. Well—he's there. The third floor, apartment 3C. You better hurry. I—I—"

The phone banged up.

"Well?" the commissioner questioned. "Interesting?"

"Maybe." Satan nodded. "A tip-off on Rusty Walsh. He's hiding out uptown."

"Ah!" The commissioner beamed. "I've wanted him, Satan; wanted him bad. A small shot, but he'll talk big. A stool pigeon gave it to you?"

Satan grinned.

"In a way, perhaps. Only I don't like the sound of 'stool pigeon' this time. I'll pick him up."

"I'll send a raiding squad." The commissioner's right hand moved toward a row of white buttons.

"No. I'll go alone," Satan said. And when the commissioner looked up, added, "You know how it is. The boys don't like my working directly from you like this. They say I hog the stage." He paused. "And I guess I do. But I like it that way. I'll go alone."

"It's important. Walsh can talk about Daggett, and I guess he'll be willing to. He was a fool to come back to the city. Daggett might use Eddie Jerome to snuff out Walsh. If some stoolie knows Walsh is in town, then Daggett will know. Better take a few of the boys. Walsh will be armed—and careful."

"I'll be armed, too. And careful," Satan said.

"Careful about yourself, maybe." The commissioner

smiled slightly. "It's Walsh I want to protect. But go ahead. You're a lone worker. I never interfere with you. Who gave you the tip?"

"You'd be surprised." Satan picked up his hat and walked toward the door. "About the Radcliff girl. Go easy on her, Commissioner. She isn't a bad kid."

"She isn't a dead kid, either; and isn't going to be."

"She'll raise a row." And when the commissioner only smiled, Satan added, "A damn big row."

"Money! Influence! Her father and I have just as much of both as Daggett has. Everything will be nice and quiet. She'll thank us for it later. But she'll go quietly now."

Satan's thin lips opened, but no words came. His feet seemed to move slowly, yet his body disappeared rapidly through the door. Out in the hall, he passed up the elevator and used the stairs. His thoughts were pleasant.

Nina Radcliff was a good kid; clean and decent. She didn't belong in detective work, of course; yet she had made good. She knew Satan wanted Walsh, knew that Walsh would talk. Yep, Satan had laughed at the kid—and now, like the advertisements in the papers, she had moved over to the piano and played a tune; a death tune for Hollis Daggett. She was a woman in a thousand; a hundred thousand, for that matter. Satan frowned. After all, he had nothing to go on. It was just instinct with him. It wasn't simply her brown eyes. That is, not the eyes themselves; or what others would see in those eyes. It was what was behind them that he believed in.

He reached the street. His shoulders moved, straightened. He was unfair to the girl; unfair to himself. Five minutes before she had just been a girl of another world who didn't mean a thing in his life. Now he knew the truth; admitted it even to himself. It wasn't Frank Hall, the man, who had such pleasant feelings about Nina Radcliff, the girl. It was Detective Satan Hall, who felt that a new and valuable cog had been added to his machine for hunting down the criminals.

However, Rusty Walsh was in the city, and Rusty Walsh would talk—and Satan knew where Walsh was. He smiled grimly. Danger? Not for him. He knew Walsh; knew his kind. And what was better, Walsh knew him.

TWO

THE DEATH CAR

■

Satan Hall dropped from the taxi almost a block away from Walsh's hideout. He walked slowly down the block, keeping close to the shabby buildings. Just another moving figure on a busy street; a figure so close to the houses that anyone on that side of the street would have to raise a window and peer out; even lean out, to spot him. Even then the dark slouch hat, the bent head, would tell little.

Satan had his plans. He knew the apartment number. The thing was simple. He'd simply buzz the apartment below; or if he got no answer there, the apartment above. That would be 2-C or 4-C; it didn't matter which. A quick dart up or down a fire escape, a raised window, a gun in his hand—and Walsh looking into his face. Satan grinned. Walsh, a rat. His kind were all rats.

He had almost reached the apartment house—was passing the little areaway on his side of it—when it happened. Instinct, knowledge, a presentiment derived from always expecting the unexpected and always living close to death; call it what you will. It happened too often to Satan to be simply luck. He turned his head suddenly.

Of course he had heard the car; he had heard many of them passing back and forth. Now, when green eyes simply looked over his shoulder, he recognized the danger; recognized the car; recognized it even before the rear curtains parted and the round black muzzle shoved out. Yes, he recognized it for what it was—a death car. The death car! He knew now why Daggett had withdrawn the demand for his removal. This was quicker; surer.

His first quick reaction was to fling his body to the sidewalk and roll toward that areaway; into it and out of the way of fire. He'd have done it if the thing he saw had been simply a rifle, an ordinary pistol or even a sawed-off shotgun. But a submachine gun would spew lead into his rolling body long before he reached that protection, if he ever did reach it.

A second's thought; a second's stunned stupidity even? No. Satan had faced death before many times. He never had to think; that is, consciously think. When he first turned his head, that Tommy gun was already through the curtains; already settling itself upon the door of a car that had slowed down almost to a stop. Perhaps subconsciously Satan's brain sent frantic warnings to the muscles which acted simultaneously with those orders.

A white face, glaring eyes, the circular drum of the Tommy gun all faced Satan at once; faced him as he spun his whole body, whirled it twisting to the sidewalk; his head still facing that car, his eyes glued upon the evil face.

The Tommy gun exploded; spat lead. There was a dull jarring thud just below Satan's left shoulder, a searing pain along his side; as if hot ice—yes, ice that was hot—were drawn across his body. And as he fell Satan saw the hands; other hands, that reached out, gripped at that Tommy gun, tried to guide it, push the nose down toward his body, now flat on the sidewalk.

There were two men, then. The one who used the gun; the other who tried to guide it as Satan crashed down. Well, it didn't matter whether one man killed you, or two; if two faces were above that gun or only one. But Satan recognized both those faces. The one who merely tried to guide that gun was Chopper Hays; the man who actually fired it was Daggett's right-hand man; the shrewd, clever, deadly killer—Eddie Jerome. Something strange in that, very strange. For Chopper Hays was an expert with a Tommy gun.

Satan's teeth showed and his eyes narrowed as he pressed the trigger of his forty-five and shot Chopper Hays almost in the center of the forehead. Was! Yes, "was" was right. Glaring evil eyes still stared, but there was the glare of death in them; recognizable even before the hole popped red between those eyes.

The face was gone. The other face was gone, also. The curtains waved, as if a struggle took place behind them. Queer, that! A struggle between the living and the dead. The machine gun popped its nose high in the air. For a moment Satan could see the hands still clasping the nose of it. The motor roared, the car jumped ahead. Satan's gun followed the speeding car. Bullets tore through the curtains where the face of Eddie Jerome had been. Satan's eyes bulged.

The machine gun dangled dangerously from between black curtains. It hung over the side of the car; a white hand still clutched the nose. Satan fired carefully. The white fingers that grasped that gun were splashed red, disappeared entirely. Heavy metal crashed to the pavement as the car rounded the corner.

The street suddenly went dead; a silence that followed for a moment the roaring shots. Then, as Satan came to his feet, bedlam started. A woman shrieked, a child cried, pounding feet hit the sidewalk, windows were opening. Satan felt his side. A messy job they'd made of it. But they generally did where he was concerned. Guys that fired at him lost their nerve at the crucial moment. A Tommy gun spitting lead at him, and no one hurt! He felt his side again. That is, no one badly hurt.

Someone said: "There he is. That's the man."

A hand rested on Satan's shoulder, a siren screeched down the block, there was the shrill blast of a police whistle. The voice that belonged with the hand said: "Drop that gun, or by God—Oh, it's Hall; Satan Hall."

The voice stopped. Satan had turned. Green eyes stared into wide blue ones, at the uniform below them; the brass buttons.

"Hell!" said Satan. "No harm done. Just a few scratches. Those mutts can't even kill you with a machine gun unless your back's turned. Don't be a dumb cop. Get that Tommy gun there in the street. Hell! man, no one got hurt."

"No?" The cop half turned, jerked a thumb over his shoulder. "Look! Poor kid, right in the stomach."

Satan turned almost as the radio car drew to the curb. He looked down at the girl. Nineteen, maybe twenty. She lay there on the sidewalk. She was very quiet. Blood stained her outstretched hand. But she didn't draw the hand away and the blood didn't bother her. Satan turned his head. Nothing would ever bother her again. That was the only good way to look at it. She was dead.

Satan cursed softly as he looked down at the girl.

A man behind him said: "And that's the way it goes. They never get the right person. It's the innocent bystander who . . . My God, man! Look! It's blood."

Satan's glance fell, and for the first time he was aware

of the warm stream flowing down his arm. But it didn't splash red upon the sidewalk—it couldn't; not then. Not while he stood above the girl.

There was the ambulance. Lieutenant Schmit; half a dozen plainclothesmen; a fat officer with a perpetual grin, who now held the machine gun and was trying to wrap it up in an old raincoat. Satan clutched his arm, spoke to him quickly.

"They were pegging at you, eh, Satan?" Lieutenant Schmit said as he looked at Satan's red hand. "Not so bad, maybe." And over his shoulder he whispered, "Have a look-see here, Doc. There's people who believe Satan can't bleed." And back to Satan: "How about you; any luck?"

"I killed the man with the . . ." Satan hesitated. "No, I'm not sure I got the one with the machine gun, but I killed a man."

"That's right." Schmit nodded. "You would, of course. Did you get a look at him?" And when Satan hesitated again, added, "Now, come, Satan! The system's a big one. This personal vengeance is all right for hoods, but we cops—"

Satan's smile was not pleasant for the lieutenant to see.

"The man I killed was Chopper Hays," he said simply.

"Hell! Then he's the man who worked the typewriter. Imagine anyone else trying it with him in the car! Why, he's a natural for a blast-out."

"Just the same"—Satan was trying to think as the doctor probed his arm—"I'm pretty sure—no, I'm dead sure it wasn't—"

He stopped. The doctor said: "Look at your other side; your shirt there. You'll have to—"

And Schmit, opening his mouth to say something about the wounds, changed suddenly as a thought struck him.

"What did they want to get you for, and why this street? What were you doing here?"

Satan turned, pushed the doctor roughly from him, ran toward the steps of the house. He, too, had forgotten why he was there. But it hardly mattered now. Rusty Walsh wouldn't be one to sit around during all that blasting on the street outside.

There was no necessity for ringing a bell in that apartment house now. Three or four people stepped back as Schmit, the police surgeon, and a couple of men followed Satan into the dingy hallway. They were on his heels as he rounded the turn of the second floor and made for the third.

"What the hell, Satan?" Schmit called irritably, then saved his breath. He was a big man, given to weight and not especially partial to running up steps. Satan was already at the door of apartment 3-C when Schmit and the others came up.

"Come on! Satan! What's the racket? Hell! man, you're bleeding like a stuck pig! Look at that floor!"

"Watch below. The roof, too, from the fire escape." Satan shot out the words.

"God in heaven!" Schmit threw up his hands. "You tell me that now, three flights up! Here! You busting in? What's the office?"

"Rusty Walsh!" Satan gagged.

"Oh!" Lieutenant Schmit pushed Satan from the door, threw his own shoulder against it, grabbed the knob, and almost fell into the room. A gasp. "You're right. There's your Rusty Walsh."

Satan saw the man; saw the body stretched out there on the floor. The throat had been ripped open and the blood had dried. It was a far more horrible, more brutal death than the one down stairs. A young police officer went to a window, pushed it up, stuck his head out, saw older men eying him and tried looking up and down the fire escape.

But Satan saw nothing brutal in that murder; that is, nothing nauseating. The death of rats like Walsh and his kind didn't affect him.

The police surgeon turned to Satan, noted the whiteness of his face; the paleness of his lips; the blood that dripped down his arm more even and steadier now.

But the doctor's mental explanation of Satan's sudden weakness, if it was weakness, was all wrong. It was not caused by the dead body of Rusty Walsh, it was not the girl on the sidewalk below, nor the wounds on his own body. Satan's thoughts were not of those things; at least, not as separate things. He had just one thought; one terrible thought.

Nina Radcliff had trapped him; sent him to his death. That he hadn't died was because he had thrown himself to the sidewalk and let a young girl take the dose that was meant for him. That he didn't realize the girl was there didn't matter; that is, didn't matter as far as Nina Radcliff was concerned.

As the doctor worked, he thought that Satan's grin was simply gameness; sort of laughing at pain. He didn't know that Satan felt no pain; that Satan wasn't even thinking of pain. He was thinking of one thing. He had been trapped by a woman; a fine, clean, decent woman who had put a pair of brown eyes on him. Pain? Hell! There was no pain; no physical pain.

THREE

A KILLER VOLUNTEERS

■

Hollis Daggett's offices occupied an entire floor in one of the finest buildings in the city. Under his name gold letters informed the curious that he dealt in high-grade securities.

In a way, he did. High-grade to him; low-grade to those who were forced to buy them. But the real purpose of those sumptuous offices was to meet influential friends; political allies; men whose names would not permit them to associate with Daggett in his more private rooms above the dance floor in the Wellington Hotel.

Hollis Daggett sat back in the big leather chair, folded fat pudgy hands across his stomach. His head was large but his face was small; that is, his features were placed directly in the center of a huge open space. It was as if a child made a snowman, then picked out a tiny space in the center of that enormous head to put the eyes, the nose and the mouth.

Daggett was a big man in more ways than one. He was a big frog in a big puddle; or rather, a cancerous growth eating at the heart of a great city. Slowly and surely Hollis Daggett had worked his way into control. Gangster; racke-

teer; politician. Now a power behind the throne; the throne
of evil that dominates all too often in many large cities.
His stepping-stones to success had been the shoulders of
friends; those he had made and broken. Dishonest politicians who were tossed aside when no longer useful; honest
ones who had been framed or had died suddenly.

Now he tapped his pencil on the desk; frowned. Hollis
Daggett's frown was peculiar. It started at the top of his
forehead and rolled down to his eyes. Little beady eyes
that didn't narrow into slits but narrowed all around into
smaller little black balls. He looked across at Eddie Jerome.

"Tell it to me, again, Eddie," he said slowly. "All of it.
Then I'll tell you what to do."

"Hell!" said Jerome. "It was a nasty job. I don't want
to argue it with you after—"

"We won't argue," said Daggett very softly. "I'll tell
you; just tell you. Now—from the beginning."

Jerome's rather good-looking face, in a hard sort of way,
ran through a series of twists that were meant to give the
impression of thought; of an inherent honesty and simplici-
ty he didn't have or didn't even understand.

"I'll tell you, mister." His words ran freer, easier when
he was puzzled as to the best way to express himself.
"When you suggested putting the finger on this Satan
person—"

Daggett's little eyes snapped, darted fire. His voice was
still low but was crisp now, with a hardness to it.

"I suggested what?"

"Well, when I thought it might be—"

Jerome stopped, leaned forward. "Hell, mister! I ain't
good at such talk. We're alone, and I don't see no sense to
it." He paused, ran a hand across his mouth. His jaw
hardened. "It's like this! Satan Hall, the dick, gets the
finger on him. The woman plays things and Satan sets his

feet directly on the spot marked X. Chopper Hays . . . But this Satan don't run, with lead playing up and down his spine. In plain words, boss, Satan turns and burns Hays down—right between the eyes.''

"Satan didn't die then, and Hays—''

"Satan, no. And Hays . . . Cripes! he went out funny!'' Jerome made a motion toward his chest and hands. "I didn't think he had real blood in him. But it was red enough. I was a mess.''

"I see.'' Daggett never took those eyes off Jerome. "The money, then. You took it back from Hays. And you're telling me exactly what happened!''

"That's it.'' Jerome hesitated. "I got the money back. I was figuring on taking this bird Satan over myself. Hays wasn't the man for the job.'' He looked long and earnestly at Daggett. "Well—here's the dough, but I could earn it easy enough.''

Daggett said: "You're paid plenty; always will be paid plenty. But I don't want you found dead with my money in your pocket. Satan's bad; damn bad, though I thought Hays would do the job. And the body!'' Daggett jerked a hand toward the phone. "I've been in touch with things, and the body hasn't been found yet.''

"No, not yet. That's right,'' Jerome agreed heartily, too heartily.

"What car did you use?'' Daggett demanded sharply.

"Nothing to worry about there,'' Jerome said easily. "A Pierce I picked up on Sixty-ninth Street.''

"Where is it?''

"Down in Pinto's garage.''

"My God!'' Daggett came to his feet. "And blood inside of it?'' And with a sudden jerk to his words, "And the body! Don't tell me it's—''

"Yep,'' Jerome gulped. "It's still in the car.''

"Are you crazy? Is Pinto crazy? This is murder! A girl dead in the street, and the car and the body at Pinto's! What's Pinto doing?"

Broad shoulders shrugged. Jerome grinned slightly.

"You told me never to argue; that you were telling *me*. I was hot; damn good and hot. Satan looked smack at me. As for Pinto, that's his trouble."

"You fool! You blundering idiot!" Daggett's face blazed with wrath. He put those beady eyes steadily on Jerome's. The killer's face colored slightly; piercing eyes shifted. Daggett said: "You better tell me all of it."

Jerome jerked his head in agreement.

"There are other angles to the thing; angles that may have to be ironed out. Oh! nothing a big guy like you can't handle, but puzzling to a little guy like me." His words were low; ingratiating. He watched how the flattery hit Daggett, was not pleased by what he saw in that face, moved his shoulders and shot his words straight. "It's like this, boss; Chopper Hays wasn't working that typewriter at the time of the blast. I was."

"You!" Daggett's little eyes blazed. He raised a hand, stretched it across the desk toward Jerome's throat, touched that throat, moved his other hand—stopped. He saw something in Jerome's face now; something that—well, perhaps the thing which had made him bring Jerome in with him in the first place. Jerome spoke, and there was nothing ingratiating in his voice now.

"None of that, mister; none of that." Jerome did not take so much as a step backward before those chubby hands fell to Daggett's sides. "I like your style. I like your stuff. I like your money. But—this Chopper Hays turned yellow. He took a flop; his hands shook. I had to go through with it at the last moment. And Tommy guns ain't my line, I guess."

"You guess!" Daggett sneered. "And he went yellow! You told him, then. Told him it was Satan he was to get, and that's what got him. You told him, didn't you? You told him, after what I said."

"Yeah, I told him." Jerome picked at his teeth with the end of a match.

"Why?"

Shoulders moved. Jerome said, and his explanation was simple, and very real to him: "It was Hays' big mouth. He shot it off to me on our way to the blast. What a big guy he was with a cannon! He didn't really have to shoot! When they saw his face they just died of fright! He was a big wind. I couldn't stand it. Yep, that's right. I told him it was Satan Hall and he'd better say it all with lead. It was after that he blew up. It ain't my fault, mister. You didn't give it to me straight. You said if Hays knew who it was he'd want more jack. Well—it wasn't jack he wanted. It was nerve. What could I do? I took the Tommy. It was sort of new to me; I'm handier with a rod. Then this yellow hood, Hays, either got panicky or got his nerve back when he saw the dick on the sidewalk and—and—well, he grabbed at the nose of that Tommy and—"

"And the police got the gun," Daggett cut in. "I know that. You dropped it and it fell to the street."

"Hays jerked it from me."

"But Hays was dead," Daggett said. "They say he was dead, shot through the head, before the gun fell."

"Dead or alive, he wrestled that gun from me. Did you ever struggle with a corpse? A corpse all covered with blood?"

"Your fingerprints were on that gun, eh?"

"No, no." Jerome lied rather stiffly, as if he meant it to be a lie. "I was wearing gloves."

Daggett looked at him.

"Why didn't you dump the body someplace, leave the car?"

"I was a sight; blood all over me. I thought it best to hole up the body for a bit. Keep things stirring and moving at headquarters before they found the body. I thought maybe you could spirit that Tommy gun out of there, in the excitement."

"That machine gun. Why?" Daggett paused, and then added: "So you *are* thinking of fingerprints!"

Jerome made a depreciating movement with his arms.

"There was a lot of blood on that gun; on my hands. I ain't no expert."

"I thought you were wearing gloves," Daggett fairly growled.

"Hell! I was—maybe." Jerome paused, looked toward the ceiling. "A guy can't be sure about such things. I just thought, if I wasn't wearing gloves, that gun might disappear— just turn up missing."

"If you weren't wearing gloves and that gun isn't missing, there will be a lot of grief for you?"

"Yeah, that's right." Jerome nodded, undisturbed. "For me, and a lot of others."

"What do you mean—a lot of others?"

"Oh! that's just talk, I guess." Jerome made his voice easy but his eyes were long slits. "I ain't the sort of movie picture hero who dies for his friends—like Walsh."

Hollis Daggett studied the man for whom he had searched the country and picked above a hundred carefully selected others. And he liked him; liked the easy freedom from panic in a situation of such seriousness. Such a man was useful; such a man was worth preserving. Such a man was worth—well, worth keeping that deadly glare out of his eyes.

Daggett's hand stretched out and gripped the hand of the killer.

"Don't worry, Eddie. Perhaps I have underrated you."

Jerome grinned.

"I could use some jack." He eyed the bills he had tossed on the desk. "And I don't think such a hell of a lot of Satan Hall." And as his fingers wound around the bills Daggett thrust into his hand, closing the killer's fingers on them with his own pudgy ones, "There's the dame, Daggett. I could frame her your way."

Daggett straightened; stiffened. Though he never admitted it, even to himself, he was conscious of his ugly, almost grotesque appearance.

"There's been many beautiful women in my life, Jerome. Nina Radcliff is a gorgeous creature." His stomach shot slightly forward, attempting to masquerade as his chest. "My only trouble has been keeping such—keeping such women from me. I can't understand it."

"Me neither." Jerome looked at the peculiar hulk of a man; the queer head; the distorted features. "If you can make 'em, anyone can. Thanks for the present, boss." He pushed the money into his pocket, then said: "What's all the grief about Satan Hall? He's only a common dick, like plenty of others. I didn't think you had any fear of the law."

Hollis Daggett pushed a finger half unconsciously along the scar that ran from his eye to his mouth. His lips set tightly. He remembered clearly the night Satan had whipped the gun down the side of his face. He said: "I obey no laws and can at least appreciate Satan, who recognizes no laws; that is, no state-made laws. He's a killer, Eddie. Just like—like any other killer."

Eddie Jerome cocked his head.

"What's it worth if he—if he ain't able to kill anymore?"

"Plenty." Daggett's head bobbed up and down.

" 'Plenty' ain't no figure to me," Jerome said, then turned. The door opened. A man stood there.

"The dame is here, and—"

Seeing the look on Daggett's face, he said hastily, "No offense, boss! It's Miss Radcliff. She's hard to handle and is burning up the office."

"Yes, yes." Fat hands rubbed together; great jowls moved as lips twisted and Daggett unconsciously ran a hand over his forehead, back across his sparse hair. "A minute, Raymond. Three—say. Then show her in. Yes— show her in. She seems disturbed?"

"*Disturbed* ain't the word. I'll show her in."

When he was gone, Jerome said: "Watch yourself, mister. That dame is poison. There's two worlds, you know. She's got it in her to be soft."

"I know, I know." Daggett turned to a mirror, straightened his tie, felt of his chin—chins, rather—ran his hand down his face. The skin was soft; he liked that. "You wouldn't understand, Jerome. This is the girl; the woman." He paused. The next words were hardly audible. "In a short while; a very short while, my woman."

"Yeah? Well, this woman has been running back and forth to the commissioner, hounding Satan Hall. Chester Radcliff, her old man, is death on you."

"She's beautiful, Jerome." Daggett held out his two hands, moved chubby fingers. "Those hands, alone, are dead clay. People speak of the hands of a great artist, but that means nothing. It's the brain behind those hands and the spirit behind that brain. The hands can make physical beauty; appreciate physical beauty, but the brain directs that beauty. This girl's mind and spirit and soul are for me to shape. She—"

Daggett paused. Eddie Jerome had opened his mouth to

speak; speak his piece on "dames" and the danger of dames. But he didn't say anything. He felt a sort of a tingle run up and down his spine. Not a shudder; at least, anything that Jerome would recognize as a shudder of repulsion. It was just something in Daggett's little snapping eyes, the rolling jowls, the twisted, curling, sensuous little mouth.

But as Daggett walked to the private door that led to the outer hall and held it open for him to leave, he finally said: "Don't let that dame take things off your mind, mister. Big things; things that are big to me."

Daggett smiled.

"Big things." He nodded. "Big things to you. A Tommy gun, eh? Don't worry, my boy. It will take me just as long as it takes to lift that phone. Good-bye."

Jerome hesitated, stepped into the hall and closed the door.

A GREAT MAN'S WEAKNESS

∎

Alone, Hollis Daggett lifted the phone. His conversation was short and crisp. He finally said: "If it's done right, over a dozen people will handle that little piece of field artillery; at least, move it around. Satan, too. What? Oh! in case that your wife and daughter, who are very proud of you, might feel differently. Let us talk straight. Your daughter's graduation from college would hardly be in tune with your entrance to Sing Sing." A longer pause, and then, "You misunderstand me. I'm not arguing; I'm telling you."

Daggett laid down the phone, looked toward the door, hesitated, then opening the drawer of his desk, lifted out a tiny mirror. For a long minute he stared into it. But before he put that mirror back in the drawer he carefully brushed his hair, even ran a finger over his eyebrows.

She was small; straight, with an erect carriage. Brown eyes blazed. She stood in the doorway, framed like a picture in the light from the outer office.

"You lied to me; lied to me." Her voice was hoarse; a

break in it. Her right hand raised and rested on her chest, slim fingers just touching the whiteness of her throat.

Daggett crossed the room, his huge form moving quickly; perhaps not gracefully but certainly not lumbering. He took the girl's hand, his fingers gripping it in an odd, moving, creasing motion. His little eyes sparkled down at her, a hand rested on her shoulder. She was propelled carefully, with an apparent lack of force, into that room. Despite his weight, his seemingly flabby body, there was great power in those arms.

His foot moved cautiously behind her. The door swung back, slowly, carefully, as if an unseen hand guided it; then closed with the almost unheard click of the latch.

"Don't speak yet, Nina." He guided her to a big chair close to the window. "Sit there in the light. You are very beautiful, child; very gorgeous indeed. Let me look at you." He nodded as he lowered her into the chair. "Yes, even anger becomes you. There! don't talk yet. Words are such dangerous things; angry words, that creep back on us later; so much later—often too late. I hope, my child, you have done nothing to—to excite the law or the enmity of your father."

"Only coming here to see you, and that—"

"I quite understand. I want you to come. I want you to see that a little evil must often be tolerated for a great good. But, there! you are distressed, unhappy, uncertain—and you have come to me. Don't speak yet, Nina. Remember that you have come to me, and that no matter how great your troubles are, Hollis Daggett will make them little."

"Satan!" she said. "Satan Hall! Is he dead?" Her hands clasped the arms of her chair as he turned his head. She came half out of the seat. "Is he dead?"

Daggett turned and faced her. It was with difficulty that

he kept that hardness out of his eyes; with difficulty, too, that he kept the lust out of them. But Daggett said: "No, he is not dead."

"Oh. Oh!" She dropped back into her chair again, put her upper teeth down on her lower lip. "I was there across the street."

"Yes. I know, I know." His beady eyes fastened on hers. For a moment she crouched back in the chair, then brushed at her eyes; sat up again.

The girl came suddenly to her feet.

"I'm going out. I am going to see Satan Hall," she said. She watched Daggett, but there was no change in his face. "You hate him, don't you? You fear him."

Daggett smiled.

"It is not given to me to fear any man." He straightened as much as it was possible for that body of his to straighten. "If I hated him, I could sweep him aside; have him dismissed from the force."

"But you—you didn't."

"You asked me not to. It amused me to please you, Nina."

"Amused you?"

"Perhaps that is not the word. It pleased me to please you. Be careful of that man. He is not exactly human." This time his eyes studied her a long time. "But no man can make a fool out of you; not a woman like you, for long."

"What do you mean?" She took a step toward him, her eyes blazing.

"I mean just that. When I do anything for you; can do anything for you, I will not want gratitude; not gratitude that comes from your emotions." He took her hand now. "I'll want only the friendship that comes from reason;

your understanding that I am and can be nothing but your friend.''

She looked at him, dropped her eyes from his face to the pudgy hand that held hers; then jerked her hand free. She tried to draw back; her legs pressed tightly against the chair.

''You? Why, my father's one of the biggest—''

She stopped. ''What could you do for me?''

''More than your father, the commissioner of police, or Satan Hall. More than any living soul could do for you. I could and would chance powerful enemies for you.'' He moved toward her; a hand ran over her shoulder, along the back of her head. Fingers pushed through soft bobbed hair. His eyes—

She jerked herself free, slid her feet around the chair, backed toward the door. She was suddenly alarmed; frightened at what she saw in those eyes, or thought that she saw—for it was gone almost at once. They were steady eyes; maybe hard; maybe even slightly cruel, but there was nothing in them of—

She shuddered once; shook her head. There was nothing to fear in those eyes; just the repulsiveness of his face must have startled her. She must have been wrong—wrong about what she saw there.

''I'm going.'' There was still a touch of the same nameless something that she had seen in those eyes bothering her, for she clutched awkwardly, perhaps involuntarily, at her chest.

''That's right.'' Daggett nodded. ''Run along. If things go wrong, always feel that you can appeal to me; always remember that I am bigger than your father, the commissioner of police''—he smiled—''even bigger than Detective Satan Hall.''

The girl nodded, didn't speak. She never knew that she

could experience fear; an unknown, unnamed, even unrecognized fear. Then it was gone—gone as she passed the desk outside and hurried from the offices.

Daggett stood looking at the closed door. Then he went back to his desk, jerked out the mirror, looked at himself. His were features that were different; character was in his face! Yes, he believed that, or made himself feel that he believed it. Character that made men fear him, and women— women . . . God, he certainly had read fear in the girl's eyes; but then—then . . .

He snapped up the phone, called a number. A soft feminine voice answered. Long after he laid down the phone Daggett smiled contentedly; sat there, his arms folded across his stomach. The woman's voice had jumped into life when she heard his name; when she found he was coming to see her. Character! That was what was in his face. Character that men feared and women . . .

Well, Gladys Riece was beautiful, attractive, and one of the most sought-after women in the city. She was thrilled by his voice. But he wasn't thinking of Gladys Riece; he was thinking of Nina Radcliff. And he was thinking how long he would have to wait—how long he would wait.

F I V E

SATAN'S SILENCE

∎

Detective Satan Hall sat very straight and very stiff. The
girl stood flat-footed before him. Small, slim, erect; steady
brown eyes on him; her little turned-up nose had a defiant
air. She nodded, too, as the green eyes settled on her;
smiled slightly when they shifted and looked out the
window. That was what she was waiting for. It gave her a
thrill to think that she could make those deadly green balls,
which struck such terror to the criminal, shift. At least, she
liked to think that she could make them shift. She said
softly: "You like me, Satan. You think I'm good and clean
and decent." And, the eyes coming back and settling on
her without the admiration she had hoped for if not
expected, she added, slightly doubtful: "You said that to
me; and you do like me, don't you?" She was sorry she
added the "don't you," but it was too late now.

Satan said: "Sure, Nina, I like you. Is there any reason
why I shouldn't—yet?"

"Yet!" She snapped out the word, was ready to make a
long discourse of it. Quick thoughts flashed in her brain,
formed a picture. Quick, hurried words were ready to pop,

but they didn't. She finally said, "Why won't you let me help you; help you in your work of ridding the city of criminals; the politics behind those criminals; the vicious practices that make such criminals possible?"

Satan smiled.

"You don't belong, kid. Things are tough enough without having a woman to worry about and protect."

She leaned forward eagerly.

"Then you would worry about me; want to protect me."

"Sure!" Satan nodded indifferently. "Your father's Chester Radcliff. He's one big banker who isn't looked on with suspicion; besides, he's a friend of the commissioner. I'd have to give you attention. That's part of the system; part of the vicious politics that make a dick's job tough. Yep, I'd have to worry about you."

"Satan"—the girl's brown eyes blazed—"I'm beginning to believe all the things I've heard about you. Just a machine; just a man with a gun and a desire to use it. They say you've never taken a vacation. Can't you even take one in your heart; just a day off for something personal; a friendship that might—might—"

"Might—what?" Satan spoke slowly. "A few weeks ago you were in love with a cheap hood, a murderer, and he died. I had to kill him to save you."

"Oh!" The girl stiffened; and then: "I want to help you, Satan. I want to pay society for the wrong I did it." And with a little quirk at the corner of her mouth, "For the trouble I caused you. I want you to know I can help, that I have taken advantage of my former welfare work, that I still associate with people who are in on the know. Don't you see? Look at me now. I've got the stuff, Satan. I've pushed my way in here; right into the private room of the commissioner of police. That shows I've got the stuff to get ahead on my own."

"That shows you're Chester Radcliff's daughter."

Brown eyes blazed.

"I don't need any father to help me. I've made you an offer. Come on! Do you take me, or do I work alone? I want to help. Give me a yes or no."

"No!" Satan didn't waste words.

It wasn't the answer she wanted or expected. Though she asked for a direct answer she had not really wanted one; at least, not as abrupt as that.

"You don't believe I can help, will pay my debt to society and—"

Satan Hall laughed. At least the girl thought he did. Anyway, his mouth opened and queer sounds came out of it.

"Listen, Nina." He pointed a long, strong finger at her. "You're talking out of a book, not out of life. Debt to society! Hell! that's your trouble. You're fed up on society. What you want is excitement, and one way or another you intend to get it, no matter who or what gets hurt."

"Excitement!" Her voice was low; very calm now. "And one way or another I intend to get it! You think— you think . . ."

She hesitated, laughed, found it hollow and stopped. "So you can't see good in anyone. You're thinking that I just want excitement, and that if I can't run with the hounds I'll run with the hares."

"With the rats," Satan corrected her. "It's not a game, and there are no hares in crime."

"So that's what you mean by 'good and clean and decent.' You think I'm—"

Satan shook his head, cut in.

"That's why I don't fancy women; they snap you up too quick." And when she would have spoken, interrupted, "I'm not a guy to duck from under." He looked at her,

and his eyes were so hard, so steady, so cold and apprais-
ing that it was only with an effort she was able to keep
from shifting her gaze. "I knew a guy once that was clean.
He used to bathe twice a day, but he got himself lost in a
desert without soap or water." A long moment; and then:
"Of course, after he was found he washed himself up
again. There! don't make a face. You've been places
where there isn't any soap. You're going to have your
chance to wash up."

The girl smiled.

"I see. I suppose I should thank you. You mean—about
my father."

"That's right. That's why you got in here so easy. He's
sending you on a trip to Europe. I know! You said you
wouldn't go. But you'll have another chance. It would be
better for you if you gave him your word to stay away a
year."

"So he's been talking with the commissioner. You
mean—I'll be forced. To go somewhere, if not to Europe."

"I don't mean anything," Satan told her. "I'm just
advising a trip to Europe. It would do you good."

"I won't go!" Her feet spread slightly now, seemed to
settle more firmly on the thick rug. "I'm over twenty-one."

Satan shook his head.

"There's a lot of people over twenty-one who've gone
places they didn't want to go. It's that money and influence you were talking about."

She raised a small white hand.

"Yes, yes." She nodded. "Father threatened me with
that once before. Now—I see. Father's money; father's
friends; the commissioner of police." She hesitated a long
time. "And you, too, Satan. I didn't think you'd be in it.
What reason would you have for wanting me out of the
picture? You are not just thinking of me?"

"No, I'm not just thinking of you. But I might have reason enough." He came to his feet, steadied himself on the arm of the chair, threw open his coat, unbuttoned his vest and very slowly opened his shirt. He was watching the girl closely; her eyes—those brown, honest eyes. And he wondered about eyes; if honesty could be registered at will, just like they did in talking pictures.

The girl saw the bandage; the red against the white. Her lips opened with a sudden little popping sound, hung so. The blood drained from her face, leaving two spots of red; seemingly brilliant in the sudden whiteness of the rest of her face.

"Satan. Satan!" She swayed forward, stretched out her hand as if she would have fallen against him. But she didn't; she couldn't. He grasped her wrist, held her arms stiffly, held her from him. Her trembling lips hardly formed the words. "Satan—you've been shot."

"That's right." He never took those green orbs off her. And now her brown eyes shifted; were certainly incapable of a direct look. "Two slugs. One right through the arm; just plain luck that it never touched a thing. This one"—his shoulders moved—"Took some excess beef off this hide of mine; no harm done. Do you know where I got the lead; just what place?"

"I—I . . . How should I?" And when he didn't speak: "Of course not."

"Well, it was on a side street over by Tenth Avenue." His lips twisted grimly as he saw her grasp the broad windowsill, lean on it. "I got a call to come down there. Important information!" And suddenly, "You don't know anything about that call?"

"No. No! Of course not. Why?"

"Why? You see, the party said it was you. Gave your

name—the woman who called; the woman who put me on the spot.''

''Was it—did it sound like my voice?'' She had turned again now and was facing him, very close to him; her brown eyes uncertain, pleading perhaps. At least, searching. Damn it! he couldn't tell what was there.

Satan hesitated. It was in his mind; on his lips, even, to tell the truth—that he had recognized her voice. But he didn't. He said: ''I don't know. I don't know. I haven't heard you much over the phone. It was just—a woman's voice, but she said 'Nina Radcliff.' '' And slowly now, very slowly as he dropped his eyes from the girl, ''Was it you?''

A long, very long moment of silence; and the girl laughed, a little shrilly.

''So that's why you treated me like this! Satan, Satan! Can't you see; can't you understand?'' She threw herself forward, her arms about his neck, her little hand against his chest. Soft hair brushed his cheek.

For a moment his arms went about her, just touched her back; but he didn't hold her, not exactly hold her. Peculiar, too. Satan didn't like women, and now—now. . . She was so young and beautiful, and—and. . .

His hand fastened on her shoulder, started force to push her away; but only started. He said, and his words sounded thick—thick even to him: ''Nina. Nina! About that phone call! Did—did you make it?''

''Me! Me? Of course not, Satan.'' She didn't intend to straighten herself; that is, didn't until both those strong arms moved suddenly and jarred her erect. ''So that's why you don't want me to help you.''

''You didn't make—didn't know about that call, then?''

''No. No, silly.'' She had her bag open now, a tiny mirror in her hand. She was dabbing at her face. ''I've been foolish about you, Satan. Very foolish.'' She looked straight at him now. "But somehow I don't care if I have.'' She stepped near him again. "Won't you say something? You can't be such a fool about women that you don't understand. Won't you say something—something to make it easier for me?''

"Sure. Sure!'' he told her. "Take that trip to Europe.''

"To Europe? For months; for years, maybe? Maybe you'd never see me again.'' And when he just grinned and she moved uncertainly toward the door, "You wouldn't care; it wouldn't mean anything to you?''

Broad shoulders shrugged. Satan said: "It might. You see, one of those bullets could have gone into my heart.''

"Satan. God! Satan.'' She swung suddenly, fear in her voice. "You don't think I called you to your—your death.''

"No, no.'' He pulled at his pointed, V-shaped chin; spoke easily. "But if you were in Europe—well, I couldn't be fooled that way. Calls apparently coming from you!''

"I see, I see!'' she said. But it was as plain in her face as it was back in her frantic brain that she didn't see at all. "But they won't send me to Europe. I won't go! I'm over twenty-one. Why not come up to the house tonight and see the fun?'' She turned abruptly, passed to the other room. Then the door swung open again and she thrust her head in; said softly, though the commissioner's secretary was far across that outer room: "Satan, you don't—don't think I made that call?''

"No, no!'' He smiled again when he reassured her. "I don't think that; don't *think* anything like that.'' And he didn't. He knew beyond a doubt that Nina Radcliff had made the call that had trapped him; was supposed to trap him to his death. And he wished that she had told him the truth; given him a desperate, or even a foolish reason. Anything but a direct lie! And why hadn't he told her the truth; that he knew she had called? It was better that she didn't know; better for the millions of citizens that he served. It was always good to be on to an enemy; an enemy who posed as a friend, and it was always better that that enemy didn't know.

But what did it matter now? The girl would be sent away. Good and clean and decent! Hell! What a mistake he had made about that girl. Mistake? Yes. Sure. Yet, did he still believe in her? No sense in that sort of reasoning; that sort of thought. Of course not. But thoughts are not always logical, or even reasonable. Satan's shoulders shrugged. He had made a bet on brown eyes. And he had lost.

WANTED ALIVE

■

Ten minutes later the commissioner hurried into the office. He looked quickly at Satan, said without preliminary: "It was Chopper Hays, all right. They picked up the body over on First Avenue. Right in the death car—a Pierce. A dozen people saw the driver climb out of the car and hurry away, but none can identify him."

"Were there any fingers missing?"

"Two," said the commissioner. "Shot clean off. Schmit said you thought it might have been someone else."

"Hoped, not thought," Satan nodded. "Eddie Jerome was using the machine gun. I saw his face, or enough of it."

"You didn't shoot him, then? At a time like that you thought of what I said?"

"You flatter me." Satan smiled. "It's a good story, but I didn't have much time to think. I just opened fire, and the wrong face came into the picture and took the dose." He leaned forward. "But we've got Jerome. I can go on the stand and identify him. Others saw him, too; people on the street."

The commissioner shook his head.

"I'm afraid that wouldn't be sufficient without direct evidence." The commissioner paused. "Of course Hollis Daggett was behind it; sent him. That's why he withdrew all his influence to have you removed. He was afraid you'd work independently and privately through me. He fears you, Satan, and decided to have you killed. He'll alibi Jerome; with important people, who will be believed by a jury. People you can't prove the lie on."

Satan's grin broadened; at least, his mouth.

"I saw Jerome firing that machine gun. His prints will be on it. Prints that won't lie; prints that will hold 'big people' for perjury unless they are convinced first that they'd better not lie. You wanted Jerome; you spoke of law. That machine gun will roast him. It shouldn't be hard to incense the public through the press. You see, Commissioner, this is no moving picture drama; no gangster war that thrills people. An innocent bystander was murdered; someone in no way connected with crime; just a young girl. There's horror to the public there; a personal horror, that this can happen to anyone; happen to them. The fingerprints on that machine gun should do the trick."

The commissioner stood facing Satan now. Satan's green eyes widened. He saw no enthusiasm in the commissioner's eyes. The commissioner opened his mouth to speak, closed it again, then said: "You've been wounded. Badly hurt."

Satan shrugged a shoulder, winced at his painful discovery that it was the wrong shoulder, then said: "We'll forget that. This machine gun; fingerprints! The district attorney could convict a man if the prints were on that gun. That's so. That's law; that's evidence—sufficient evidence, isn't it?"

"Yes, of course. If we had the prints and the gun."

"So that's that." Satan nodded. "Eddie Jerome gripped that gun tightly. His fingers are plainly outlined in blood; smeared in the blood of Chopper Hays. And on the top of that I can stand up in court and put the finger on him."

"One man against the testimony of many. You're a prejudiced witness; a man who has sworn to get the one closest to Daggett."

"Look here, Commissioner!" Green eyes were sparkling, thin lips were tight. "You wanted evidence; you wanted a conviction. That gun will make witnesses change their evidence if they know in advance. Well, let me have it, Commissioner."

The commissioner half turned his head, then looked back straight into the eyes of Satan. He said slowly: "There will be no fingerprints because there is no machine gun. There! don't talk. It just disappeared."

Satan Hall showed no surprise.

"So early in the case; even before it was threatening evidence. Think of that now!"

"You don't seem surprised." The commissioner's voice was indifferent, his features placid; yet with a certain paleness to his face, a peculiar glint back in his eyes. Satan knew and understood. Inside, the commissioner was a seething volcano.

Satan's laugh didn't help any, and his answer less so.

"I've been too many years in this game to be surprised. Evidence! Witnesses! The right people controlling money and death can always make evidence and witnesses disappear, change sworn testimony, and clear-cut memory becomes a foggy, useless thing." This time Satan's grin was peculiar and rather pleased. "That's why the talking pictures always have detectives with their hats on. They're afraid of losing them."

"We'll find the man who sold out the department; who

got that machine gun. I'll crack down hard this time. Yes, we'll find who got that gun."

"Who got it, but not who paid for it." Satan leaned forward. "But you'll be lacking the evidence against Jerome. Do you still want to see Jerome face a jury—or see him my way; face up on a slab, where his kind belong?"

"I'd still like to see him face a jury. McCray, Daggett's man, who would have talked, is dead. Walsh, who would have talked, is also dead. Jerome, who will talk to save his own hide, is free. Yes, I would like to see him face a jury. But it's not personal with me now. Jerome is out to get you; no two ways about that. If you have to kill him, you have to kill him."

Satan thought a long moment.

"No," he finally said, "I don't have to kill him. I'll play the detective just this once, and I'll give you and the district attorney and a jury of the people the evidence that's needed; that the law demands. Enough to roast Jerome for the murder of a girl."

"Good. Good!" The commissioner was smiling now. "I like to hear you talk like that, Satan. The missing gun! We'll find it, no doubt, fingerprints carefully removed, and trace it perhaps to Chopper Hays."

"Hell!" said Satan. "I'm going to trace that gun directly to the fingers of Eddie Jerome." He hesitated a long time; then said: "You'll keep quiet about the gun, Commissioner, for a while."

The commissioner smiled.

"It's not a story I'd be apt to tell around."

"I don't mean that. I mean Daggett and Jerome. If they don't fear the gun anymore, Daggett won't be so particular about Jerome's alibi. I'll check that first, in the way of form."

"Yes, yes." The commissioner pulled at his chin. "Don't do anything foolish, Satan; an arrest, I mean. The technicalities of the law never bothered you before. Remember—knowledge may serve you for personal vengeance, but knowledge is not evidence and only evidence convicts in a court. Take care of yourself. If you need me tonight, I'll be at Chester Radcliff's."

"His daughter, eh? You're going to act tonight?"

"Tonight. At once."

"She might embarrass the department; you, and her father, eh, if she keeps up such company?"

"It would embarrass her more if she were dead. She's a fine girl, Satan; straight and clean. I don't want to see her dirtied." And with a grin, "She's stuck on you. But she's young and foolish. She's going on a cruise around the world."

"Boats touch ports, and she'll make trouble."

"This boat won't. It's been chartered by her father."

"She'll have to come back sometime. When?"

"That will be up to you."

"Me?"

"Yes. When Jerome isn't around to act for Daggett, and when Daggett isn't around to act for himself. Too bad. Wonderful girl. Wouldn't harm anyone but herself."

"Wouldn't, eh?" Satan looked at him. He was wondering. Then, with a little grimace to his thin lips: "I'd like to see how she takes it."

"Fine!" said the commissioner. "Her father thought of that, too. She talks a lot about you, and helping you. He thought if you were there it might make it easier for her." And after a moment: "You wouldn't interfere. You think it's best for her to go?"

"No, I wouldn't interfere." And sort of grimly: "Sure I think it's best for her to go."

"Fine!" The commissioner stared at Satan, came closer, took in each feature of that peculiar face, finally jammed a finger against Satan's chest. "I wouldn't take you as one to attract women; and such a woman."

"No, no. I'm glad I don't attract many." Satan's lips parted.

The commissioner pondered.

"Peculiar; a girl like that—and those who attract her!"

Satan jarred erect; then laughed.

The commissioner laughed too; said, slightly red: "I wasn't thinking of you, Satan. I was thinking of someone else."

"That's all right." Satan came to his feet. "I was thinking of someone else, too."

But neither one of them mentioned the name of the man with the little beady eyes; the tiny features in the center of a huge head.

The commissioner was watching Satan closely now, wondering if he had heard the stories; the stories that were forcing a young girl on a private cruise around the world.

Satan was mad when he closed that door; mad at himself. But he was smacking his lips. He was actually feeling pleasure at the idea of being there when Nina Radcliff was shipped off to Europe. It was a good thing too; a damn good thing. So he was simply a killer, eh? They didn't like that. Well, he'd give them the evidence that would roast Eddie Jerome and see what satisfaction they got in dragging a helpless man to the electric chair instead of just lifting his dead body from a public street.

THE LAW

■

Chester Radcliff was visibly nervous when he followed Satan into the large living room. The commissioner was the only other occupant of that room. He turned, caught the look in Satan's eyes and jerked his head toward a tiny hallway; a closed door beyond it.

Radcliff said: "You're a hard man to know, Detective Hall, but Nina talks about you a great deal. You saved her life, to say nothing about the money you saved me." And after a moment: "You're not here to interfere?"

"I told you, Chester, why Satan is here," the commissioner cut in. "It will give Nina more confidence. She looks on him as a friend. It should take away the feeling of being held a prisoner by her own father and myself, her oldest friend. She'll see our point."

"That's fine." Radcliff rubbed his hands, looked directly at Satan. "You're going to help—talk to her?"

"No," said Satan, "I'm not. I'm curious, that's all. She interests me; her connections interest me. I want to see how she'll take it; if she'll go."

"She'll go." Radcliff set his lips tightly. "Tonight! I've

decided on that.'' He nodded toward the hall, the door at the end of it. ''She's in there now, making her decision. I've made mine; she knows that. If she'll give me her word—why, it can be a real pleasure cruise. With friends— friends she used to know.''

''Did she give you her word?''

''No, she didn't.'' Radcliff paced the room. ''She seems different; perhaps resigned. At first it was threats. You remember?'' He looked at the commissioner. ''She never would speak to me again and all that. Now she just smiles at me; said she wished to think until eleven o'clock. Something about seeing if I were as big as I thought I was. I didn't like the way she put it. It was almost as if she expected''—Radcliff smiled slightly—'''some of this cheap nightlife gang she's been going with to storm the house and rescue her. She's got silly ideas about things lately.''

''Has she?'' Satan's tone made the question emphatic.

''Good God!'' said the commissioner, ''you don't expect—'' he walked to the front window; pulled back the shade. ''Have a look on the street, Satan.''

Satan shook his head.

''I saw them when I came in. You're very thorough, Commissioner. Perhaps you, too, believed some such thing.''

''Hardly. Hardly!'' The commissioner pulled at his chin. ''But I'm giving her plenty of protection.''

''That's why you asked me to come?''

The commissioner smiled, said, ''Hardly,'' again; went to a chair and sat down. The little door opened, squeaked; there was light in the tiny hall. Satan saw the girl plainly; the whiteness of her face, that untamed hair sweeping from beneath the tilted white hat; brown eyes that were wide. She was dressed for traveling and carried a bag in her hand.

Her father crossed to her, tried to take the bag. There was relief in his face. His words were pleasant. "Good girl. My girl." He put an arm about her shoulder when she held tightly to the bag. "You've decided to go then, yourself?"

"Yes." She stood very stiff and straight. "I've decided to go—myself. Don't touch me!" She shrank from his arm. "I'm going alone; away from this house—away from you. Don't touch me!"

Radcliff stepped back as if she had struck him. He leaned on the table, looked at the commissioner, saw no help there, turned back to his daughter.

"I'm sorry, Nina, but you're going away. A year, six months, perhaps even a shorter period. You've only got to promise things, you know."

"Promise to let you lead my life; promise to look at my duty through your eyes. I wanted to do things, help people, fight the very crime that nearly destroyed me, be some good in the world. Now you're driving me into that very life."

Radcliff laughed. At least, there was a grating noise far back in his throat. He said: "It may be my fault. Maybe I have neglected you. I gave you all the freedom any girl ever had. And the return? But no more of that. If you haven't any more sense a year from now than you have at present, you stay away. Well"—he glared at her now—"do you go quietly?"

The girl just looked at him. She didn't speak at first, then she turned her head to the commissioner, to Satan. It was to Satan she spoke.

"So you came to see the fun. You came to see what money and influence could do." And ended bitterly, "You told them that I trapped you!"

The commissioner straightened, Radcliff showed surprise. Satan Hall did not speak. The girl bit her lip.

"You didn't tell them, then? But you came here to see me beaten. You're afraid, and you want me to go?"

Satan said, ignoring her question: "You promised to put on an act. I came to see it."

"But you want me to go." She hesitated, listened. Some of her poise suddenly left her. "You talk of right and wrong and freedom and law. Well—I'm free, a citizen, and twenty-one. Who's to stop me leaving this house; going where I please; doing what I please?"

The commissioner said: "You're getting yourself all worked up, Nina. There is no need of it. Someday you'll thank us. Freedom doesn't give you the right to harm other people. You're hurting your father now. Your grandfather built up the name of Radcliff, your father made people respect it more. Now, you want to tear it down. You're a bright girl; you won't be foolish." He turned his head slightly as the door bell rang. "I promised your father that you'll go—straight."

"All right," she said. "You've had your chance." Brown eyes shone bright. "I don't think you can make good."

The commissioner was smiling easily when the door opened and the butler put his head in.

"It's a Mr. Aaron Whitlock," he said, and after a bit, "He said you'd want to see him."

"But I don't want to see anyone, and—"

A little man pushed in. He carried a small briefcase and sported a pair of heavy gold-rimmed glasses on the end of his hooked nose. He spoke before Radcliff could open his mouth. He knew how to make his words count and demand attention.

"It's about Miss Nina's cruise and the newspaper interest in it, and the yacht up at Larchmont," he said quickly; and then, while Radcliff was recovering from his amazement, "the commissioner, eh? How fortunate! And Detective Hall—Satan Hall. I've never had the pleasure of meeting you in court." And with a grin that split up the entire lower part of his face, "But then, you seldom bring me clients. Ah! Mr. Hall, we criminal lawyers would have little practice if all detectives were like you. A detriment to our profession; a positive menace!"

Satan grinned in return. He knew the little man; knew of him, as everyone in the city did. A criminal lawyer. The criminal lawyer. One who helped frame the laws that protected him and made him a criminal lawyer instead of a lawyer criminal.

"Maybe I'll give you a client," Satan said. "Eddie Jerome. You know him?"

"Jerome?" The little man seemed to think. "Yes, I've met him. A shrewd businessman, I believe. You think perhaps he'll need me?"

"And how!" was all Satan said.

Aaron Whitlock closed his lips tightly, blinked closely set eyes, shook his head, finally nodded it.

"But perhaps you're right. Jerome is an impulsive fellow; apt to fly off the handle." A mouth broadened again, yellow teeth showed and the lawyer laughed pleasantly. "You're not thinking of murder, Satan? That's my strength, you know. The unfortunates who, because of one misstep, are persecuted for the missteps of others—unless, of course, those unfortunates come to Aaron Whitlock and ask him to defend them."

Satan's green eyes were steady.

"I was thinking of murder, yes."

"Really!" A moment's pause. "Not yours, I hope. Be careful, Satan. There would be extenuating circumstances in your death. It's open gossip in certain circles that you don't like Jerome! Self-defense! Persecution! Really, quite a case if he should kill you."

"It won't be for my murder, and I'll bring him in alive."

"Fine! Excellent!" The little lawyer bent his shoulders, rubbed his hands, dug a finger into Satan's chest. His gray eyes twinkled, but they were cold. There was no warmth in them.

"I'd be no match for you up a back alley, my boy; but in a courtroom . . . Dear me, dear me! I'd make a . . . Hello, what's this?"

Aaron Whitlock looked back as the commissioner's hand fell on his shoulder. The commissioner said: "Come to the reason for your visit."

Gray eyes grew hard and steady. Aaron Whitlock's body followed his head. When he straightened, he was almost as tall as the commissioner. When he spoke now, his voice was sharp, indignant and authoritative; his words crisp.

"My business," he said, "can hardly be with you. I presume, in your capacity as police commissioner, you are here for the same purpose that I am."

"And that?" said the commissioner.

"To keep a family misunderstanding, a slight difference of viewpoint on the broadening influence of travel, from becoming a public scandal; a nasty, vulgar display of prominent personalities in court." And when the commissioner would have talked, the lawyer said: "I think my business is entirely with Mr. Radcliff."

Radcliff coughed.

"And just what is that business, and whom do you represent?"

"Miss Radcliff." A discolored tongue wet pale lips.

Whitlock carefully opened his briefcase and extracted a number of legal papers, of various sizes and shapes.

"First"—he ran his finger over the papers—"we have Miss Radcliff's birth certificate. A mere formality, as far as you are concerned, Mr. Radcliff." And as Radcliff's face reddened, "And here's an order to prevent the—the—"

He raised his glasses slightly. "What a charming name! To prevent the Viking from leaving the yacht club. The captain's name is Mott—Victor Leward Mott. That court order, of course, is signed by a Westchester county judge. I have other writs of a surprising and perhaps unpleasant nature." His smile now took in the entire room.

"And just what do you intend to do?" It was the commissioner who spoke as Radcliff looked over at him, his lips set tightly, his fingers opening and closing at his side as if he were controlling himself from stretching out those fingers and fastening them upon the scrawny, corded neck of the little lawyer.

"Why—nothing, I hope." Whitlock's eyes opened in mild surprise. "It would be a nasty mess for the papers; embarrassing for your bank, Mr. Radcliff, and your associates. But I'm not really thinking of all that; simply the interest of my client."

"The interest of your client!" There was a sneer in Chester Radcliff's voice; that is, from the viewpoint of one who did not know Radcliff well. Those who did know him understood that he was too big a man to sneer.

"Well, yes—of course." Aaron Whitlock was still affable. "Miss Radcliff informs me she is not a good sailor; suffers from seasickness. I'll see that she doesn't take a cruise."

"I know you and your kind." Chester Radcliff leaned forward, towering over the little lawyer. "Suppose I have you thrown out of this house."

The little man nodded pleasantly.

"That, of course, is a personal matter which does not concern the interests of my client. Regarding the young lady! At the very least, it's abduction, Mr. Radcliff. No doubt what you propose to do is excusable, and perhaps it will be most leniently dealt with by the court. But it's a nasty scandal. The tabloids particularly will gobble it up, and"—he ran through the papers in his hand again, smiled— "before you threw me out of the house, of course I would leave another little paper; one which our newswriters treat with such facetiousness—our old friend the writ of habeas corpus; the order of the court that the body of Miss Radcliff be brought before it."

The commissioner was between the two men. He said to Whitlock: "Just what do you intend to do with all these legal documents?"

"Intend?" said the lawyer. "I can't answer that. But I hope to return them to the briefcase and carry them away with me." He paused, smiled over at the girl. "As the papers are heavy and I am not very strong, Miss Radcliff will no doubt be kind enough to carry the briefcase for me."

"She . . . You expect her to leave this house with you— now!" Radcliff stormed.

Aaron Whitlock nodded.

"I expect her to leave here with or without me; go where she pleases. You have lawyers, Mr. Radcliff, very able lawyers. They will advise as to your going before the court and requesting the commitment of your daughter to some institution. It will be for me, in her interest, to see that a commitment is not granted. The scandal will be deplorable; but that is up to you."

There were words after that. Chester Radcliff's high-pitched, threatening; the commissioner's soothing, soft-spoken, but jerky. It was Satan who broke the tension. He laughed, came to his feet.

"So that's the law!" he said; looked at Radcliff and jerked a thumb toward the girl. "If you could get her committed with Aaron Whitlock behind her, then most of the killers wouldn't be walking the streets free today." He went toward the door, paused, his hand on the knob, and turned back. The green in his eyes fairly shone now. He raised a finger, pointed it straight at the girl.

"She got the stuff, Radcliff," he said. "The stuff that makes for good or bad, and no one can work it out but herself. You lay off that kid, or you'll be hiring Aaron Whitlock some day to defend her as an accessory to murder." And with the door half open: "A tip to you, Aaron. I'm willing to take you on in open court. I'd like to try a new game. So—stay up tonight."

"Tonight! Why?" Aaron Whitlock was puzzled; it showed in his face. He wasn't afraid, yet a tiny chill ran quickly up his spine. Satan knew no law, recognized or obeyed none. Did Satan wish to find out who was behind him; who had sent him there? Satan had peculiar ways of finding out things, and Aaron Whitlock couldn't stand physical pain. He said, before Satan was fairly through the door: "You—you suspect someone is behind me. Want to know who?"

Satan shook his head.

"I don't simply suspect; I know. That kid was as surprised as any of us when you walked in. Oh! she knew; at least, hoped some racket would be worked, but didn't know just how. Besides, that last-minute push-in of yours was drama; and I know who likes drama and who thought such drama would make a hit with the kid. Yep. I know who paid you and sent you. Your steady and best client— Hollis Daggett. And what's more, I know why."

The girl stepped forward, spoke before Whitlock could. "Why?" was all she said.

Satan looked at her but said nothing. Aaron Whitlock got his question in.

"Why do you want me to stay up all night?"

"Because," said Satan slowly, "I'll be arresting—not killing, understand—simply arresting Eddie Jerome for the brutal murder of an innocent girl. Good night!"

Satan stepped into the hall and closed the door softly behind him. A detective grabbed his arm as he was leaving the house.

"Big things going on, eh?" he said. And when Satan pulled away, "Don't be so high-hat. Who gets the police escort tonight?"

"No one," said Satan. "Absolutely no one."

EIGHT

ON THE DARK SIDE STREET

■

Satan was down the steps, walking slowly from the house. So that was the law the commissioner wanted respected and enforced! He chuckled and wondered if the commissioner was so keen about it now. Laws were made to be broken; lawyers were trained to interpret those laws so that they could be broken. But this time the law was good. Imagine a girl like that being sent away from temptation! Brooding the entire trip; building up a hatred of her father, of society. Why not let the girl work it out herself? Why not—

Satan's lips parted, green eyes slanted more. She had almost worked him out of his troubles that very day; trapped him like any common hood, and then simply lied about it. In plain words, the criminal code. Admit nothing, tell nothing, let the law prove it if they can. Which they can't, most times.

The side street was dark as Satan turned the corner; that is, he was starting to turn the corner when a taxi drew up, pulled quickly to the curb. The driver called to him, entirely unconscious of the fact that the nose of a gun held far back beneath a jacket wavered the fraction of an inch between himself and the interior of his car. The driver said: "Hop in. There's a party wants you." As Satan moved into the light the knowing grin faded from the taximan's face. He drew back behind the wheel, sucked in a deep breath. He didn't kid with such a face; didn't wisecrack either. He just said nothing.

A voice spoke from inside the car. It was low; no more than a whisper.

"Please get in—quickly."

Satan walked to the cab, climbed on the running board, swung his body back. Most of the time he was hidden from possible fire from that car, but the casual passerby would not have noticed his movements as out of the ordinary; they were so quick, so decisive.

The girl gasped when Satan's face followed his right hand and the gun into the cab.

"Oh!" She stiffened. "Hurry. There is death waiting for you down that block."

The girl was alone in the cab. Satan turned his head slowly, looked down the street; the darkness of it, the quiet of it, the dotted lights in many windows. Then he opened the door and slid into the cab, dropped down beside the girl, looked at her two hands that were folded in her lap, holding a pocketbook. The taxi moved on. The girl said, in a hurt sort of way: "It's not a gun; it's a pocketbook." And when Satan didn't lift his eyes from her hands, "Perhaps you would like to look inside." With a derisive motion she stretched out the bag, gave a little exclamation of surprise when he took it, opened it, felt around inside, returned it to her.

"You think I'd kill you—shoot you?"

"No. I don't."

"Then why the doubt? You were looking for a gun in that bag?"

"Sure." Satan nodded in the darkness as the cab went downtown. "Wiser guys that I—lads who knew lots more about women—have been shot by them. What I thought wouldn't do me much good if you emptied a gun into me."

"I thought"—her voice grew soft again—"that you said I was good and clean and decent."

Satan said simply: "Lead in the belly would hurt just as much if you were good and clean and decent. Anyway, you got soiled; had your chance to wash up tonight and didn't take it."

"My chance!" She laughed. "The chance for someone else to give me a wash, you mean. I'll take my own baths, thank you. Do you know why I came after you?"

"Yes. You wanted me to answer that question. Why Hollis Daggett kept you from going away."

"That's not true." She hoped that Satan couldn't see the red that suddenly sprang into her face. "I wanted to help you. If you'd gone down that side street you would have been killed."

"I went down a side street today and didn't get killed."

"Satan"—a little hand rested on his large one—"tell me the truth. You believe I sent you to your death today?"

"Hardly, since I'm here with you—and alive." Satan laughed. A metallic sound, grim, hard. "But you telephoned me to be there, didn't you?"

"No!" she snapped the word at once. A long minute of silence. The girl felt rather than saw those peculiar green eyes in the darkness. Finally she said, "I did telephone you, but I didn't know; didn't understand." Fingers tightened on his wrist now, a tousled head was close to his shoulder. "I didn't have to tell you that."

"No," said Satan, "you didn't. I recognized your voice on the phone, beyond a doubt."

"And you didn't tell Father or the commissioner! You did believe in me a little then; think a little of me." Soft hair was against his cheek.

"Hell!" His shoulder moved so quickly that the girl's teeth clicked; her head jarred against the side of the cab. "I wasn't thinking of you; I was thinking of myself. No guy likes to be laughed at; to be a sucker."

"Oh!" she said. "Why do you think I'm telling you now?"

"Simple. The first crack didn't go over. You're trying to straighten yourself out for a purpose."

"Yes, I am—I am." She spoke rapidly now, as if she must get it all out before she changed her mind. "You're different from any man I've ever met. I like you, Satan. Yes—God help me! I—I more than like you. I want to help. I want to be more than just the daughter of a rich man. I want... Can't you see? I didn't want to be a sucker, either. I didn't want you to know someone made a fool out of me. Anyway, I heard talk that Rusty Whitlock was there, and I telephoned you. They cut in on the wire, or simply—"

"Used you as a sucker," he said.

"Then you do see; do believe. Satan, Satan. I was afraid if you knew the truth you'd never like me; never let me work with you. You believe—believe me now?" She raised her hands, placed them against his face, pushed up his head, forced green eyes to look straight into brown ones that showed now and then in the passing streetlights.

In and out, like an electric advertisement, those brown eyes flashed. It was a good face; and her story was plausible, of course. She was new in the game; in the racket maybe. It would be easier to use her than to force her. Satan had seen that demonstrated at her father's house a few minutes before. But he said: "You want me to believe that you were just a sucker."

She hesitated; and then, very slowly, hardly audible: "If—if you can like a sucker again." She was a little afraid of his silence. "It might have been just a bad break, you know. Remember—tonight—just now—I saved your life; kept you from being killed on that side street."

"Tonight!" Satan laughed. "I had no previous intention of going down that side street, so no one could set a trap for me there. I turned into that street on sudden impulse, to avoid being overtaken by your father or the commissioner. You'll have to get another story of why you came after me."

"Well"—she stiffened—"why do you think Hollis Daggett helped me?" She would have gone on; tried to persuade Satan to tell her, but he answered abruptly.

"He wants you."

"Oh!" She laughed a little. "Satan, he's old enough to . . . well, he's much older than I am. But he's a big man—and I suppose that's flattery. But for Hollis Daggett to be in love with me—"

Satan stared at her a long time, finally said: "There's a great difference between love and lust."

"Satan"—she touched his arm—"Hollis Daggett would hardly be one to attract women. You know that; I know that."

"But Hollis Daggett doesn't know that, or won't believe that, or will find ways to make himself attractive; perhaps in the belief that there are other things less attractive. Stay away from Daggett and Jerome."

"So you, too, want to lead my life; give me orders?"

"I'm giving you a warning," Satan told her flatly. "There's going to be fireworks. Jerome is going to roast and he's going to talk before he roasts. The hot seat is big enough to hold even Daggett. It won't be pleasant for you or your father or the commissioner if you're dragged into the mess."

"It's nice of you to think of me," she said stiffly.

"I'm not thinking of you; I'm thinking of the citizens that pay me. It's going to be a dirty mess. Get out of it; get from under. I won't spare you any, or anyone else." And when she started to cut in about trying to help and wanting to do something, he ran on. "You did something; something today. It isn't pleasant to hear, kid, and you didn't mean it. But by your interference you stuck the finger on that girl just as if you stood behind the gun and pulled the trigger."

"Satan!" The name was jarred from her. She caught her breath, then called to the driver to stop, waited until he pulled to the curb. "I've liked you, Satan. I've humiliated myself, but that's more than I'll take from any man." She leaned over to the door, jerked it open. "Come on. Get out!"

"Sure. Sure!" Satan moved slowly. "You're soft. I gave you the truth, even if you couldn't take it. But don't get swept into the mess."

"That's right. That's right." She was mad now; it was in her voice, in the back of her throat, in the blazing brown eyes. "You and my father and the commissioner drove me into the 'mess' tonight. You know Daggett. He protected me from those who should have helped me; he wanted a promise in return. He got that promise."

"Yeah?" Satan stood on the curb, his body twisted, one foot on the running board.

"Yeah?" She mimicked him "That's why I followed you; picked you up. To tell you about my word of honor. Don't grin. I've never broken it yet. I thought you'd understand and help; force me not to keep that promise; keep me, so I couldn't.''

Satan's head bobbed up and down.

"That's woman's logic," he said. "What was the promise?''

"The promise was that if I were free, I would come to Hollis Daggett tonight. I thought—hoped—you would keep me from being free." The door closed with a bang as Satan moved quickly; jerked his fingers back just in time to save them from being crushed.

Satan made a movement toward the cab as it pulled from the curb, then shrugged his shoulders. Hell! The whole thing was a mess. He had saved the girl's life, and kidlike, she built romance out of it. Her father; the commissioner! They only drove her deeper into the mud; proved Daggett a bigger man than they; than the law. The law which they worshiped; tried to beat, and found that it bounced back and smacked them in the face.

The girl . . . brown eyes! But there were thousands of other girls with brown eyes in the city; one with brown eyes who lay on a slab in the morgue. They wanted law, eh? They were going to get it. Jerome would talk; Daggett would be dragged in. And with Daggett's downfall the whole criminal structure; the impregnable organization of crime and politics would crash; crumble in a cloud of dust that would smother many big, respected names; tear false gods from their pedestals.

Satan Hall hopped another cab and was driven straight to the home of his friend, Lieutenant Morrisey. His words were short and to the point. He wanted to know about the witnesses to his attempted blast-out and the death of an innocent girl. Innocent girl! That was a good phrase; the district attorney would make something out of that.

Morrisey said: "There's three who saw the actual murder and saw Jerome in the car. I rustled up his picture, and they can identify him. But hell! Satan, there will be an alibi that Daggett will build up, and it will be big; big men that a jury will have to believe. That machine gun, now, with his prints! If we only had that, it would cinch the case. But without it—"

"Never mind that gun; we'll have it. About those witnesses. Got them?"

"Two were willing to take the money and live in Jersey. And just about time! A couple of heels were looking for them; runners from Aaron Whitlock. The third, a broker called Clarence Floyd Duncan, won't budge. He promises his testimony, and that he'll identify Eddie Jerome on the witness stand. He thinks he's above being 'intimidated.' Anyway, that's his front."

"Okay!' Satan nodded, satisfied. "Where's Daggett right now? You've kept an eye on him?"

"Yes. He's been in his rooms above the dance floor in the Wellington Hotel. Sort of an office, with more than one 'out.' There's gossip that he really owns the Wellington, but no one can put a finger on that."

"No one wants to!" Satan snapped. "Jerome around?"

"He went into the Wellington and hasn't come out. Why the big interest tonight?"

"The commissioner wants law and order; the press wants law and order. They're going to get it. I'm bringing in Eddie Jerome for murder, and I'm bringing him in tonight."

"But why the hurry?"

Satan grinned.

"I promised Aaron Whitlock a client. I don't want to disappoint him."

"You told Whitlock!" Bushy eyebrows raised. "He'll tell Daggett, and Jerome will know. They'll be prepared."

"That's why I told Whitlock. Daggett will have to prepare his alibi hurriedly; he won't have time to get the big names who will have to be persuaded, coerced, and blackmailed into it."

"But the gun?"

"I'll have that tonight."

"You think Jerome has the gun, or that Daggett's got it?"

And when Satan said nothing: "You think they'll keep it; that Daggett will keep it until the fingerprints on it can really be identified—that if Jerome's fingerprints aren't on it, they'll return it for evidence?"

And after a moment's thought, "I don't think Daggett will keep it to hold over Jerome's head. It will be his own head that will be in danger if Jerome is convicted. Anyway, he wouldn't keep that gun where you can get it; and if he did, the fingerprints could be wiped off it with a single swipe. You—"

"Don't worry about that gun, nor the fingerprints," snapped Satan. "I'm going to make that arrest tonight."

"Now—at once?"

"Now." Satan paused. "After I get my legal warrant, and have a look at the dead girl at the morgue."

"God! Satan. Why that?"

Satan's lips set to a single grim line.

"It makes me work better."

"But you'll—you'll kill him, Satan. Kill him sure. It's a young face; rather a sweet face."

"Yes, I know. I want to see it again." He swung in the doorway and faced Morrisey. "They don't like my methods; they don't like my ways; they don't think death is a deterrent to crime. By God! what do the people want?"

"The people like the sensational, of course, Satan. They—"

"They'll get it. They'll get it! Sensational, eh?"

"And the girl, Nina! What of her? It's tough. She's a good kid."

"That's right, that's right. A good kid. Well, that's the law, too; the law they want enforced. If she stands in the way of justice tonight—God help her."

Satan turned and left the room. Brown eyes seemed to dance before his green ones; brown eyes that had something in back of their depths.

Fifteen minutes later the attendant at the morgue, who had brought in and taken out hundreds of bodies over the years, shuddered slightly. The experience was new to him. He was a man with little, if any, imagination and never before had he seen a living devil stand above a body, even lift the eyelids and for a full minute stare unblinkingly into dead, brown eyes.

His attempted jocular remark that he hadn't seen any of Satan's stiffs lately sounded flat to him. But that didn't matter. Detective Satan Hall didn't answer; didn't even look at him; didn't even appear to have heard, as his feet beat over hard stone and he left the house of the dead.

NINE

THE MACHINE GUN

■

Hollis Daggett looked over the large flat desk at Eddie Jerome, who toyed with the irons before the blazing logs in the great stone fireplace. He said: "Knowing what you did, you came here. Why?"

"Why not?" Jerome returned easily. "After all, it was your racket; putting Satan on the spot. If your killer went yellow and if some dame, out of curiosity, furnished the background, can I help it? Whitlock got hold of me, or someone from his office. Said Satan was going to arrest me tonight. You were told, weren't you?"

Daggett jerked his head at the phone.

"Yes, I was told. Now, why did you come here?"

Eddie Jerome leaned far over the desk.

"I'm a sociable fellow, mister; a damned sociable fellow. I like people around; like friends." And very slowly: "I ain't a guy that would burn alone."

Hollis Daggett grinned.

"You're worried, then? You haven't got the proper confidence in me."

Jerome looked at the huge flat desk; the white paper

spread upon it, the black machine gun that rested there; he even saw the red stains, especially around the trigger guard.

"What's that doing here?"

"That's the gun, isn't it? The murder gun the police want?"

"You oughta know." Jerome hunched his shoulders. "All Tommy guns look alike to me. But what's the idea of it being here? It's hot; damned hot."

Hollis Daggett got up and walked around the desk, laid an arm on Jerome's shoulder.

"We'll put the gun back; have it turn up someplace. You shouldn't have lied to me about your prints, Jerome. They're down in the cop's files, but they're not on that gun."

"No?" said Jerome. "Not on the gun?" His eyes widened. "You're not trying to frame me—keep that gun over my head, for later?"

"No, I'm not." Daggett looked at him steadily. "I can't understand Satan's bluff; Satan's threat to arrest you to-night. Have you told me everything—everything that happened?" Little eyes were round and bright and steady in that great face.

"Sure. Sure! Everything!" Jerome said indifferently. "Why?"

"Because"—Hollis Daggett's words were very steady— "there are prints on that gun; decided prints. They are not yours. They must be the prints of Chopper Hays. I haven't got his here, so I can't tell. But I'm sure they are not yours. I'll have this tomorrow."

"That's funny, but good." Jerome's face brightened; and suddenly, "You know your stuff, mister; but since when have you become a fingerprint expert?"

Daggett smiled, waved toward one of the numerous doors.

"Professor Darryton is in that room; he's one of the best experts in the city."

"So that's how it is." Jerome screwed up his face. He was puzzled, yet he liked the way things were going. He was sure; positive, five minutes ago, that his prints would be on that gun. He said, "You build me an alibi; a good one, and without the prints on the gun Satan has no case. Hell! he must know that. Why his sudden threat of arrest? Why this threat to bring me in alive when he can't begin to prove a case?"

"Bluff!" Hollis Daggett said. "Bluff, with something behind it. He hates me, and you are close to me. He wants to throw us off guard. By God! Jerome, I think he intends to shoot you to death, resisting arrest."

Jerome jerked erect. His lip twisted, his face blanched suddenly. He looked toward the several doors along the walls, heard a slight sound above, looked up.

"What's that?" he asked.

Daggett smiled, walked to the side of the room, opened a narrow door, called: "Come down, Nina."

Feet moved across the floor above; feet hardly audible on thick rugs.

"That dame here?"

"Yes, sure." Hollis Daggett smoothed back his hair, pulled at his vest, looked at Jerome. His little eyes sparkled. Women were his one weakness; his weakness because he wanted to impress others that it was his strength.

Feet beat on stairs, one of the numerous doors opened, Nina Radcliff stepped into the room.

"You know Eddie," Daggett said as he took her hand and with exaggerated courtesy brought her to the center of the room. "You were there tonight, my dear. You heard

Satan Hall's threat to arrest Jerome. You think he meant it?''

"I know he meant it." She straightened her little body and glared at Jerome. "And I believe he did it, Mr. Daggett. I—"

" 'Hollis,' my child. 'Hollis.' " Daggett's tiny round mouth made funny little grimaces when he smiled. "We mustn't stand on ceremony when we understand each other so well now." The grimace became a smirk, the girl drew back; rather, seemed to draw within herself. Her entire body tightened in a peculiar way.

"It was he." The girl pointed at Jerome. "I heard him talking, and—"

"And you fell for it, eh?" Jerome moved threateningly. "You phoned Satan, you double-crossing little twist!"

Daggett said quickly: "Tush, tush, Eddie. Nina and I understand each other." He patted her hand. "Just each other! It wasn't Jerome, my dear, who had anything to do with that poor girl's death. We have proof it wasn't."

The girl spoke. She was confused, bewildered.

"But you told me you wanted Walsh arrested. You said it would prove that he knew nothing; could know nothing about you—and then he was found dead! Satan thinks I . . . Oh! don't you see the position it puts me in? I don't know what to believe; whom to trust, Mr. Daggett."

" 'Hollis,' my dear, 'Hollis.' And you should know who to trust after tonight; after the—shall I say the bad friends I made in order to help you? Your father is influential, the commissioner is his friend. Don't misunderstand me." He held her hand tightly now, looked into those brown yes—and he had hard work controlling his voice, hard work not to grip those slender fingers too tightly. "I would make such enemies a hundred times over to feel that you are my friend."

"Satan told me it was something else. I can't explain, can't say it; but that was why you brought me here."

"I brought you here because I wanted you near me. The Wellington is a hotel, like any other hotel. Your rooms are your rooms; engaged by you."

"But why do you want me near you? Why the door down here, to your—to these rooms?"

"Your freedom might be very temporary. The commissioner's influence is far-reaching; you might be spirited away. Here I can protect you. There! Run above."

"Satan will be coming here tonight?" she asked.

"I don't know, but it won't bother you. Sleep well!" He led her back to the open door; the little flight of stairs. "If you're nervous, lock the door above the stairs. Good night!"

When she was gone Jerome said: "Why have her here? Why bring her down to see me? She ain't your kind. Hell! she thinks you're an old gentleman—old, and gentleman." Jerome started to laugh, and stopped. It wasn't the time for mirth. He read that in Daggett's face; realized, too, in a hazy way why Daggett had brought the girl down. Something like a boy showing off. But his eyes widened as Daggett held up a key and looked toward the stairs.

"There'll be an understanding between us in the morning," he said.

"Yeah?" said Jerome. "You think there will?"

"I know there will." And eyes growing smaller, "Women as well as men must recognize that I'm the master. Now to business."

Jerome looked toward the stair, twisted his face, realized that in the morning the girl wouldn't care much—one way or the other. Daggett's conquests of women were well-known to him; open gossip in the hot spots. It was at times a rather brutal conquest.

But Jerome only said: "About that typewriter! Going to leave it there if Satan comes?"

"I think so. I think so." Daggett ignored the sudden pugnacious movement of Jerome's jaw. "It's this way, Eddie. The police have nothing on you. Satan's been hounding you because I built you up. Now, what's to prevent you and me hiring detectives to locate that machine gun; locate it after the police mislaid it so as to stick the crime on you? See the point? Satan was one who could have gotten rid of that gun; he had the opportunity. The gun will be traced to Chopper Hays. Hays is dead. Blooey! All an attempt of Satan Hall to misplace evidence that would clear you. Here—"

Hollis Daggett turned, threw open a door, raised his huge hand, bent a finger. A slim, long man with glasses came in. Daggett waved a hand.

"Professor Darryton!" he said to Jerome.

"It's all very irregular." The fingerprint expert was hardly at ease. "I don't understand it."

The phone rang. Daggett jerked it up; said: "Well?" And after a moment, "Why, certainly. An officer on official business is always welcome. Send Detective Hall right up." And slamming down the phone, "We'll take the wind out of his sails. You stay there, Professor." A huge hand shoved the spectacled man into a chair. "We'll let this Satan Hall make a fool of himself."

"Just what do you mean by that?" Eddie Jerome looked toward the different doors, moved uneasily on the balls of his feet, involuntarily slipping his right hand beneath his left armpit.

"A false arrest!" Daggett sat down behind the desk; his manner was crisp. "We have our expert, the professor; the gun as evidence. You've got the number of it?" And when Darryton nodded. "That's fine!"

"I don't think," said Jerome slowly, "I could go for an arrest at this time. Satan don't like me; he wants to frame me for that bit of killing. And you know what happens to guys downstairs in cop houses."

"Nonsense!" Daggett smiled. "You—"

"I don't think," Jerome said again, and his lips twisted into a ugly grimace, "that my arrest would be good policy for me—nor for you, mister."

Daggett waited a full minute before he spoke. Finally he said: "Okay, then. We'll play it your way."

FINGERPRINTS

■

Satan Hall stood at the foot of the broad staircase that led from the dance floor and dining room below, to Hollis Daggett's quarters above. Twice he turned and looked back at the dancers; listened a moment to the music, then he took a bit of cardboard from his pocket and stared at a picture torn from a late paper. It was a nice picture; a picture of a pretty girl. She was smiling and looking up at a young man. She was looking at the young man whom she was to marry next week. But she wouldn't marry him; not next week, not ever. A short while before Satan had seen that same girl; that same face. It wasn't smiling then. It simply glared white under a light, on a slab in the morgue.

Carefully he laid an oblong legal paper on top of that picture. His own smile was not pleasant. A judge had grumbled about signing that warrant; just a slip of paper that said a certain man known as Eddie Jerome was wanted for murder.

Satan knew that his quiet entrance was not entirely unexpected. Figures moved from distant tables; two or three men who crossed the room talked to others in the high-backed booths. A man came leisurely down the stairs. Pete McNally, a well-known gunman who more than once had beaten the rap for murder. McNally nodded, and Satan touched his arm.

"I suppose you heard," Satan said slowly, "that Eddie Jerome is wanted for murder. That is, he is wanted alive." And when the man only looked at him and grinned foolishly, Satan said, "But it's only Eddie I want alive. His friends" —Satan pounded a finger against a flat chest—"like you, ain't wanted—ain't wanted *alive*. Remember that."

A big bruiser of a man met Satan at the first landing. He pointed to a door close by.

"Mr. Daggett's in there," he said. "Just walk right in."

And Satan did. He opened the door, stepped inside and closed it behind him.

Green eyes took in the three men, widened slightly as they saw Darryton, narrowed again as they lighted on Jerome leaning against the mantel above the blazing fire, a cigarette hanging from his mouth. It was Daggett who spoke. He had slipped a pair of glasses from inside his vest, put them on his nose, twisted the thick black ribbon slightly and said: "Detective Hall. Don't see much of you these days." He ran a finger along the nearly healed scar, which showed only a dull white purple down his cheek, snapped out his watch. "Something important, no doubt. The hour, you know!"

"Didn't know about it, eh?" Satan stepped to the center of the room, jerked a finger at Jerome. "It seems like the people of the state aren't satisfied anymore with dead rats; rats weighted down with lead. It seems they aren't satisfied unless they can smell flesh burning—human flesh." He tossed the picture and warrant down on the desk. "That's the body; that's the warrant. That's right! I want that punk, Eddie Jerome, for murder. I'm taking him now."

"Really!" Daggett laughed. "You're too good a detective to be laughed or kicked out of the department. Jerome's a friend of mine, and I won't see him framed. Yes, the truth leaked out about the missing machine gun. Private detectives located it for me. It's here on the desk. Didn't you see it?"

"Sure, I saw it—the machine gun." Satan nodded. "What about it?"

"That," said Daggett, "is the gun that killed the girl."

"Says you!" Satan looked contemptuously at the gun.

Daggett leaned back, stuck thick thumbs in the armholes of his vest.

"Experts have a way of proving things. The gun, no doubt, will be traced to Chopper Hays. The ballistic boys can tell from the slugs in the girl's body just what gun they were fired from. Jerome's prints are not on the gun, but other prints are." Daggett leaned forward. "The prints of Chopper Hays."

"Does he say that?" Satan looked at Darryton. "Did you find Chopper Hays' prints on that gun?"

Darryton cleared his throat, found hard work speaking, finally said: "I found that the prints on that gun most decidedly do not belong to—er—that man there." He pointed to Jerome. "There can be no doubt of that. As for this Hays! Really, I haven't seen his prints yet."

Daggett smiled.

"But undoubtedly they will be there. It might be most embarrassing, Detective Hall, if certain people swore on the stand where that gun—that machine gun, which dealt death to an innocent girl—was actually found, and who hid it; hid important evidence in an attempt to frame an innocent man; send him to the electric chair." And with the smile broadening: "Really, Satan, I thought better of you. Hate and bitterness, and the feeling that in some way through Jerome you could hurt me, has warped your judgment. Don't you know; didn't you realize that, unless Jerome's fingerprints were actually on that gun, no jury would consider convicting him—with his alibi?''

"That's right," said Satan. "I knew that."

"Ah! And did you ever think that it might be proven that the gun was actually found where you put it; that you lifted that gun?''

"Sure!" Satan nodded. "You wouldn't have much trouble in proving that I lifted the gun."

"Perhaps, after all"—Daggett's voice was soft—"it mightn't be so good for you if you took Jerome"—he tapped the warrant—"for murder."

"No. It's against all my principles," Satan agreed, "to take Jerome for murder." And before Daggett's smiling words could come in, he added, "The dirty yellow rat! If I had my way I'd shoot holes in his rotten carcass." He paused, stretched out a hand, stopped the mumbling fingerprint expert who was saying something about leaving— and doing something about it, too.

"Stay back there." Satan strode to the desk, jerked the black bag from the expert's hand, pounded it down on the desk. "Get busy, fellow. You know fingerprints. I'll give you a souvenir of mine."

Not understanding, the expert watched Satan dust the powder on the sheet of paper, smack his hand, his spreading fingers, onto the surface.

"Get your glass, fellow; get your glass." It was a full minute before Satan could make the trembling man understand, by pushing his head from those prints on the paper to the ones on the machine gun. But when the fingerprint expert did speak, it was Jerome and Daggett who couldn't understand; fully understand at once.

"That's correct, gentlemen," Professor Darryton was

saying. "The fingerprints on the machine gun are the prints of this man here. Yes, there can be no mistake about it. Both are the fingerprints of Satan—Detective Satan Hall."

And this time there was a dead silence and no interference when the slim man, hastily grabbing his case and more hastily shoving things into it, headed to the door, flung it open, and closing it with a bang behind him, was gone.

Eddie Jerome stiffened against the mantel; Hollis Daggett came straight up on the end of his chair, both his hands flat on the desk. Fascinated, he watched the gun appear in Satan's right hand; just an empty white hand that seemed to waver slightly, then hold something black; something long and deadly and menacing as Satan moved back to that door, spun the key, straightened, grinned.

Hollis Daggett said, or rather, just breathed the words: "What does it mean? What do you mean?"

"It means," said Satan, "just what I said. You won't have any trouble in proving I took the murder gun; the Tommy gun. It means that I'm not a book-reading detective and that I realize that a case only begins after the arrest of the murderer is made. The taking of the murderer is nothing; it's the convicting of him that is the real work; sometimes impossible work."

"So"—Daggett's glasses hovered on the edge of his little nose, pinching the skin tightly—"that's why you kill." Involuntarily his eyes drifted to Jerome. Not consciously, just involuntarily. He knew he was looking at Jerome; but yet, he seemed forced to do so.

Satan's words came through tightly set lips.

"I kill because I have to kill. I kill because the state and the people are better served by killing. I kill in self-defense."

"And you make it self-defense." Daggett was trying to think; think fast. And thoughts simply raced in his mind;

kaleidoscopic pieces. All there, perhaps, but refusing to put themselves together.

Jerome wet his lips.

"You intend—You're here to kill me."

Satan half turned, walked to Jerome, jerked a gun from beneath his left armpit, patted his right, tossed the gun across the room. It hit the rug, turned over, skidded across polished wood and lay against the paneled wall close to the narrow door. Then Satan spoke.

"Not me, Eddie. I'm not giving you a chance, tonight. If you show fight, you won't die. I'll just shoot your legs from under you, like *that*."

A single shot.

Eddie Jerome, who had suddenly lurched toward Satan, jumped back—fell back. Quick pain struck his leg, flew upward. He twisted slightly, clutched at a chair, sat on the arm of it. His curses were not threatening; soft and whining. He glared at Satan, but there was fear more than hate in his eyes.

"None of that, Satan; none of that," Daggett said.

"Why not?" Satan grinned. "The state employs expert surgeons. They'll fix him up. Nurses will sit with him day and night, give him every attention, every comfort—so he can burn. If he wants more of it—"

Satan raised his gun. "I've got lots of time and the music is loud downstairs." And suddenly he switched his gun to Daggett. "If you want to lose a couple of fingers— why, press one of those buttons."

Daggett frowned, moved his hand quickly, raised his head, shook it slightly at Jerome, put vulturelike eyes on Satan.

"Tell me about it, Satan," he said slowly.

"Sure! I've got nothing to hide," Satan slammed in. "You and your friends rode me; the papers rode me; then honest officials rode me; yep, even the commissioner.

They wanted a man, not a body. They didn't know or ignored the fact that only a dead murderer is a reformed murderer. Well—I'm giving them a case; a real case; the kind they want.

"I copped that machine gun and put another in its place—blood and all—for your bought betrayer of the citizens to steal. And I put my prints on the second machine gun. As for the real murder gun! Yes, I've got it! Got Jerome's prints on it. I've got real witnesses; honest lads that can go before a jury and swear to that gun. I have witnesses hidden away who saw Jerome as well as myself. Saw him use the Tommy gun."

Daggett's tongue made a little circle about his tiny mouth.

"Can't we—you understand, Satan—talk this thing over; sort of—"

"Sort of fix it for Jerome, eh?" Satan leaned forward. "Jerome, who tried to get me!"

"Well—yes." Daggett never took his eyes off Satan. "Fix it for a price." Daggett's foot moved—moved toward an electric button beneath the desk. But he didn't press it. That might mean killing Satan; killing him there in his office. He didn't want that; couldn't think of doing that— at least, not while there might be other ways.

Money was one. Money was the best way. But Satan was talking.

"Yes—we can fix it for a price, I guess," Satan said, "if Jerome will pay it."

Daggett smiled. After all, Satan was human. Yet, even as he smiled and looked into those green eyes, some doubt struck him. But Satan had said "for a price." Daggett spoke easily now; smoothly, friendly.

"Jerome's my friend; just as I wanted you for a friend once. I take care of my friends. I like you, Satan; always liked you. It was just that you rubbed me the wrong way. Well—it's a big thing, the way you put it. You'll see how I stick to my friends—to Jerome. Name your figure, and make it a stiff one.''

Satan nodded very slowly.

"That's right. But you have nothing to do with it, Daggett. It's Jerome who can pay the price. You see, it's like this. Inside, Eddie Jerome is a rat; a dirty, slimy rat. Look at him now; look at him whining there! When the jury comes in and the judge says he's to fry, and the stink of his own rotten carcass is burning in his nostrils, he'll talk. Yep, Jerome can talk himself out of that chair by talking you into it. Look at him, Daggett! Look at him. By God! you're going to burn!''

Daggett's lips set tightly; small eyes came even closer together, rounded into tiny circles of hatred. But he didn't lose his head. He looked at Jerome, and Jerome cried, "By God! Daggett, I won't go with him. I can't. He'll torture me; torture hell out of me, and—and—''

With a sudden shrill whine, "If you let me go; if he tortures me, maybe...God! if he tortures me I might talk—talk about you.''

Hollis Daggett turned his eyes to Satan, took in his position close to the little door from which the girl had come; shot a side glance at another door almost directly behind Satan, and with a little grimace, pressed his foot down on the button beneath the rug. He'd have to kill Satan now. His orders were for the men he had hidden behind that door to shoot; to open that well-oiled door noiselessly and shoot to kill. There was no other way.

ELEVEN

DOORS OF DEATH

■

Things happened. Two doors opened almost at once; the one the girl had used and the one Satan stood so close to. But Satan heard neither door.

Two men raised guns directly at Satan's back; two fingers tightened on separate triggers, then loosened. There was something suddenly between them and Satan's back. It was a human figure; a girl. Nina Radcliff stood directly in the path of their fire and Nina held a gun; a gun that she had picked up from the floor beside that door; a gun that she had seen Satan throw there as she peered through the tiny crack.

Nina Radcliff jabbed that gun directly against Satan's back, said in a forced, dead voice: "Drop your gun, Satan—or you'll be killed."

For a moment Satan held his gun; held it directly on the big body of Hollis Daggett, and in that moment of stunned surprise the girl was under his arm, knocking up his gun as he fired.

With a new hope, a new courage, born of seeing two men with guns in that doorway, Eddie Jerome acted quickly. He swept the tongs from the fireplace, stepped forward on his good leg and swung those tongs above the girl's head.

The tongs landed viciously on the side of Satan's head. He stumbled forward, turned, saw the face of Eddie Jerome, tried to lift his right arm; his right hand with the gun in it. And the tongs came again, swinging higher this time; up and down. Straight down on his forehead! Satan had a sudden thought as they struck, or before they struck, maybe. Nina Radcliff had made a fool of him; a dead fool. After that, no thoughts. A fall; a long fall. A fall with no end to it. And then there was an end; a sudden end. He was conscious again.

Satan was sitting there in a chair. Through the haze of mist and blood he saw the two men by the door, heard Daggett speak to them as he bent over the big chair and went through Satan's pockets; even patting his arms and legs.

"All right, boys, get out—say nothing." He turned to the girl when the two men had left. "You're a wonder, child. They would have killed Satan, and I don't want him dead just yet." And pinching the white, bloodless cheeks of Nina Radcliff, "That'll repay him for calling you a 'poor dumbbell.' But don't do it again. If one of those others had stuck a gun in his back it wouldn't have worked. They would have had to kill him, and he would have killed me before the lead ripping into his back paralyzed him."

"That's right." Jerome hobbled across the room, leaving a trail of blood on the carpet, cursed loudly, struck Satan across the face. "Bright guy, eh? Just another sucker for women." And when the girl pulled at Jerome's arm, "Better beat it, sister. You're in things now; right up to murder."

"Murder!" The girl gasped. "You're going to kill him?"

"And how!" Jerome nodded vigorously. "If you were at that door you got an earful. He'll be dead. If anyone can recognize him as Satan Hall, the great—"

"Now—now!" Daggett stood up straight, Satan's gun in his right hand. "Don't you bother about him, my child. You did very well. We are going to protect you. No harm will be done Satan here; just as assurance that he won't bring you into it." Daggett shook his head. "Very serious for you, Nina. But I am your friend; I'll take care of you."

Satan opened his eyes, stared straight at the girl. His lips opened and closed. He didn't speak then; he didn't need to. Red flashed into the girl's face, to leave almost at once; turning the sudden white to a peculiar creamlike yellow.

"Satan—Satan!" she said. "Don't say it now."

Thin lips grew long and narrow, eyes hardened to hateful green balls. And Satan spoke; his words were thick.

"I don't need to say it. You can see it; read it. You two-timing little—"

Daggett took her arm, started to pull her away. She jerked herself free. Brown eyes blazed; her voice was coarse, rough, like other women of the night Satan knew. She fairly shouted: "You wanted to frame them. Him— Hollis Daggett! Hollis, who did more for me than my own family, than you! Think what you want! Damn you, think! I—"

She raised her hand, brought it down across Satan's face, half fell forward, was sprawled over him there in the chair.

A few seconds, maybe less, her arms were about him; at least, behind him as she steadied herself. The same hair was against his cheek; wet—yes, wet with his own blood. She was talking, too; at least, he thought he heard sounds— sounds that might be words, far back in her throat.

And she was gone. Daggett was leading her to the little door. Satan heard the door close. He heard something else. Her words still ringing in his ears.

"Fight" and "truth" and "licked," or was it "not licked"? And, damn it! something about "a gun." Also not trying "to take Jerome alive." He shook his head. It couldn't be right; just the throbbing in his head, the taste of blood in his mouth.

Jerome said to Hollis: "That fixes up the girl for you. Can we get away with this? Will we tie him up and get to work? That gun; that evidence! He knows where it is. He's got to tell."

"We can't tie him up," Daggett said. "Oh! the room is soundproof and all that, but things might go wrong. The cops might suddenly break in. Satan threatened to get you tonight. Even the commissioner might wonder what happened to him. If they broke in—"

Daggett paused, looked at Jerome; the tongs still in his hand. "He's unarmed," he finished suggestively.

"That's right." Jerome nodded. "I could crush his skull, at that."

Daggett winked at Jerome, lifted his gun, came close to Satan.

"Jerome's impulsive; he can be nasty," he said. "I'm for you, Satan, but I can't control—can't be expected to control a lad who sits on the edge of the electric chair. Why not tell him where the machine gun is? Where those witnesses are?

"Forget the whole thing and walk out of here a free man, with big money in your pocket?"

Satan set his teeth down hard, said: "If I'm dead or

alive, he roasts. The only difference is—I won't see him.
You'd better step from under, Daggett. You've got lawyers. Try the law."

Daggett shook his head.

"You tried the law tonight, Satan, and see what happened?
But I've got a lot of money," Daggett added softly as he
tried to push Jerome back.

Jerome said: "To hell with that stuff, mister. Let me at
him. I'll make him talk."

Satan's eyes widened. Jerome didn't have the tongs
anymore. He carried in his hand the highly carved poker
from the fireplace. It was glowing at the end.

Daggett stood between the two men.

"You're going to kill me now," Satan said. "You'll
have to."

"But that would be foolish, Satan. What of Jerome,
then?"

"One or two murders! What difference does it make to
Jerome? He'll run out like the rat he is, and you'll supply
him with money like the rat you are. Then later—"

"Hell!" Jerome coughed in. "Let me at the yellow
flatfoot. Keep that gun on him, mister. How do you like
that?"

Daggett was shoved aside. Jerome moved his body
forward. Hot steel shot out. Satan involuntarily moved his
head; moved it just in time. Flesh burned close to his left
eye. Jerome said: "You wanted the smell of burning flesh,
eh? How do you like it?" He poised the poker again.
"Where's that machine gun?"

Daggett said: "Now—now. Easy, boy." But there was
nothing of command in his voice; in his words. More,
perhaps, a simple warning for Jerome not to overplay
things in the beginning.

The poker came closer. Satan braced himself in the

chair, his back tightly against it, his eyes shifting from the gun in Eddie's left hand—Satan's other gun, to the now dulling glow of the poker's end. Yes, he braced himself, his hands tightly down on the side of the chair seat; against the springs; against—by God! against cold steel; the cold steel of a heavy-caliber revolver.

Steel. Steel! Brown eyes! The girl had said, "Fight." And as the fingers of his left hand closed about that gun he knew what she had meant; knew that she had first stuck the gun in his back to save him from being shot to death by the two men in the other doorway; knew that the slap in the face had been a fake—a pretense of anger that gave her the opportunity to fall over him and so plant the gun in the chair.

But the hot poker was close, almost touching an eyelid. This time he jarred his head so quickly back and down that iron burned against his forehead. Not so hot now; not such a searing of the flesh.

Satan's left hand shot up from that chair; blue-black steel flashed. Mechanically, even instinctively, it drew a bead right between hateful cruel eyes. And he did it. Lowered and twisted that gun even as his finger closed upon the trigger and Jerome screamed to Daggett to shoot.

Satan was on his feet, his right hand crossing over his left, clutching at the hot poker. He gripped it, too, tore it from Jerome's hand as Jerome crashed back from the slug in his shoulder.

Hollis Daggett jerked up his gun, and that was all; for Satan's great right hand, burning with the fire of that poker, tore and struck with almost a single motion. Daggett staggered, clutched at the desk. It was the heavy end of the poker that hit him. Hollis Daggett fell forward on his face.

Jerome was still staggering back when he fired; emptied his gun wildly and frantically at the glaring face of Satan, before him. He didn't know if he hit him; couldn't tell, for Satan's face was a single mass of red but for the eyes in it; glaring devilish balls of green fire.

No, Jerome didn't know if he hit Satan, not did Satan know. His body jarred twice, he thought; once, anyway. But his feet were far apart and he stood swaying on them. Then his shoulders bent, his lips parted, smacked back again as Jerome's gun clicked; clicked harmlessly twice— three times—before Jerome knew the truth. His last shot was gone.

Satan clutched the poker and moved slowly forward. Jerome screamed, cried out to Daggett. There was fear, terror in his voice, in his eyes, in the twisting body that sought to avoid the advancing man. And Jerome saw the tongs he had discarded, gripped them, turned, started to back across the room away from the man; the man with the gun in his left hand, heavy iron in his right and that devilish, bloody head that moved slowly toward him, propelled by uncertain yet steadily moving feet.

Jerome crouched low, saw Satan move to the right of him, as if Satan didn't see him; saw Satan drag an arm and sleeve across his eyes to wipe the blood away. Then Satan swung directly, faced him. Satan's head went up, green flickered like a cat's eyes in the night. Jerome cried out again. He was not dealing with a human being, but a fiend from hell.

"Alive. Alive!" Satan cried out, pointed his gun direct- ly at Jerome's head, hesitated a moment, then flung the gun across the room.

"Alive," he muttered again, and moved forward.

They were both big men; both strong men, and Satan had been weakened by loss of blood. And Satan didn't strike at once. He reversed the poker in his right hand, so that the sharp end with the curved iron a few inches from the point was toward Jerome.

Eddie Jerome struck first. The heavy tongs crashed down on Satan's left arm and bounced onto his head. Satan's knees buckled, straightened again. He swept up the poker with the curved hook.

Yes, Jerome was the stronger then, by far the stronger physically. But he looked through a mask of red blood into green eyes and was afraid. Besides, Satan laughed; a weird, eerie sort of sound the first time Satan struck. After that he continued to laugh. There wasn't any reason why he should laugh as he struck and hacked the terror-stricken rat to his knees.

Satan's thoughts were far from funny. He was thinking of the dead girl with the slugs in her body; even of the man she was going to marry, and that her eyes were brown. But he laughed just the same.

TWELVE

THE THING ON THE STAIRS

■

Downstairs the music played softly. Youth and age danced to its charm. Young bodies clung close; soft, warm, red cheeks brushed hard, pale ones.

Pete McNally came down those great broad stairs and spoke to a couple of men in evening dress who lounged against the banisters. With apparent unconcern they caressed armpits. Pete said in a low, husky voice: "Satan's been up there a long time. Soundproof or no soundproof, something screwy is going on in that room." He stopped, knitted his eyes, looked toward the entrance to the dance floor. A man waved twice. "Hell!" said Pete. "Something wrong outside. The police are here. I'll have a look-see in that damn room if I've got—"

Pete stopped again, turned. A man had laughed at the top of those stairs; at least, something had laughed; something that wasn't human. And Pete saw Hollis Daggett; saw him dart down a few steps into the light and stand before a figure in the blackness. He heard Daggett, too, caught the plea in his voice, the shriek half of fear; more, perhaps, of horror.

It was then that Daggett threw up his arms and stepped backward; at least, he started to step backward. But he didn't step; just threw out a leg grotesquely, stumbled, pitched downward, and striking on his back, turned over and hurtled down those steps to the floor below.

Pete McNally clutched for his gun, held his hand so beneath his coat. His eyes bulged, his mouth hung open. The thing he saw filled him with an unknown sort of terror; paralyzed him like a nightmare. His hand simply fastened to his gun, but he didn't draw it; couldn't draw it.

He knew from the green in the eyes of the thing that staggered down those stairs and the fact that the detective had gone up, that the man—the thing, rather—was Satan Hall. But that wasn't all that held McNally. It was the other thing; the beaten, senseless thing that pounded from step to step behind Satan; the thing that Satan dragged.

He didn't even remotely guess then that the shapeless mass was Eddie Jerome.

And Satan was talking; mumbling to himself or to the others—or just mumbling, a word here and there. "Alive" and "Burning flesh" and "It's what the people want!"

No one tried to stop him; no one tried to shoot him. No one gave a second look at the great hulk of the underworld king who lay at the foot of those stairs. The music stopped; people watched, fascinated with horror, the unsteady, faltering steps of that battered, beaten man who dragged another; another bloodstained form behind him.

The tension broke. A woman screamed; a man tore from the room. Someone cried out shrilly, and Pete McNally finally started to draw his gun.

A calm voice at the foot of the stairs said: "I wouldn't do that, Pete." It was the commissioner of police speaking.

A less calm voice shouted: "Drop that gun or I'll plug you full of holes!" It was Lieutenant Morrisey.

Satan laughed. The commissioner spoke. His voice didn't shake. It was clear—calm. He felt certain he was facing a madman.

"Resisting arrest, eh, Detective Hall?"

Green eyes stared a long time at the commissioner. They never wavered. Finally, with a convulsive movement that took every bit of strength in his spent, body, Satan jerked the unconscious form of Eddie Jerome around in front of him. He half raised a hand in salute, said: "Wanted for murder. Wanted alive. Wanted—"

Morrisey stepped up two steps, looked at Satan, said in an awed voice: "Unconscious. Out on his feet, and *on* his feet."

But it was the frail body of the commissioner that braced itself and caught Satan as he fell; held him too. At least, long enough to let his battered body sink gently to the floor.

Satan opened his eyes once just before they took him upstairs to the operating room. There was lead that needed removing. The commissioner waved others back. Satan said: "Well, will they fry him? Will he live to fry?"

The commissioner shrugged his shoulders.

"He'll live. The arrest was a—a brutal affair. I'll stand behind you, of course. But the evidence, without the machine gun, won't be sufficient to convict him."

Satan grinned; straightened his face at once. It was not in condition for smiling. But he told the commissioner about the gun.

"The prints are Eddie Jerome's. I've got the witnesses who saw him in the car. And he'll talk; talk words all over his mouth about Daggett. Yes, I know he will. I found out tonight. He's yellow; a dirty, nasty yellow." And after a moment, when a white-coated figure moved toward the bed, Satan added, perplexed, "How did you happen to be at the Wellington at just that time?"

The commissioner coughed behind his hand, said: "I was telephoned to come. A woman. I don't know who it was." And closing one eye, "Don't worry about Nina. She won't be brought into it."

"That's good. That's fine!" And rather weakly, as the doctor gripped his wrist, "Do your stuff, Doc. I've got to live. I've got to live to see a guy die."

The doctor nodded, laughed.

"After what you took tonight, there isn't a surgeon here who could kill you."

Satan heard the nurse at the door say: "But he's not seeing anyone. No, no! I said—"

Satan opened his eyes as Nina Radcliff thrust her way in the door. Her manner was brisk; her little body erect, with a swing to it. Poise, he thought; yet back of that poise a sort of nervousness. Her voice cracked, too, when she saw his face, but she spoke her words as she had planned them; must have planned them.

"Hello, sucker." She took his hand. Hers was cold. And then, as she didn't plan to say but did say just the same, "You called me that once, you know. Now—we're even."

"Thanks for the gun." Satan gripped her hand. "I nearly didn't find it."

"I'm sorry about the slap in the face." She stammered, tried to pull her hand away. "I came to tell you that we're even now. You saved my life and I saved yours. That makes us even. You know it."

"Is that all you came to tell me?"

"What else?" Slim shoulders raised slightly.

"Maybe that you're—that you sort of washed yourself up tonight."

The girl laughed. It was rather high-pitched.

"I'm washed up with you," she said, "if that's what you mean. I don't like suckers, either."

She jerked her hand free, and suddenly realized how easily she did it; how weak Satan really was. She noticed the whiteness of his face, the sudden pallor to his lips; and the lids that blinked above green eyes, finally dropping and hiding them.

Satan said, in a voice that sounded distant, faraway: "Is that all you came to tell me; that you don't like—suckers?" His voice died slowly, as if he were dropping off into the sleep of exhaustion.

She hesitated a long moment. The hand on the sheet was very white; very still. There were deep scars on his face, and strips of plaster. Nothing much of his face there but thin, hard lips—slightly parted now, as if he did not have the strength to close them. She looked down; was sure his eyes were closed, his breathing regular; then said very softly, and her voice broke: "No, I don't like you, Satan. I couldn't ever just *like* you."

She leaned forward suddenly and kissed him full upon the lips. And she was gone, hurrying out the door; not sure then if Satan were asleep, not even sure that he was awake.

Satan lay there on the bed. If he slept, his dreams were pleasant, for he smiled. And if the smile hurt his face— well, it just hurt his face, that was all. For it stayed there a long time.